EVA CHASE

Wrathful Wonderland

The Looking-Glass Curse
Book 2

Wrathful Wonderland

Book 2 in the Looking-Glass Curse trilogy

First Digital Edition, 2019

Copyright © 2019 Eva Chase

Cover design: Sly Fox Cover Designs

Ebook ISBN: 978-1-989096-30-7

Paperback ISBN: 978-1-989096-31-4

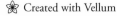 Created with Vellum

CHAPTER ONE

Lyssa

You know you're in Wonderland when you wake up in the morning and the first thing you feel is gratitude that your head is still attached to your body.

I rolled over in Hatter's guest room bed, rubbing my neck as if some part of me needed extra confirmation. Bright mid-morning sun streamed through the window, but my definitely-connected head was still bleary. We'd been up pretty late last night.

We'd taken on the Queen of Hearts and won—maybe not a full victory, but a big one.

A smile curved my lips. I pressed my face into the plump feather pillow, its chamomile tea scent filling my nose. Say whatever you wanted about Wonderland's downsides—tyrant queen, regular beatings and beheadings, weird monsters lurking around the fringes—no one could deny the beds were freaking comfortable.

Part of me wanted to drift off into another hour or so of sleep. But because I was responsible, practical Lyssa Tenniel, a larger part of me was pointing out that I was lucky I'd gotten to sleep at all. The White Knight had given us a device to provide a warning if the Queen's guards came charging up the stairs to Hatter's apartment. It might not have gone off overnight, but it still could at any moment.

We had an awful lot to do before I could feel safe here. Or before I could get back to my real home, where beheadings weren't even a thing.

With a grumble at myself, I pushed back the covers and hopped out of bed. Pain prickled up my forearm along the stitched-up cut I'd gotten when under attack by a guard a few days ago.

I'd slept in the tank top and khakis I'd been wearing when I'd arrived in Wonderland yesterday evening, and the thought of leaving them on any longer made me cringe. I eyed the borrowed dresses in the wardrobe in their bright colors and bold patterns that my best friend Melody would have swooned over, picked one of the less flashy ones, and headed to the bathroom.

We didn't even know yet whether everyone who'd been part of last night's mission had made it back. Sally, the woman who'd come with us into the palace gardens and run off to distract the guards, hadn't met up with us at the wall during our escape. If *she'd* made it home, it'd been alone. Theo was probably already checking on her.

Across the hall from the bathroom, Hatter's bedroom door stood a few inches ajar. I hesitated, hanging the dress on the hook beside the sink. Every other morning I'd been here, Hatter's door had either been firmly closed, because he was up and marking that room off limits, or wide open, because he was still sleeping and that was how it always reset, like the fateful night ages ago just before the Queen had trapped Time to quell the growing rebellion, when he'd fallen asleep in his armchair waiting for bad news.

We'd freed Time in the wee hours of the morning. This might as well be his first brand new day in Wonderland in decades.

I couldn't resist. I padded across the hardwood floor and eased the door farther open.

The only other time I'd looked in on Hatter sleeping, he'd been slumped in that chair beside the bed, fully dressed, as apparently he'd woken up every morning across all those decades Wonderland remained stuck repeating the same day. The position hadn't looked all that comfortable.

Last night, he'd made it to the bed. He lay on his back, the covers bunched across his chest, his angular face tipped into the pillow and the spikes of his dark blond hair veering this way and that in even greater disarray than usual. He'd bothered to take off his hat and his suit jacket, at least, but his maroon tie still hung loose beneath the rumpled collar of his dress shirt. Old habits were hard to break?

The sight of him brought a flutter of warmth into my

chest. Well, the sight of him and the thought of what he might or might not be wearing under the covers. It was hard not to think of his smile last night when I'd asked him to kiss me and the intensity of his mouth claiming mine.

I wavered, torn between the urge to climb right into that bed with him and the uncertainty about how he'd respond. We hadn't done anything more than kiss yet. And the last time I'd been in his bedroom, he'd ushered me out very quickly.

Hatter was obviously a light sleeper. I didn't think I'd made a sound more than taking a breath, and he stirred. Raising his head, he stared at the bed around him, totally bewildered. Then the light of understanding dawned on his face, taking him from scruffily good-looking to pulse-thumpingly hot in an instant.

His gaze darted up to find me, and his expression turned wary but not unwelcoming. I guessed I couldn't blame him for being a little uncertain too. We'd had a chaotic time together.

"Um," I said. "Good morning."

"It is, isn't it?" he said, pushing himself higher on the bed. He considered the covers with an awed chuckle. His shoulders had relaxed when he looked up at me again. "We really did it."

I had to grin. "We did."

"I suppose this is going to take some getting used to."

His tone was warm enough that I decided to just go for it. I walked over and sat on the edge of the bed just a foot away from him. My heart beat faster, but the spark of desire in his green eyes encouraged me. I curled my fingers around his loosened tie.

"Just as a tip," I said. "Generally people take these off when they go to bed."

"Hmm," Hatter said. "It's a good thing I have you here to advise me on these matters. I seem to be out of practice."

"Happy to help in any way I can." I tugged the tie looser, and Hatter leaned toward me. He smelled amazing, like lime and wood smoke, bright and dark at the same time. Like Wonderland.

"Amazing that I ever managed without you, looking-glass girl," he murmured, his dry tenor dropping low enough to send an eager shiver down my spine.

"It really is," I said, a little breathless, and then our lips collided.

Hatter tucked his arm around my waist to pull me even closer. His mouth was so hot and sure I nearly drowned in the wave of need that swept through me. All I could do was hang onto his tie like my life depended on it.

He kissed me again, more deeply, my lips parting with a pleased sound to let his tongue sweep over mine. His deft fingers trailed up my side. They teased over the side of my breast, edging closer until my nipple was aching for contact. His thumb flicked over the peak, and I whimpered into his mouth. Heat pooled between my thighs.

I slid my hand down over the taut muscles of Hatter's broad shoulders and his contrastingly lean chest. I was just a moment or two from discovering whether he wore boxers or briefs when a joyful shout pealed down the hall.

"New day, here I come! New dresses. New shoes. Lands, I can change the furniture in my fucking room now!"

Hatter and I had jerked apart at the sound of his daughter's voice. Her bounding footsteps thumped down the hall past the door I'd thankfully nudged shut behind me when I'd come in. My lips twitched in amusement at her solo celebration.

Doria had joined in on the mission last night, but only on the sidelines and at the beginning. Hatter had woken her when we'd gotten back to the house so she'd know we'd returned safely and victorious. She sounded even happier now that the news had sunk in.

"Pops!" she called from downstairs. "There's no breakfast. We need something special for today."

Hatter rolled his eyes at the nickname and gave me one last quick kiss that tasted like an apology to both of us. I got up as he scooted off the bed and was a tad disappointed to discover he'd slept with his pants on. He leaned out into the hall. "Give me five minutes!"

"Fine, but I'm only cutting you slack because you were out saving the world yesterday."

"Teenagers," he muttered fondly, turning to his wardrobe.

If Hatter had actually been as young as he looked, he wouldn't have been more than a teen himself when he'd become a father. He'd told me he'd adopted Doria when she was two, twelve years ago. But he wasn't actually as young as he looked, thanks to Wonderlandian weirdness. I still wasn't totally clear on the timelines, but I wasn't sure how much it mattered.

Definitely not as much as the fact that Hatter appeared to be going to change his clothes without asking me to leave the room. Maybe I'd get the answer to that boxers vs. briefs question after all. I dropped into the armchair next to the bed, and my eyebrows jumped in surprise. The padded velour upholstery was so cozy I wanted to tuck myself right into it.

"This chair is actually pretty comfy," I said. Still not an ideal sleeping spot, but better than I'd expected.

"You can have it," Hatter tossed over his shoulder. He pulled a suit out of the wardrobe—the dark violet one he'd been wearing the first time I saw him—and set it on the bed. "I never want to sit in that thing again."

Fair enough. I *could* move it to the guest bedroom if I wanted to. Either of us could, with time moving properly again.

"I guess you can get rid of things now," I said. "And not have them pop back to where they used to be overnight."

"A feature of our new reality that I'm very much looking forward to," Hatter remarked.

My gaze traveled automatically to the folded paper sitting on one of the bookcases across the room. A folded paper with a charcoal sketch of the house I'd inherited less than two weeks ago from my grand-aunt Alicia.

Aunt Alicia had drawn that sketch for Hatter after she'd fallen through the same mirror I had into

Wonderland, some fifty years ago. From the vague letter she'd left for me, I'd gathered our family had a strange tie to this place. I touched the ruby ring she'd also left for me, confirming it was still hanging from its chain under my shirt.

Aunt Alicia hadn't left Wonderland in the best state. Apparently she'd made promises about helping with the rebellion against the Queen of Hearts and then chickened out at the last moment, leaving the rebel group that called themselves the Spades in the lurch. Hatter had commented the other day that he'd have thrown out her sketch if his room, like the rest of Wonderland, hadn't been stuck in time.

Hatter followed my glance, and his hands paused around the tie he'd finally taken off.

"You could get rid of that if you wanted," I said tentatively. I knew he'd been harboring a lot of resentment over Aunt Alicia's betrayal of Wonderland. I also knew he'd had something of a crush on her back then. It was a little weird, thinking that, even though nothing had ever happened between them.

"I could," Hatter said slowly, and paused in a way that sent an uncomfortable twinge through my stomach. He'd probably had feelings for dozens of people before me. *I* had feelings for at least two other men in Wonderland right now, and he didn't see anything weird about that. It shouldn't have mattered.

But I didn't have those Wonderlandian sensibilities by nature, and an irrational little piece of me wanted him all to myself.

"The thing is," Hatter went on, catching my eye, "it isn't Alicia's house anymore. It's yours now. It's where you are when you're not here. When you were gone, the last time…" He hesitated again as if struggling to decide on the right words. "It made the wait easier, being able to look at that picture and know you were safe there."

Oh. My throat felt suddenly tight. He hadn't even known if I'd come back, the last time. He'd yelled at me about the probability that I wouldn't. But even then, it'd mattered more to him that I'd gotten out of danger.

"Better to keep it, then?" I ventured.

A smile touched Hatter's face—small, but enough to crinkle the corners of his eyes the way I loved. "I think so."

I had the impulse to drag him right back into the bed, breakfast be damned, but before I could act on it, Doria let out another shout. A frightened one.

"Dad!"

At the panic in her voice, Hatter blanched. He dashed for the hall, snatching up the top hat sitting on the dresser as he went, as if he'd need it to face whatever trouble awaited. I hurried after him.

Doria was standing by an open window in the living area, peering out. Her fingers gripped the ledge tightly as if she needed it for balance. Her face had paled beneath the fall of her dark brown hair.

Hatter rushed to her side. "What?"

She pointed mutely toward the street outside. He looked, and his expression stiffened.

As I came up behind them, a resonant thudding

reached my ears. A voice was hollering something in the distance, too far away from me to make out the words, but something about the harsh tones of it sent a prickle of uneasy recognition down my spine.

I moved toward the other window to get a better view, and Hatter caught my arm.

"Stay back," he said, worry crackling through his words. "We can't let anyone see you. The guards are still looking— You need to put that powder Theo gave you in your hair."

I'd meant to do that during the shower I'd almost forgotten about taking. My gut balled tight. I edged a little to the side but no closer toward the window. From that angle, I could make out a sliver of the street.

Rows upon rows of guards in the palace's red-and-pink pleated tunics and bulging red helmets were marching by along the cobblestone road. As I watched, one came into view in the midst of the procession with a long pole thrust up in the air.

Doria clapped her hand over her mouth with a squeak of horror. Hatter flinched.

I risked easing half a step forward, and my stomach flipped over. Oh, God.

It wasn't a pole—it was a pike. And I could now say with total certainty that Sally hadn't made it home from last night's mission. With each bob of that pike, her braid swung from her decapitated head.

CHAPTER TWO

Lyssa

I stumbled backward, bile rising up my throat. The image of Sally's severed head stayed imprinted in my mind: eyes glazed and staring, skin grayed, neck rimmed with raw red flesh.

This was Wonderland, where people cavorted and laughed… and died.

"Lyssa," Hatter said. My legs wobbled, and he grasped my shoulder. I turned, pressing my face to his chest. Drinking in the bright-and-dark smell of him. His arms came around me and tightened when I shivered.

"That's what they do to Spades," Doria muttered, her voice rough. "To anyone who doesn't fall in line."

"They only parade them around when it's a Spade," Hatter said. "And not usually with the entire damned Hearts' Guard in attendance."

The spectacle was horrifying enough when I'd barely

known Sally. It could have been Doria's head up there, or Hatter's. It could have been mine if I'd been a smidge slower when the guards had chased me the other day.

"It's not just the Guard," Doria said, with a hitch in her breath that made me raise my head. I still couldn't see much of anything through the window, but the voice from outside carried to us more clearly now. And I did recognize it. Its throaty, commanding tone cut through the stomp of the guards' marching feet.

"People of Wonderland," the Queen of Hearts proclaimed. "This poison calling itself 'the Spades' has seeped around us for too long. They break the peace I have prescribed and force you all to suffer. It is time to stamp them out once and for all! We cannot tolerate it. We must not tolerate it! They will not dare trifle with me again."

"I wouldn't count on that," Doria murmured, but she'd drawn back from the window ledge as if afraid the Queen might reach her even there.

I needed to see the Queen, this villain who'd kept Wonderland's people trapped in the space of a day for nearly fifty years, whose shrieks of dismay had pierced my ears last night. I eased out of Hatter's embrace and crept closer to the window. Hatter made a warning sound, but he didn't stop me.

The Queen of Hearts sat in a golden throne with a heart-shaped back, borne by several of her guards. The immense skirt of her salmon-pink dress billowed out over the narrow platform. Her hair was styled in the same coppery loops I'd seen in a painting of her in the palace, coiled toward the base of her tall gold crown. Her scarlet lips were pursed, and her wide-set eyes gleamed with a metallic shimmer that apparently hadn't been just the painter's artistic license. Her gaze roved over the street as if it could have sliced through the walls around her just by looking at them.

When her gaze swept toward the higher floors of the buildings, I backed up with a shudder. Her voice heaved from her lungs again, so loud I'd have thought she was using a loudspeaker if I hadn't seen her hands were empty.

"You bring this on yourselves," she said. "You harbor these criminals; you look the other way. These beasts killed my *son*. They claim they fight for you. Well, let us see how true that is. Are they willing to give up their own lives when it's merely yours on the line?"

At a jerk of her hand, one of the guards broke from their formation and slammed open the door of the nearest shop. There was a cry, and he emerged dragging a young woman—a girl, really, not much older than Doria's fourteen.

An older woman appeared in the doorway—the girl's mother? She stared white-faced and tight-lipped but unmoving as the guard lashed a metal cord around the girl's wrists. He tossed the prisoner onto the back of the throne's platform with an audible thump. The girl let out a pained gasp.

The Queen smiled.

"I will collect more of you each day until the Spades come forward to take your place—or until our dungeon is full," she said, sounding almost gleeful now. "If there's no sign of them by then, you will face the punishment for their crimes and cowardice in their place. Do *not* try my patience. If you know anything of these miscreants or the new Alice Otherlander, bring word to the palace, and you will be rewarded for your loyalty."

The procession marched on. The Queen's last words echoed through me, confusion dulling my horror.

"The new Alice Otherlander," I repeated. "Does that mean me? Why would she call me 'Alice'? Why *new*?"

Hatter's jaw worked. One look at his face was enough to tell me he knew the answer.

"We didn't tell you before," he said. "We already had so much to explain, and that part wasn't really relevant—it's all the Queen's paranoia. In some ways you know more about it than I did."

"I think I still need you to tell me the parts *you* know," I said.

He drew in a ragged breath. "Before your grand-aunt, there were two other women who came through a looking-glass into the Pond of Tears. Both of them were named Alice. Alice, Alice, Alicia, Lyssa… The Queen might not even know what your name is yet, but she's gathered enough to assume you're the next in that line. And for whatever reason, she thinks the pattern is part of a plot to overthrow her."

"For the same reason she decided the Spades must have killed the Prince way back when," Doria said, hugging herself. "For the reason that she's *totally fucking insane*."

I wouldn't mind seeing the Queen of Hearts

overthrown now, but it wasn't like I'd come here to do that. I hadn't even meant to come here at all the first time. But Aunt Alicia had suggested our family was tied up with the mirror and Wonderland. How far back did that connection go? There had been Alices farther back in the family tree she had hanging in the library. Were they all Tenniels from longer ago?

Mom had said something about that, hadn't she? That my grand-aunt hadn't wanted her and Dad to name me after her. Was the name somehow part of the connection?

Too bad I couldn't really investigate the family side of things while I was stranded here in Wonderland.

"Okay," I said. "So basically, my name just makes her want to chop my head off even more. I guess you're right —it doesn't make that much difference. I'm still in a lot less danger than that girl she grabbed."

Doria sidled closer to her father's side. "Do you think she'll really do it? She'll fill the dungeon with regular Clubbers and then kill them all if we don't turn ourselves in?"

"Hey." Hatter turned to her and touched the side of her face, giving her a look filled with so much fatherly firmness and caring that it turned my heart into mush, watching them. "She's not getting you, Mouse. The White Knight will hear about this. He'll dream up one of his grand plans, and we'll stop as many heads from rolling as we can. Yours is *definitely* staying right where it belongs."

Doria still looked nervous, but a sly glint lit in her eyes at the same time. "*We'll* stop? Does that mean you're officially back with the Spades?"

Hatter gave her a grim smile. From what I'd seen and gathered, he'd been doing everything possible to keep himself and her apart from the rebel group since he'd become her father—until last night. As he'd sprinted across the gardens and prodded the palace's locks open with his hatpins, it'd been clear he was in his element. But that didn't mean he'd changed his mind completely.

"We freed Time," he said to Doria. "We have a real chance now. And I'd rather run those risks than watch you do it. *You* are going to be even more careful than usual while the Queen's on a rampage."

"I'm not promising anything," she said.

He sighed. "I didn't figure you would."

"Maybe I can help somehow, because of that whole Alice thing," I said. "If the Queen feels threatened by me being here... even if I'm not really the threat she thinks I am... there's got to be a way to use that. And I've got this too." I fished the ring out from under my shirt and popped off the gold filigree case around the ruby to show it to Hatter. "This is what Aunt Alicia left me along with the letter. She seemed to think it was important."

Hatter cocked his head as he studied it. "The gem is a match for that symbol you found on the ruin out by the Topsy Turvy Woods."

"I know," I said. "When I asked Chess about the symbol there, he said the Queen freaks out about ruins like that—she orders them destroyed if she hears about them. She's afraid of something to do with them too. It could all be connected. Aunt Alicia never said anything to you about the ring?"

"Unfortunately, no. I didn't even realize she had it." He frowned. "Theo might be able to tell you more."

His tone was a little reluctant. Hatter and the current White Knight had something of a contentious relationship, partly because Theo continued to let Doria pitch in with the Spades and partly, I suspected, because of the circumstances around Hatter's abandoning the group years ago. But Theo did seem to be the most knowledgeable person in Wonderland, maybe because in his public role as Inventor, he had a license to dig into any matter that came up.

I'd already meant to ask Theo about the ring. I'd forgotten about it during the rush of our mission and our victory afterward, but there was no other urgent task to get in the way now.

"I'll head over to the Tower then," I said.

"First get that powder in your hair, and get yourself into proper Wonderlander clothes," Hatter said. "I'm not letting the Queen get a hold of *your* head either."

The dyeing powder Theo had given me darkened my pale blond waves to a light ash brown. Definitely a different look. I stuck the rest of the package on the bathroom shelf —he'd said I'd need to re-dye it every couple days to make sure the color didn't fade too much. Then I pulled my hair back into a bun so it wouldn't be obvious how long it was. No one was going to identify me at a glance as the Otherlander the guards had been looking for.

When I came down in the borrowed dress with its pattern of rich greens and pinks, Hatter and Doria were sitting at the dining table with a platter of scones, and they had company.

"Chess!" I said, a smile springing to my face. Of the three men I'd found myself drawn to since I'd arrived in Wonderland, Chess was both the most enigmatic and the most likely to raise my spirits.

He gave me his characteristic playful grin that showed just a hint of his fang-like teeth. His whole face had a feline look to it, from the shape of his eyes to his prominent cheekbones, features that made even more sense now that I'd discovered he could literally shift into the shape of a large tabby cat when he wanted to. He'd sworn me to secrecy about that talent.

"Glad to see you too, lovely," he said in a light voice. "After the commotion, I felt the need to stop by and confirm all was as well as well can be."

"She's heading to the Tower," Hatter said. "Maybe you can make sure she doesn't get into any trouble along the way."

I wanted to say that I didn't generally get into trouble just walking down the street, but the truth was, I had screwed up a couple times during my last trip here, and with the Queen of Hearts gunning specifically for me, I didn't exactly mind the idea of having a guard of my own. Especially one as built as Chess was. Even with the loud yellow shirt he was wearing covering most of his torso, you could tell the guy had muscles upon muscles.

"If you were thinking of going that way anyway," I

said, and swooped in on the scone platter. Hatter had gotten a couple of my favorite flavor: vanilla-cranberry-pine. He caught my eye with a pleased glint in his as I scooped them up, the sweetly tart scent already making my mouth water. "And I'll take breakfast with me. Thank you!"

Chess made an elaborate gesture with his hand as he dipped his head. "I promise to return her to you with all pieces intact."

"You'd better," Hatter grumbled.

"You'd better make sure you both stay in one piece too," I shot back before I followed Chess out the door.

Chess sauntered through the city as if he didn't have a care in the world, but he managed to be stealthy at the same time. We rambled down winding alleys that took us on a more direct route toward the silver spire that shone against the clear blue sky up ahead. Theo's office and apartment were up near the top of that tower.

"I do believe every time I see the Queen, her skirts have added another layer," Chess murmured to me. "Perhaps soon they'll swallow her up and save us the trouble."

As much as the sight of the Queen had chilled me, my lips twitched at the image he'd drawn. "I guess you saw her pretty regularly when you used to hang out with the Diamonds?" I said. He'd told me he used to visit regularly with the diamond-brooch-wearing courtiers who lived alongside the royal family in and around the palace.

"Ah, I preferred to steer clear of her even then. She does put you off your whatever-you-happen-to-be-having.

And the only point in going to the palace is to have quite a lot."

"Hatter said she thinks I'm here to overthrow her," I said.

"It's an easy thing for her to predict," Chess said. "Nearly everyone wants to. The issue isn't the motive but rather the means."

He looked down at me as we walked into the Tower. The dimmer light inside didn't dull his bright auburn hair. "You needn't worry, Lyssa," he said. "A Spade dug in is there to stay. We've danced around her for ages."

"She caught Sally."

His glib demeanor faded for a second. "Sally was on her own," he said. "We'll see that you always have company, wanted or not." He punctuated that last comment with a wink.

We came to a stop in the tight but tall elevator shaft that appeared to run up the height of the entire building. My arm brushed Chess's, and my mind darted back to last night, after our victory, when I'd told him I wanted him too and he'd offered himself for a kiss.

He hadn't touched me in any purposeful way the whole walk here. Chess never seemed to worry much about anything, but it was hard to tell what was going on beneath his jokes and wordplay. Had he enjoyed that kiss as much as I had? Or was he regretting it now that the moment and the victory high had faded?

I wasn't used to being this flustered by three guys at once. But there was something so compelling about all of them in their different ways.

"About last night," I said, willing my tongue not to tangle. "The part at the end… I didn't mean for you to feel at all pressured. If you're not sure it's really such a good idea or whatever—I won't be offended."

Chess blinked at me. Then his eyebrows lifted as he must have made sense of my rambling. "You're talking about the kissing part. You're worried I might have decided I object?"

My cheeks heated. "Um, yeah, basically. I don't expect that you *have* to be into me that way. I only want that kind of company if you really want it too, you know?"

The smile he gave me then was a softer version of his usual grin, his expression so tender it sent a giddy quiver through me.

"I think this once I can produce an answer as straight-forward as you could ask for." He raised his head to speak to the elevator. "Twenty-seventh floor. Chess coming calling with Lyssa."

With a lurch, the cushion of air beneath us hurtled us upward. In the same moment, Chess traced his fingers over my cheek and lowered his mouth to mine. His kiss was as sweet as it had been last night, as tender as his smile. My heart leapt with it and with the rush of the air moving past. When he eased back as the elevator slowed, my head spun for a moment as I recovered my balance.

Yep, that was all the answer I needed right there.

"All right then," I said. "I'm glad we got that sorted out."

Chess let out a laugh that practically sparkled and nudged open one of the doors to Theo's office.

And here was the third man I'd been kissing last night.

The White Knight had the kind of presence that filled a room, no matter how many other people were around him. As we came in, Theo looked up from where he was standing by his sleek white desk in the stark white room, where he'd been talking with the redheaded twins who'd helped yesterday's mission. His stance was casual, the motion of his head subdued, but even if you'd never met him before, you'd have been able to tell he was calling the shots. Clothed in his usual white collared shirt and gray slacks, his tall muscular frame wasn't as brawny as Chess's, but it exuded confidence and power.

"I was hoping you'd make your way here this morning, Lyssa," he said in his smooth baritone, with a smile that felt just for me. His dark brown gaze swept from me to Chess. "And Chess, you've got perfect timing. Can you scout out a secure location for a meeting this afternoon? Dee and Dum will round up as many of us as they can."

"As your Knightliness commands," Chess said with an extravagant flourish that ended in a salute. He blinked out of sight as his hand dropped to his side, leaving behind only the flash of his grin for a second before it vanished too.

Chess could turn invisible at will. A man of many talents.

The twins ambled to the elevator, presumably to follow him. The one wearing an orange polo shirt with blue slacks and bowtie shot me a quick smile. The one with a blue shirt and orange slacks and bowtie glanced at me and then away. I wasn't sure which was which, but they weren't identical in friendliness.

Theo came over to join me. He took in my expression, one of his chestnut curls falling across his forehead as his eyes searched mine. His face wasn't perfect, his Roman nose slightly crooked, but that imperfection only made his handsome face more striking.

"The procession came past Hatter's house," he said, not bothering to make it a question.

The memory of the parade of guards and Sally's head bobbing in their midst made my throat constrict. I nodded.

Theo's mouth twisted. "I wish you hadn't needed to see just how vicious Wonderland can be. As you can probably imagine, the Queen's declaration has to put a temporary hold on our plans to get you home. We need to decide how to respond to her threat quickly."

"Of course," I said. It hadn't even occurred to me that he'd be worrying about how to get me to the one remaining mirror he knew of, the one deep within the palace of the Hearts, not with this menace looming over the people he'd dedicated himself to leading.

Now that he'd mentioned it, a pang filled my chest. Melody had been so worried about me when I'd returned home bleeding a few days ago. My mom fretted about me even when I wasn't facing down swords and daggers. If they realized I was missing, completely vanished from the only world they knew of…

But while I was here in Wonderland, time seemed to pass much more slowly in the Otherland where I belonged. I shouldn't be gone for long enough for anyone to worry back home until a couple weeks had passed here. If getting to the mirror took longer than that... I'd tackle that problem when I got to it.

"I do have something for you." Theo retrieved a container about the size and shape of a toothpaste tube from his pocket. "This salve should heal most of your wound so it won't cause you as much pain—and it'll be less noticeable to searching eyes."

I shouldn't have been surprised he'd have taken the time to take care of that with everything else going on. Part of the Inventor's job was coming up with plans, and Theo seemed to have a plan for everything.

"Thank you," I said.

He motioned for me to hold out my arm. The stitches stood out against the angry red line that ran from my wrist almost all the way to my elbow. Theo squeezed out a dollop of a swirling green-and-white gel that even looked like toothpaste.

A cool tingle spread through my skin and down into my muscles as he gently rubbed the gel down the length of the wound. The stitches and the redness faded. By the time he reached my elbow, the cut that had been gushing blood four days ago was little more than a thin pink line across my pale skin. Nothing visible from a distance; nothing noteworthy.

Theo's hand lingered on my arm. He was standing just a foot away, close enough that the warmth of his body tingled over me too. I had an awful lot of tantalizing memories of him—when he'd pushed me up against the tunnel wall for an incredible kiss last night, when we'd had the best sex of my life floating beyond gravity in one of his Inventor rooms here.

But as much as I enjoyed those memories, I wasn't here to get distracted all over again.

"I actually came because I might be able to help you deal with the Queen," I said. "When I went home the second time, I opened the box my grand-aunt left me. There was a ring in it that I think is important somehow, in a way the Queen wouldn't like."

Theo's thumb paused where it had been brushing over my arm in a comforting caress. "A ring?" he said.

"I'll show you." I fished it out from under my shirt. "It appears to have some kind of Wonderland magic."

CHAPTER THREE

Theo

I t took every ounce of control I had to keep my expression relaxed while Lyssa undid the clasp on the chain around her neck so she could slide off the ring. Could it really be what I thought?

And if it was, how could we use it?

She clicked open the golden shell that guarded the stone. My bright office lights reflected through the square ruby setting, flashing crimson as she handed the ring to me. A tiny point protruded from the otherwise smooth surface of its face.

My fingers tightened around the gold band. It hadn't been lost at all—or not completely, in any case.

"You said your grand-aunt left this for you?" I said, my voice sounding far away to my own ears.

"Yeah, just the ring and a letter that didn't explain much." Lyssa grimaced and tucked a stray strand of hair

behind her ear. "But I know it has to do with Wonderland
—I saw a symbol just like that gem on a ruined wall out
near the Topsy Turvy Woods. It was on Aunt Alicia's box
too. Well, the symbol also had what I thought was a
teardrop in the middle of the gem, but I think that's
because—if you prick your finger on that point—"

She reached out as if she meant to demonstrate
herself, but I couldn't resist the urge to tap my own thumb
to the ruby's surface. The sharp protrusion nicked my skin
with a pinch of pain, and a drop of blood fell on the
stone. It lay there dully for a second before leaching away
into the gem.

What else could I have expected? This ring wasn't
meant for me. It wasn't meant for anyone still living.

"Oh," Lyssa said, sounding surprised, as if *she'd*
expected something different. "Maybe my eyes were just
playing tricks on me before. Can I…?"

I handed the ring over, wondering what she meant.
She touched her own thumb to the point. Blood welled
from her skin onto the gem—and the ruby lit up from the
inside as if someone had sparked a torch within it.

Every muscle in my body went rigid. No. No, it
couldn't be. That was impossible.

I hadn't bitten my tongue, but a coppery flavor crept
across it as if the blood had fallen into my mouth instead
of onto the stone. My stomach listed. I found myself
staring at Lyssa's face as if I'd find an answer written there.
The trouble was, I didn't even know what to look for.
How could I when… when…

"I don't know why it did that for me and not for you,"

Lyssa said. "So weird." She looked up, and her blue eyes widened. "Is something wrong? Is that a bad sign or something?"

Damn. So much for control. I sucked in a breath with the most blasé chuckle I could summon, forcing the clash of emotions inside me as far down as I could shove them.

She didn't know. She didn't know anything, and that meant I could still decide how this discovery played out. I could make sure it did help us rather than hurt us, as much as possible—all of us, including Lyssa.

"I certainly hope not," I said. "I'm not sure what to make of it. What did your grand-aunt say about the ring?"

"Just that she wanted me to have it. And she said some vague things about how our family was tied to Wonderland and some purpose that she realized she had. I'm not even sure how much that has to do with the ring specifically."

My body relaxed a little more. My thoughts were still spinning. "Quite the mystery, then. Did she say where it came from?"

Lyssa shook her head. "After seeing the same symbol on that ruin, I have to think she got it in Wonderland … That wall looked like it'd been around since way before her time. Although I guess if there were other Alices from our family before her, who knows?"

Hatter or Chess must have finally filled her in on the pattern of Otherlander women who came through the looking-glass. A pattern that apparently wasn't a coincidence after all. I reached for the easy composure that would have had the right words to say next slipping off my tongue, but I couldn't quite find it. Nothing I'd heard or been told lined up with the spark of that ruby as it drank Lyssa's blood.

Lyssa snapped the protective casing back into place around the gem and restrung the ring on her chain. "You don't know anything about the ring or that symbol in general, then?" she said, sounding disappointed.

She'd been counting on me to have answers. That was what nearly everyone in Wonderland counted on me for, one way or another. I'd encouraged that reliance, but suddenly it felt like a weight on my spine.

I needed to think, but I couldn't with her right here waiting. If I was going to tell her anything, I had to do it now.

Without any definite intention, my hand rose to stroke over Lyssa's hair. She leaned into my touch automatically, her expression softening. This woman was made of courage and honesty, and she trusted me. I'd been willing to give her up, to see her home last night, despite all the good I'd thought she might be able to do for Wonderland. She deserved to be able to make her own choices.

But if the ruby shone true, then she might be our key to saving everything.

One small kernel of certainty rose up through my confusion. It wouldn't help any of us if I laid the full truth on her right now. We weren't ready to challenge the Queen on that scale yet either way. Lyssa had to spend more time with us here before she could make a real choice anyway—before she even had the option of going home. I'd spent my entire life trapped. I didn't want to inflict the same sensation on her.

Let her settle in here, let her see what this land could be, let *me* have time to work out the matter for myself, and then perhaps she could hear it without panicking. Once word got out, if she took a wrong step, she might be dead before she had the chance to make any choice at all.

If we were to challenge the Queen, this discovery opened up new avenues nonetheless. Even as I grappled with the idea at all, part of my mind was already spinning plans. I'd proven myself in the job of Inventor honestly, at least.

"I've heard legends about the blood-marked ruby," I said, picking my words carefully. "It's been said that there are tools of battle marked with the symbol that contain some sort of magic. It could be that ring activates their power? From what I understand, the Queen of Hearts wasn't able to destroy those artifacts, so she disposed of them in the distant parts of Wonderland, as well as she could hide them. If that *is* more than legend."

Lyssa's face brightened so quickly that guilt twisted my gut. "Tools of battle," she said. "Something we could use to push back against the Queen—to stop her from going through with the awful plan she announced?"

"There's a chance," I said. "It would take time to find the artifacts, though, assuming they exist at all, and we'd need to determine where to search. There's much more to Wonderland than you've had the opportunity to see. I'll need to investigate further."

"What about Mirabel?" Lyssa asked. "She's told me

things about the past—and the future—that ended up making sense. She might be able to see something about the ring or those tools, right?"

I'd have preferred to speak to our White Queen on my own, but now that Lyssa had mentioned it, I'd rather have her feel involved than put her off. "She very well might," I said. "We could stop by right now."

It was a short hop in the elevator to the next floor. Mirabel called out a cheerful, "Come in," at my knock. We found her in her room of many chairs, curled up on her favorite sofa with her knitting. Her needles worked at a languid pace on what looked like a shawl-in-progress. It didn't appear any recent dreams or memories had stirred up to agitate her.

She sat straighter as we approached with a welcoming smile. She'd left her hair down today, and the golden-brown curls spilled over the broad neck of a white woolen dress she must have knitted too. A faint sound like softly tinkling chimes drifted through the room with its various pastel shades.

"You found him," she said to Lyssa, looking pleased.

Lyssa glanced at me. "I came asking about you yesterday before I found the meeting." Her gaze slid back to Mirabel. "I mean, if that's what you're talking about."

It was often difficult to tell. I wasn't sure Mirabel generally knew herself. She tipped her head vaguely and motioned for us to sit down. "It's the best I can do to help," she said.

With the way her mind worked, dislodged from time and catching glimpses of past and future, she might very well be more prepared for our conversation than we were. Unfortunately, she didn't have much sway over where her thoughts wandered. A result, at least in part, of the blow she'd taken to her head years before my time. The rippled pink skin of the scar peeked from her hairline at her temple.

She could moderate how many of her thoughts she shared, though. I made a small downward gesture with my hand as Lyssa and I sat in neighboring chairs. *Keep any remarks limited.* Mirabel caught my eye and gave me a tiny nod.

"I don't know how much you already know about why we're here," Lyssa said. "But Theo's told me that there are tools we might be able to use to take on the Hearts—ones that have a symbol of a 'blood-marked ruby' on them? They could be hidden somewhere in Wonderland. I thought you might have some idea where we should look." She showed Mirabel the ring. "I have this too. It seems to be connected somehow."

"When Lyssa pricks her finger on its surface, the ruby glows," I said in a measured voice.

Mirabel's eyes flickered, and she knit her brow. "Ah," she said with a rough laugh. "I see."

Lyssa leaned forward. "You do?"

"That is—" The White Queen stopped and collected herself, setting her knitting in her lap. "Let me see what I can remember."

"Anything about the tools would be especially helpful," I said.

"Yes. Yes." Her eyelids drifted down until they were

nearly shut. She swayed a bit to the side, her fingers smoothing over the skirt of her dress, her lips tensing.

"They have been found too," she said after a moment in a wisp of a voice. "The sword, the scepter, and the shield. I don't think they offered the strength you were hoping for. But they led you to the truth of your heart."

"The sword, the scepter, and the shield," Lyssa repeated. "Do you know where I'll find—where I found them?"

"Where she searched before, before she'll flee," Mirabel murmured. "The one who came after, who'll leave the ring. She could have—but she ran. The course was clear ahead. He'll wait for her."

She winced and opened her eyes. "Thank you," Lyssa said quickly. "That's a lot. That's—I think that's somewhere to start. You must mean my grand-aunt Alicia, I think? She's the one who left the ring for me. She ran away from Wonderland." She turned to me. "Aunt Alicia didn't tell me anything in her letter about searching for something here, but I can ask Hatter. He might know if she went farther out into Wonderland and where."

Perfect. A clear lead—and a reason for her to leave so I could sort myself out. I got up with her and walked her to the door. But watching her smile, so pleased to have a way to help *us*, every bone balked at the idea of letting her simply walk out.

She hadn't asked for a part in any of the troubles we'd ended up laying on her, but she'd jumped in feet-first. So sweet yet determined that my heart squeezed, looking at her.

I wouldn't let any harm come to her.

"Keep that ring out of sight," I said, setting my hand on her shoulder. "If the Queen of Hearts has reason to fear it, it'll only make you a greater target. Do you want me to escort you back to Hatter's?"

"I think I'll be okay," Lyssa said. "I'm learning all the sneaky routes from Chess. You've got a ton of other things to deal with without babysitting me. I'll be careful."

It was the answer I'd wanted, but I still found it hard to let her go. No matter who else she might be, she was still Lyssa, the woman who'd shared her struggles with me so openly, the woman who'd come apart with pleasure in my arms just a few nights ago.

I couldn't help myself. I didn't just care for her—I wanted her, too.

I brought my fingers to her jaw to lift her chin, and she bobbed up on her toes to meet the kiss I'd been about to offer. The fresh smell of her, like a spring breeze, filled my lungs. Her mouth tasted like tart vanilla, and her lips moved against mine so pliantly it took another gargantuan effort of self-control to ease back.

She beamed at me, her cheeks flushed and her eyes sparkling. Another jab of guilt bit into my gut.

The moment Lyssa had descended the elevator, I poked my head out into the tunnel and said, "Third floor, follow." A second later, Griffon slipped out of the apartment there with a nod of acknowledgment to me. He'd make sure she stayed safe until I could join her again.

When I turned back to Mirabel, she'd gotten up from

the sofa, her knitting left behind. "The ring," she said. She didn't really need to say more than that.

My mouth tightened. "Yes."

"So it finally came back."

She didn't sound surprised. She hadn't looked surprised until I'd mentioned the glow, and then only briefly.

"Did you know?" I had to ask, even though I realized I might not get a straight answer.

"I... I might have and then forgotten. It can all be so hazy." She looked me up and down, and I suspected her gaze caught more than the surface of me. Her voice came out gentle. "You must have heard the stories, baby brother. You knew."

My hands clenched at my sides. "I believed it was over, far back in the past, before any of us. It's different hearing it in that distant way and then seeing right in front of you the proof that the tragedy hasn't actually ended. How can I— I hardly know where to start."

"Does it matter that much to you what she signifies?"

"It means I have more wrongs to right than I realized," I said. "And the worst of them may stand in conflict with each other."

"No one can fix everything," Mirabel said. "They weren't your wrongs."

"But they are, too. If I ever want to really lead..."

That was the deepest truth of it, wasn't it? I hadn't let myself dream often of the future time when we might have displaced the Queen of Hearts entirely, when I might steer Wonderland from a throne rather than from the shadows. I would be the obvious choice when the Hearts in the palace fell. I shouldn't have cared about that, but I did.

Of course, nothing I'd learned today had to change that if I laid my plans right.

I swallowed hard. *That* one answer was clear. We needed Lyssa to stay. It was best for Wonderland, and best for everything I might have wanted for myself. And yet I couldn't commit to it.

It was the best possible outcome anyone here could have asked for—anyone except, perhaps, for Lyssa.

CHAPTER FOUR

Lyssa

"Magical artifacts?" Hatter said. "Blood-marked ruby? I've never heard legends about any of that."

I leaned onto the table across from him. He was nimbly attaching a twinkling veil to a wide-brimmed sunhat in the back workroom of his shop. The small space had a dry velvety smell to it. I could practically taste the felt on the shelves—as well as Hatter's skepticism.

"That's the whole reason you suggested I talk to Theo, isn't it?" I pointed out. "Because as Inventor, he's heard all kinds of things not everyone has?"

Hatter made a disgruntled sound that I took to mean he accepted my point but wished he didn't have to. I hesitated, torn between memories of the way he'd clammed up when I'd asked him about his history before and the itch of curiosity.

We'd cleared the air between us, hadn't we? If I could make out with a guy, be perfectly prepared to sleep with him, I should be able to ask a simple question. How many times had Melody gotten on my case about trying too hard to be the "cool girlfriend" who never brought up anything uncomfortable? *A good guy will want to talk things through. A not-good guy doesn't deserve you, Lyss.*

I braced myself for his reaction. "I know you have issues with the way Theo has let Doria help out the Spades," I said. "But you used to work together, didn't you? Back when you were a regular part of the group. Is there some other bad blood between you—did something else happen?"

Hatter glanced up, the surprise in his eyes reassuring me. "No," he said. "Well, nothing he did, exactly. My priorities changed. It made me start wondering exactly where his priorities are. But I can't say he's done anything *wrong*. He certainly knows how to draw up a plan. I can recognize that he's on Wonderland's side as much as anyone is."

He gave me a crooked smile. "You know I've been doing some re-evaluating lately. I suppose I should ease off on him while I decide whether he really has been incautious or it's all been over-caution on my side of things."

"That's very generous of you," I said in a teasing voice, and Hatter fixed me with one of his glowers, with enough warmth behind it that it made me a little tingly. Focus, Lyssa.

"It seems like Aunt Alicia might have gone looking for

the artifacts," I said. "She did find the ring, anyway. Did she ever mention going farther out into Wonderland?"

"Not that I remember." Hatter gave the veil one last tuck and moved on to an arrangement of flowers on a fascinator. "But she could have traveled around without me knowing about it. I only saw her through her involvement with the Spades."

I frowned. "And no one else from those days is still around. Theo made it sound like it'd be pretty hard to track these things down without a starting point. I wish she'd left instructions or something."

Hatter paused, twirling a peacock feather between his thumb and forefinger. "There is actually one other person she often ran with back then who's managed to keep his head," he said slowly.

"What?" I straightened up with my fingers splayed on the table. "Why didn't you tell me before? You said everyone else was gone."

"Well, he…" Hatter grimaced. "Carpenter has changed a lot since those days. I'd imagine the main reason he's kept his head is he's put it and the rest of him in service of the Queen. The work he does these days… I don't know how he stomachs it. He'd probably turn a Spade in sooner than lend them a hand. We can't trust him. But he might have some idea of Alicia's travels that I don't."

"We have to go talk to him then," I said. "We don't have to tell him it's anything to do with the Spades. Tell him we want to help the Queen too or whatever. It's not like you've been part of the rebellion for a while anyway."

"*We* are not doing anything," Hatter said firmly, pressing another feather into place without even needing to look at his hands. "If he gets even the slightest suspicion that you're related to Alicia, he'll be carting you off to the Queen. I don't want you getting within a mile of Carpenter."

My stomach dropped. "But if I could find the artifacts—"

"I'll go," Hatter said. "On my own. He knows me. He won't be as suspicious. I should be able to approach it in a way that won't clue him in to our purpose." He attached the last of the feathers and considered the spread with an approving eye. Then he raised his head again. "I can go today. We're in a bit of a bind for time, aren't we?"

Gratitude swept through me so quickly it clogged my throat for a second. "I— Thank you. Are you sure you'll be all right going by yourself? If this guy is on the Queen's side now as much as you said… You didn't want to be part of anything to do with the Spades at all just a couple days ago."

It was my idea he was following up on. He shouldn't have to take on all the risks.

"Hey." Hatter came around the table and took my hand. His bright green eyes held mine. "I trust that if you think this is a lead we should pursue, there really is something there. I convinced myself for a long time that keeping out of the rebellion was the best thing for the people I cared about, but it didn't get us any closer to freedom. That mission last night did. Honestly, it felt good to dive back into the action."

I'd been able to see that in the eagerness that had energized him as we'd made our way through the palace. His words didn't completely erase my guilt, though.

"I'd just feel horrible if anything happened to you because of me," I said quietly.

"You don't need to worry, looking-glass girl," Hatter said with a wry smile. "I'll be fine. Believe me, I survived many exploits far more dangerous when I lived and breathed the Spades. I might be dipping my toes back in, but I'm not going to tempt danger unnecessarily. My days of being Mad Hatter are long over."

Mad Hatter. That was a side of him I definitely hadn't seen yet. He sounded so sure of himself that I let myself nod. I'd only be putting him in more danger if I insisted on coming along, wouldn't I?

"Well then," I said, "for luck." I slipped my hand behind his neck and kissed him.

Hatter kissed me back with a restrained hunger that left me giddy. When he drew back, his eyes were sparkling.

When we passed through the shop, Doria was sitting on the counter, peering at herself in a layered confection of a hat draped with silk. The mint-green shade didn't totally fit with her ruffled black dress, as she apparently decided for herself. She tossed the hat back onto the shelf and hopped off the counter.

"I have to run an errand," Hatter told her. "Stick with Lyssa? I don't really want either of you wandering around on your own with the Queen in her current mood."

"Whatever you say, Pops," Doria said.

He ruffled her hair in response to the nickname. "I'll be back tonight, hopefully not too late. Why don't you talk with Lyssa about the thing we were discussing earlier?" He glanced at me. "I'll see you soon with whatever answers I can pry out of him."

He set off with a tip of his hat and a swish of his suit jacket.

"The thing?" I asked Doria.

"Come on," she said, motioning to the stairs.

In the apartment, she led me on up to the fourth floor where she slept. The top level of the building was set up like another apartment in itself, with an open concept kitchen-living area about half the size of Hatter's main one and two bedrooms down the hall. Doria went into the master bedroom at the end, where an unscreened window looked out over a bit of roof and the back alley. The bedspread on the queen-sized mattress was rumpled, but I knew no one had slept here in years.

Doria set her hands on her hips. "This was my parents' bedroom," she said. "My birth parents, I mean. Dad was thinking you should sleep in here instead of the guest room downstairs, so you can hop out the window onto the roof right away if the Knave or whoever comes by again. We can clean things up now that Time isn't stuck anymore."

My pulse hiccupped as I looked at her. Doria's birth parents had been killed when she was a toddler by the order of the Queen of Hearts—because of their involvement with the Spades, from what I'd gathered. When we'd escaped onto the roof to hide before, I'd seen the shapes of their long-absent bodies left under that bedspread, frozen in time like the rest of Wonderland. They were gone, but this room had remained as if they'd never left.

"Are you okay with that?" I asked.

Doria shrugged. "That's what Dad asked me too. It's really not that big a deal. I don't even remember them, you know? This is all just... stuff. Anything I want to keep, I'll stick in my room. I can do that now." She grinned and then reached for the bed covers. "For starters, these haven't been washed in about fifty years."

Thanks to the resetting of time over those years, no dust stirred up as we stripped the bed and remade it with fresh sheets or when we moved to the desk in the corner and the wardrobe beside it. We picked up the few pieces of worn clothing that had been left draped on a chair or a knob. I brought a glass ringed with wine and a plate dappled with crumbs over to the kitchen.

Doria grabbed what must have been her mother's jewelry box and all the darker dresses out of the wardrobe. I hauled the ones she'd picked out for me to borrow back upstairs from the guest bedroom. We shook out the rug over the edge of the roof and left the window open so the warm breeze could drift through. It carried a faintly buttery smell from the bakery down the street where Hatter bought his scones.

Doria studied the stacks of folded shirts and slacks that had been her birth father's with a cock of her head. "I guess I'll ask Dad if he wants any of these, and otherwise we'll take them to the clothing shop," she said. "They're not really his style." She hesitated. "Maybe I'll just keep one shirt. To hang on to it."

"Of course," I said. "I think it's good to hold onto a few things, for when you want to remember—or at least think about them." I sank down on the edge of the bed. "I —I lost my dad too, when I was eight. I've still got a pair of his old gloves tucked away in one of my drawers back home." Big sheepskin ones, so soft when my dad had picked me up and spun me around when I'd been little. Whenever I smelled them, I remembered those first winters—the couple I could remember from before his illness—perfectly.

Doria sat down on the other end of the bed, leaning against one of the wooden posts with her legs drawn up in front of her. "What happened to your dad?" she asked.

"He got sick," I said. "Cancer. I guess that's not really a thing here." Chess had told me there were no illnesses in Wonderland. I groped for a way to explain it. "It's basically—this thing starts growing inside you, crowding in on all the parts of you that you need to breathe and process the food you eat and… everything. We have treatments in the Otherland, but they don't always work. And when they do, sometimes it's just for a little while, and then the cancer comes back."

I didn't like thinking back to those memories—of Dad slumped so sallow and frail on the sofa or in his bed.

Doria grimaced. "That sounds awful."

"Yeah," I had to say. "It really is. He was sick for almost three years before he passed on, and he was really weak and in pain a lot of that time."

"You still had your mom, though?"

More than Doria had hers. "It was hard on her," I said. "For a while she went kind of… vacant. But she was *there*, and she got better, over time." Until then, I'd been the one who held the family together through her listlessness and my older brother Cameron's rages.

Kind of funny that here in Wonderland, where I literally had powers no one else did and a tyrant queen had spent decades crushing everyone's spirits, I had way more support than I'd been able to count on back then.

I couldn't let these people down. There had to be something more I could do to free them completely.

Doria hugged her knees. "Sometimes it pisses me off that I don't remember them at all," she said. "But sometimes I'm kind of glad. It would probably hurt more if I had a clearer idea what I was missing. Which doesn't mean I'm not still *really* pissed off at the Queen."

The corner of my mouth twitched upward. "Obviously. I guess there are upsides and downsides either way. At least you do have one really good dad, even if he hasn't been keen on everything you want to do." No one could see Hatter with Doria and fail to notice how much he loved her.

Doria smiled too. "Yeah," she said. "Parents are supposed to be annoying, right?" A spark of mischief lit in her eyes. "Speaking of which…"

"Uh huh?" I prompted with a raise of my eyebrows when she trailed off.

She twisted the corner of the bedspread in her hand. "Dee came by the shop and told me there's a meeting for all the Spades happening in a bit. I was planning on going."

Which meant either I convinced her not to or I went with her, if I was going to stay with her like Hatter had asked. From past experience, I didn't think the former option was going to pan out.

"I don't think he'll get angry at you for coming with me like he did last time," she added quickly. "He knows I'd go anyway. He even started coming to the meetings with me."

That was true. "I guess he didn't actually say we shouldn't go out anywhere," I said. "Only that we should stick together. And… if the Spades are making plans, I'd like to be in on them too."

Doria's face lit up. "Then it's settled," she declared, jumping up. "We'd better get going. It's almost time for the meeting to start."

CHAPTER FIVE

Lyssa

I t was kind of a shame that Hatter was missing the current meeting of the Spades, because Doria and I headed up the steps at the back entrance of a costume shop and found ourselves joining what looked like a giant tea party. A bright red table stretched the length of the room, set out with plates of cakes and cookies and pots of tea. I watched one of those pots lift up of its own accord to fill a cup it deemed had gotten too low.

Tall stools with low backs stood all around the table. The refreshments circulated a lot like the rotating conveyor belt at Melody's favorite sushi place, but instead of the food traveling around while the diners waited, the food stayed put and the chairs glided from spot to spot.

Actually, "hitched" was a more accurate word than "glided." The rotation stopped and started at an

unpredictable pattern and with a grinding whir that gave
me the impression the inner workings were starting to fail.
Yellow sheets papered over the place's broad front window,
and dust bunnies had gathered in the corners. The sugary
smell that laced the air was a little stale. But then, a
happening café wouldn't have made a very good secret
meeting spot.

Theo stood by the head of the table where the stools
shot straight around to the other side. He was the only
figure in the room not in motion. Twenty or so others
perched on the stools. Chess gave me a wave, and Doria
bounded over to the empty stool next to the redheaded
twins.

There were a *lot* of empty stools. Something like half
of them were unoccupied. My heart sank as I hopped
onto one between Chess and a burly guy I recognized
from the pre-mission meeting yesterday evening.

No wonder the Spades were having such a hard time
taking on the Queen of Hearts. The memory of this
morning's procession lingered in my mind—all those rows
of marching soldiers. Even if only half of the people Theo
might have counted on had shown up today, they couldn't
have risen up against the Hearts and won, not on
their own.

Looking at the faces around me, most of them drawn
and grim, I could tell they were well aware of that
fact too.

I hooked my feet behind the rung on the stool's base
to help me keep my balance as my seat lurched to the
right. There had to be some reason for hope. We'd just

ended one of the Queen's most awful acts of oppression. The Spades could make plans that spanned more than one day, build up more resources…

But the Queen's parade and proclamation probably felt much more real to them than our victory. They hadn't even gotten to experience one completely new day yet.

A couple more people trickled in, and then Theo cleared his throat. His warmly commanding baritone carried over the rasp of the mechanical chairs.

"You all know why we're meeting again so soon, and why I wanted as many of you here as possible, so let's not waste time rehashing this morning's events," he said. "Chess, you had a look around the palace grounds?"

"A look and a listen," Chess piped up from his seat beside me. Even *his* grin looked a bit strained. "From what I heard, the Queen has stayed true to her word and locked her current prisoner in the palace dungeon. That is, four floors beneath the ground level, with guards at every level in between."

"Attempting to break anyone out of there would be a suicide mission," the man at my other side said.

The pained set of Theo's mouth suggested he agreed. "Dee and Dum, your observations of the Hearts' Guard in the city?"

One of the twins sat up a shade straighter. "They've cut back on the patrols. Just ten guards that we saw making the rounds—talking to the Clubbers, making friendly." He wrinkled his nose. "They aren't so much trying to catch us outright as trying to make a point about why the rest of the city shouldn't count on us."

"Turning the Clubbers against us right when we might have had a real chance of convincing them to rise up," a woman across the table from me muttered around a mouthful of cookie.

"We can't forget that we struck a major blow against the Queen's rule last night," Theo said. "As difficult a problem as she's presented us with, we've *gained* ground. All this gambit means is that we need to rally our forces and gather more power to our side as quickly as possible."

His gaze found mine for an instant before my stool yanked me past him around the table. More power—like the artifacts he'd talked about. If one of them was a weapon—if Aunt Alicia's ring would allow us to use it— we *had* to find them. The Spades needed an advantage the Queen couldn't match. And we needed it before her dungeon filled up with innocent civilians.

With another jolt of the stool, I found myself facing a woman with a pointed face and beady eyes like a ferret. She stared straight at me, frowning.

"Why is the Otherlander still here?" she demanded. "The Queen is cracking down on us even harder because of her. We've got enough to worry about without that hassle too."

My fingers curled tighter around the edges of my seat. It hadn't occurred to me that I might be unwelcome here.

"I came back because I thought of a way I could help reach the watch," I said.

"And Lyssa did help us," Theo said, a stern note entering his voice. "We couldn't have freed Time without her. *Because* she was generous enough to put herself at risk so that we could break free of the cycle we'd been stuck in, she's now stuck here with us until we can see her to another looking-glass doorway."

"I'm doing everything I can to make sure I don't draw attention," I added, and motioned to my dyed hair, my clothes. "The Queen won't even know I *am* still here."

A mutter carried from farther down my current side of the table. "If the Otherlander really wants to help us, she should turn herself over. That would satisfy the Queen for a little while—or at least distract her."

My head jerked around, a chill seeping through my skin all the way to my gut. I couldn't tell who had spoken, but none of the faces I could see in that direction looked disturbed by the suggestion.

Chess caught my elbow, his grasp both steadying and protective. When I looked at him, he wasn't so much grinning as baring his sharpest teeth.

Theo's jaw had clenched with a flash of his dark brown eyes. His voice came out low but with a clear warning, so potent it sent a warm shiver under my skin despite my discomfort. "I sincerely hope we aren't turning to the same tactics as the Queen, volunteering others to make their sacrifices for us," he said.

"Of course not, White Knight," several of the Spades hurried to say. Flickers of horror passed through some of their expressions. But there were others who still looked tense, as if they weren't willing to speak up but didn't exactly have a problem with that one speaker's suggestion.

Chess's hand stayed on my arm. I swallowed hard, but my stomach was full of ice.

These people had been working together for years— for decades. I'd dropped into Wonderland for the first time ten days ago. Just with my name and where I was from, I'd provoked the Queen's paranoia and maybe driven her toward the measures she was taking. I couldn't really blame them for feeling uneasy about my presence, could I?

If I did turn myself in to the Queen, would that fix anything? A prickle ran along my neck at the thought. I'd be giving myself over to the same fate Sally had met. It *would* be my head on a pike paraded through the city.

And then what? She'd be happy for a few days before going back to crushing the rest of Wonderland? No. As sick as I'd felt hearing her call out for my capture this morning, I couldn't believe that sacrifice would be the right move in the long run, if I even had the spine to make it. Not now. Not while we still had other reasons to hope.

"There's another plan I'm working on," I said, with a glance toward Theo, looking for guidance. How much would he want me to say about the ring and the artifacts before we had anything more specific to offer? "I'm going to leave the city looking for something to give the Queen a good reason to be scared of me. So, I won't be here to get you in trouble, and if it works, I'll come back with a way to turn the tide in the Spades' favor."

"I'm assisting Lyssa in this venture," Theo put in. "I believe it's the best chance we have to overcome the Queen's rule completely."

"But that doesn't solve any of our problems today,

does it?" a rough voice said. A man with a horse-like mane, coarse and strung through with gray, bowed his head where his seat was approaching Theo. "Tomorrow the Queen is going to take more Wonderlanders for her prison. Can you say you'll have this plan ready to see through before her prison is full and she takes all those people to the chopping block?"

"Every day we stand back, the Clubbers will turn more against us," the ferret-eyed woman said. "How many of them might have looked the other way before but could point the finger at us now?"

Theo exhaled. "I won't lie to you. The results are still uncertain, and it will take time for us to discover how far we can take them. Which is why we are meeting here today—so we can decide together how we go forward."

A momentary hush fell over the table, leaving behind only the whir of the stools and the clink as someone set down a teacup.

"Could we bring more Clubbers over to our side now?" I asked tentatively. "They have to see how horrible the Queen is being, that she's the villain here. If all of the people who show up at Caterpillar's Club every night march on the palace, we'd have a chance."

"We've tried to inspire them to the cause," the man beside me said. "As more heads have rolled, fewer new ones have been swayed to our side. It's not that they don't see who the villain is, it's that they dislike the consequences of standing up to her."

The Clubbers needed a sign—like an artifact. Like magic. But we needed to give them that *now*.

"I'll go," the gray-haired man said. He set his gnarled hands on the tabletop, letting them slide when the stools shifted again. "I'll turn myself in to the palace in exchange for that girl. We can end this ridiculous challenge right now."

The ferret-eyed woman stared at him. "Smith…"

"I've only ever contributed bodily strength to the rebellion," Smith said, his voice weary but firm. "And my supply of that is dwindling. I've had a life longer than so many who've fallen to the Hearts' blades. We can prove that we won't let innocents die in our place and stop this horrible scheme of hers in its tracks before she can demand more than one of us. That will buy us time. It may convince a few of the Clubbers to find a little courage in themselves."

Every particle in my body balked at the idea of this man giving himself over to be killed. "This group is so small already," I said. "Can we really afford to lose anyone?"

He gave me a pained smile that he then turned on the rest of his comrades. "If we wait even until tomorrow, she'll demand more of us as a 'fair' trade. I've seen this moment on the horizon for years. I didn't know it would come this way, but at least it'll serve Wonderland more than if I was simply caught by a guard over the wrong comment overheard."

There had to be a better answer than that… didn't there? My gaze darted over the faces around me, but an air of resignation had come over the gathering. Theo left his spot at the head of the table to grip Smith's shoulder.

"If that is the choice you wish to make," he said, "it *is* yours to make. We'll make sure you're remembered often and well."

Even he couldn't see a way around this? I opened my mouth, wanting to protest more, but no real arguments came to me.

Who was I to argue anyway? The actual Spades were accepting this solution as if there was nothing so strange about it. Suddenly I could see why Hatter might have had qualms about the group's guiding philosophy.

They could be cutthroat in their own way when they wanted to be. They were willing to give up a life if it seemed to benefit more people than it hurt.

Doria had said there was no way the Spades could have killed the young prince, but watching this scene play out, I wasn't so sure she was right. If they were willing to send one of their friends to the slaughter, why would they balk at killing one of the Queen's children?

Smith stood up, and the rest of the Spades slid off their stools to gather around him, offering fond words and grateful gestures. I'd just gotten up awkwardly, not sure whether I had any place joining in, when a man with a lizard's head spun around where he'd been peering past a gap in the window's papering.

"There's a guard heading toward the building. Scatter!"

At those words, the group broke apart in an instant, everyone rushing toward the stairwell. My heartbeat stuttered as I caught up with Doria. Theo reached us a second later, his hand coming to rest on my back, his expression tense.

"The Tower is closer than Hatter's house," he said. "Come with me."

He motioned to the twins too. All of us hustled down the stairs and into the alley behind the shop.

The other Spades scattered in various directions, slowing their pace and taking on a casual demeanor as they spread out. Theo led the four of us through a gap between two buildings so narrow I had to walk sideways to fit, across the street to another alley, and then out onto the cobblestone road just a short jog from the silver spire the White Knight called home.

He knew his way around the city like Chess did. I guessed that shouldn't surprise me. The thought of Chess made me glance around, but the other man hadn't come with us.

Chess should be safe. He could simply blink out of view if a guard came too close.

Somber silence filled the elevator shaft as it propelled us up to the twenty-seventh floor. When we reached Theo's level with its doors on every side, Doria rubbed her hand over her face and glanced at the twins.

"Since we're here anyway... It's been a long time since I got to challenge you guys in the games room. Who's up for blowing off some steam?"

"Sounds extremely satisfying to me," the more smiley twin said. His brother didn't look as enthusiastic, but he glanced at Theo as if for permission.

"Be my guest," Theo said. "You *are* my guests for the

moment. I'll rouse you when it's safe to leave."

Doria stopped long enough to inform me, "I'll be fine. The worst thing that'll happen is the evil eye from these guys when I whoop their asses." Then she pushed open the silver door as if she knew exactly where she was going. The twins tagged along behind her, one of them laughing as he challenged her prediction of whose ass would be whooped.

Theo eased open the gold door. It opened into the hallway outside his office. I glanced around, disoriented— I'd gotten into the habit of choosing the bronze door, and it always took me right into the office-slash-workroom— and Theo's arm came back around me.

"You look like you need to sit down," he said gently.

I let him usher me into the lounge room we'd relaxed in before. My spine stayed stiff as I sat down on one of the cozy sofas. Theo sat at the other end, studying me.

"I'm sorry you had to hear some of those things," he said. "No one there would really try to send you off to the Queen. They're just frustrated, hardly thinking straight. We barely had a few hours to feel we'd accomplished anything before she found a new way to box us in."

Could he really say with so much certainty that they hadn't meant it? He might never consider lowering himself to those tactics, but I'd felt the hostility in that room, even if it'd been brief. I had the urge to ask him about the prince's murder and the responsibility the Spades shrugged off, but showing I doubted him felt like an insult. He'd indicated before that he didn't believe the Spades had anything to do with that death either.

It didn't matter anyway. By all accounts and all evidence, the Queen had been awful before her son died, and no one death could justify the torture she'd put all of Wonderland through.

"I know," I said. "Is there really nothing else we can do except let Smith get himself *killed*?"

Theo's mouth twisted. He didn't need to tell me how much he hated the solution he'd accepted. *He* would never have agreed to killing anyone in retribution, especially a kid.

"Sometimes the best we can do is make a small concession to prevent a larger tragedy," he said. "I don't like it, and if no one had offered themselves, I'd have gambled on us retrieving the artifacts in time—on them making enough of a difference. But I won't stop someone willing."

A lump rose in my throat. I didn't want to die, but the situation we were in was a lot more my fault than Smith's.

"I feel so useless," I said. "The Queen is angry about me, and I'm not doing anything to change that."

"You're doing everything you can," Theo said. "What did you find out from Hatter?"

"He's gone to talk to Carpenter," I said. "He isn't sure whether he'll know anything—or tell Hatter anything —though."

"But he might." Theo eased forward so that his knees rested against mine and took my hand. "I know Hatter. He wouldn't go trekking across the land on too slim a chance. So you wait, and when he comes back, then you can move forward."

"What if it's still not enough?"

"You've already done more than anyone in Wonderland has managed to accomplish in nearly fifty years," he said. "Don't you dare beat yourself up for not having even more answers than the rest of us do."

So much passion rang through those words that most of my doubts disintegrated. I was doing it again—feeling like I had to take on the responsibilities for everyone around me. For an entire country, now, instead of just my family. I dragged in my breath and managed a smile. "Okay. I'll work on that."

Theo's thumb traced a line across the back of my hand. The warm contact brought back the memories of all the even more enjoyable ways he'd touched me just a few days ago. But his gaze was still fixed on my face, his eyes dark with concern. "I know you have plenty of other reasons to be unsettled. What do you need right now, Lyssa?"

With him touching me like that, looking at me with so much determination and affection, the answer rose straight from the core of me.

"I need you," I said.

Something shifted in Theo's eyes, almost as if I'd surprised him. Then he moved forward, his hand sliding to my waist, the other rising to tease along my jaw. When his mouth finally met mine, I was starving for him.

I could have this. For now, while I waited to find out what else I could give, I'd have whatever he would give me.

CHAPTER SIX

Hatter

I smelled Carpenter's workplace before I saw it. A ring of tall craggy rocks sheltered the Oyster Cove, but the mingling odors of salt, seaweed, and raw flesh drifted along the paved path that led out there. I breathed through my mouth, more and more shallowly the closer I got.

If it hadn't been for the smell, the cove would have looked appealing enough at a glance. The blue-gray water lapped the shore along its crescent of pink sand. In the distance, across the larger endless expanse of sea, a few scattered clouds were turning purple as the sun sank toward the horizon. The wind made a cheerful whistling sound as it passed through the gaps in the rocks.

All perfectly pleasant until you noticed the wooden cart pulled off to the side with a headless body lying prone within it.

Carpenter was down at the edge of the water next to a dimpled metal track that stretched from halfway up the beach to deep within the water. He'd put on more bulk since I'd last seen him, years ago, but his legs were still just as short. His rounded gut pressed into his knees as he crouched down. I didn't know how he could bear to eat at all, let alone in excess, carrying the memories of his time here.

Another form moved in the water. Walrus surfaced, his coarse gray skin dotted with liver marks, the wet collar of his shirt clinging to his wide neck.

"This one's ready!" he announced in his guttural voice. "Sending 'im up."

He gave a heave, and the water rippled as a marble platform surged along the track to the shore. Carpenter spread his meaty hands to catch the end. A greenish-black casing, which in my humble opinion more closely resembled an immense seedpod than an oyster's shell, sprawled across the entire length of the platform, water trickling off its ridged surface. Carpenter hauled the platform all the way up the sand and then stepped around to the side.

I cleared my throat, walking out of the shade by the ring of rock. "Carpenter. I heard I'd find you out here this afternoon."

Carpenter's egg-shaped head came up. He still had the same short brown beard, grizzled now with flecks of silver. His hazy blue eyes, like a pale reflection of the water, widened at the sight of me. The grin that crossed his face looked more amused than anything. That seemed to bode well for this visit.

"Hatter!" he said. "It's been a long time. What in the lands brings you all the way out here, far from your city comforts?"

The ribbing note in that question wasn't entirely friendly. A reminder to keep my guard well up, even if I saw reason for optimism.

"I realized what a long time it had been," I said. "And I thought you might be missing some of those comforts. When was the last time you got your hands on one of Baker's mince pies?" I held up the box tied with cloth that I'd picked up from the bakery before heading out here.

Carpenter's face brightened just as I'd hoped it would. When we'd been friends, I'd seen him down as many as five of those pies in the course of a meal. It was both a gesture of good will and a callback to the past times I wanted to get him talking about.

"Let me finish up here," he said. "I've got an oyster to hatch and another to plant. Do you want to help?"

The question felt like a test. I didn't want to, in the strongest possible terms, but I needed to win points with my former comrade, not lose them.

"Why not?" I said, as if I found nothing about his work unsettling. I set down the boxed pie and then my suit jacket on top of it, rolled up my sleeves, and forced myself to walk right up to the pod-shell-thing across from him.

"Grip it right here," Carpenter said, tracing a seam that ran along the ridge at the top of the casing. He dug his fingers into that narrow gap. I followed suit farther down, restraining a cringe at the cool slimy texture. "Now pull!"

He yanked the one side of the casing toward him, and I tugged on the other side at the same time. The thing split down the middle with a sputter of gas and a thicker stench like fermented seaweed. I dodged to the side as it crumpled by my feet.

A pale body with pearly skin lay in the slick remains of the casing: a young man, black-haired and slim, his eyes closed. Carpenter knelt down.

"It always takes the pearl-heads a while to come to," he said casually, and smacked the man's cheek a few times with the back of his hand.

The man's head listed to the side. Then his eyes fluttered open. He stared vaguely forward with a few slow blinks. His body twitched, and he turned to look at me. His dazed expression made my stomach clench. Whoever this man had been before, nothing remained of him now except a blank slate ready to receive orders.

"You, pay attention over here," Carpenter said with a loud clap. "I'm your boss until you get to the palace. Listen up."

The pearl-head's face swiveled toward him. Carpenter motioned him up, and the man pulled himself off the casing onto wobbly legs. Carpenter tossed him a burlap tunic. "Put that on. Then get yourself into the cart and sit down. The palace folks will give you a proper uniform when they decide what to do with you."

As the man absently pulled on the tunic, Carpenter

strode to the cart where the headless body was lying. "Give me a hand?" he said to me.

My stomach balled tighter as I joined him. I could guess from the body's overall shape and the timing that I was looking at the part of Sally that the Queen hadn't put on display.

It wouldn't be her when Carpenter and Walrus were finished with her, just a dull-minded drone. The woman I'd bantered with before I'd left the Spades, who'd charged into the palace gardens last night ready to take on every Heart, had already left this body. The head that regrew in the watery chamber wouldn't be more than a facsimile of her looks, nothing of her spirit.

That knowledge didn't make me feel any less sick about grasping her shoulders to carry her with Carpenter to the platform.

He tucked the folds of the deflated casing around her until her body was completely hidden. Then he nudged the platform back into the sea. Walrus shifted into place to receive the casing and fix it to the equipment beneath the surface.

A bit of grit had stuck to my hands from Sally's body. I'd have given anything to wash them, but the cove's water hardly seemed any cleaner. At least I'd won those points with Carpenter. He brushed his own hands together and gave me a warm smile.

"Let's have that tart," he said.

"How long does the new head take to grow?" I asked as we headed to the back of the beach by the rocks, pretending an approving interest in his work.

"Depends on the body," Carpenter said. "If it's a weak one, or too young or too old, we don't bother at all. With the decent ones, it could be a week, maybe two, or anywhere in between. We've usually got a few down there at any given time. Can't always replace 'em as quickly as she removes 'em."

He snapped his mouth shut after that last word and glanced toward the water as if checking to see if Walrus might have heard that almost-criticism of the Queen. His co-worker hadn't yet resurfaced. Carpenter let out a chuckle as if it'd been a joke all in good fun. As if even jokes couldn't cost you your head these days.

The palace needed servants, and the Queen had the disturbing habit of running through them—and running them through—a lot more quickly than their natural lifespan should have been. Waste not, want not. Even the pearl-heads could be re-pearled if their bodies had held up, from what I'd heard.

"I'm glad to see you're well," I said carefully. I'd have had to take care with this subject even if I had really been here as a friend. "I have to admit one of the reasons I thought to come out here was, ah, concerns prompted by recent events. No ground feels completely secure when the atmosphere is constantly shifting, does it?"

I wasn't sure how much Carpenter knew about the Queen's proclamation this morning, but the tightening of his mouth told me he understood what I meant well enough. He gulped a bite of the pie, crumbs sprinkling his beard. "I make myself of use," he said, by which I figured he meant, there weren't many willing to do this job, so the Queen might not be in too huge a rush to displace him.

"You do indeed," I said, managing to hold back the dryness that wanted to creep into my voice. "I admire your ambition. It's only…" I glanced toward the water as he had. Still no sign of Walrus. I lowered my voice anyway. "I've heard a little talk about the previous Alice, saying she came out near this cove. That would have had to be before you had anything to do with this place, of course, but I'm not sure, when emotions are running high, all those details would be considered."

Carpenter paused in mid-chew. He swallowed, but he'd turned a bit sallow. "No questions have come my way," he said, seeming to gather his confidence. "Perhaps the suggestion has already been dismissed."

"Perhaps," I said, about to lead into my real gambit.

A faint splash brought both our gazes up. Walrus's gray head had broken through the water's surface. "Is he still here?" he asked in his ponderous voice, presumably meaning me.

"An old friend," Carpenter said. "The work's done, isn't it?"

Walrus let out a huff of breath. My skin prickled. I couldn't prod Carpenter with him listening. Especially when he was studying me with shadowed eyes.

"What's his business anyway?" Walrus muttered.

I gave him a smile and raised my hat. "Hatter. I do have a few that can work in the water, if you're ever so inclined."

He grimaced as if the thought disgusted him, but to

my relief, he pushed away from the cove. He swam for a few strokes above water and then dove back down.

"He isn't a bad sort," Carpenter said after a moment. "Just not very interested in being company."

"Fair enough." I hesitated, waiting until I was sure Walrus wouldn't re-emerge, and then shook my head, making my tone as rueful as I could. "That story about Alicia is crazy anyway, isn't it? I expect I knew just about everything that went on back then, and she never left the city."

Hope lit inside me the second Carpenter's chest started to puff up. Even when he'd been a Spade, he'd never passed by the chance to one-up someone else if he could. I'd purposely exaggerated my confidence to provoke his self-importance—and apparently there'd been something on that subject to provoke.

"You didn't know so much as you think," he said with a smirk. "That last time she came through, she snuck out to the Checkerboard Plains. Asked *me* to show her the way to the train."

"The Checkerboard Plains?" I said incredulously, tamping down on my eagerness so it wouldn't show. "What would she have wanted out there?"

Carpenter shrugged, leaning back against the jagged rock and devouring another chunk of pie. "She was all mysterious about it, like she liked to be. I got the impression the idea came from something she saw or heard while she was in the Otherland, but she didn't say what. Not that it matters now, does it?"

His tone darkened on that last question. I laughed as

casually as I could. "If it didn't back then, I'm sure it doesn't now."

Something she'd seen in the Otherland—something from one of the previous Alices who'd traveled to Wonderland, the same way Alicia's notes had directed Lyssa? The information was a start. At least we'd narrowed down the scope of any investigations we took on.

I had enough wits not to leave the moment I'd gotten that answer. "Is it true the orangeberries grow better out here?" I asked, and let us ramble through another half hour of meaningless conversation.

The sun brushed the surface of the sea, and Carpenter stood up. "It's getting late," he said. "A long walk back to the city. I could give you a ride as far as the edge of the palace grounds if you don't mind joining me and my pearly friend in the cart."

The cart where the body of a friend had been lying just an hour ago. A creeping sensation ran through my nerves. But it would be ridiculous to turn an offer like that down if I wanted him to believe I was at ease with his current line of work.

"Perfect," I said, girding myself. "Thank you for the lift."

The sky was stark black with a scattering of stars by the time I reached the hat shop. I hustled up the stairs to the apartment, trying to be both quick and quiet. It turned out neither mattered that much.

Doria was curled up in the wing chair by the table, her hands circling a cup of tea. The smile she gave me managed to look accusing—and a little bleary.

"You said you wouldn't be home too late," she said, waving the half-full cup at me. The milky liquid nearly sloshed out.

"I believe I said I *hoped* I wouldn't be back too late," I said, coming over to lean on the back of the chair. I tugged one of the braids mixed in with her hair, and she made a face at me. "You didn't have to wait up."

"I missed the main excitement yesterday. I wanted to have a front row seat if anything interesting happened tonight." She cocked her head at me. "Did you get some answers?"

"I think so," I said. "But nothing all that exciting. Sorry to disappoint you."

She sighed and motioned to the dish rack, where another teacup was drying. "Lyssa meant to wait up too, but I had to order her to go upstairs after she almost fell asleep on the stool."

Of course our looking-glass girl would have insisted on washing her dishes even then. "She's been through a lot in the last day and a half," I said. "I'll give her the news, such as it is, tomorrow. Now I'm ordering *you* to bed. Off with you!"

"Yeah, yeah," she muttered around a yawn.

As she headed up, I turned on the alarm device Theo had given us and pointed it at the apartment's front door. Then I ordered myself to my own bed. It'd been a couple of long days for me too.

After all those years, it was hard to imagine I'd once slept in this bed every night. Remembering Lyssa's morning greeting with a grin and a flicker of heat, I pulled off my tie. I did have actual pajamas around here somewhere, didn't I? I hadn't bothered with them in years since I'd always been reset back into that damned suit anyway.

There, folded in the drawer in the base of the wardrobe. They were nicer than I remembered, a silky fabric with purple and green stripes.

I burrowed my head into the pillow and let the memory of Lyssa's presence sitting next to me on the bed paint over the images of the Oyster Cove and Carpenter and the cart ride partway home. The taste of her lips. The heat of her hand moving down my—

I jerked awake without any sense of having fallen asleep. The sheets had tangled around my legs. A voice was hollering loud enough to carry from the street outside…

That was the Queen's voice.

My pulse hitched, and I scrambled out of bed in an instant. The light drifting into the hall was only a touch brighter than dawn's pallor. I hurried down to the living area with its large windows.

Looking outside, all my nerves jolted with the thought that our world had been reset after all. The rows of guards, the Queen on her throne, it was all as it had been yesterday morning.

Except not. As my heartbeat thudded on in my ears, I remembered that the sun had been higher when I'd watched this horrible spectacle with Lyssa and Doria. The sky had been unclouded.

And the head on the pike brandished in the midst of the parade had been Sally's, not this one with the mane of faded hair I recognized as Smith's.

Oh, no. He must have offered—and of course our White Knight had accepted.

The Queen didn't sound anywhere close to appeased by the fact that the Spades had answered her challenge. "This is barely a start," she was ranting, waving her hands from her ported throne, her face flushed ruddy. "Where are the rest of the Spades? How will they atone for the crimes they've committed against all of us? Yesterday I took one. Today I take two. The deal remains the same. Let's see how long they can pretend to be heroes."

Even as she spoke, one of the guards was grabbing a man who'd been watching the parade with his door cracked ajar. An elderly woman already lay bound behind the throne.

"Oh, God," Lyssa murmured.

I startled. I'd been so focused on the Queen that I hadn't heard our Otherlander coming downstairs. She stood a couple steps back from the window, a caution I appreciated even as I wanted her all the way on the other side of the room. The color had drained from her face. Horror shimmered in her eyes as her gaze shifted to meet mine.

"Everyone thought she'd stop with this tactic if she got what she wanted yesterday—if the Spades proved they wouldn't let other people die in their place," she said in a thin voice. "Smith gave himself up to buy us some time. But she doesn't care. She's going to keep at it anyway. He didn't change anything, and we're still in the same awful position we were before."

I rubbed my mouth as if that would draw the right words out of it to set Lyssa's mind at ease. But *my* mind wasn't remotely at ease. My spirits were sinking.

What I'd done yesterday hadn't been enough either. There were too many people I didn't know how to protect.

"Yes," I said. "It appears we are. Let's see what we can do about it."

CHAPTER SEVEN

Lyssa

I walked into Theo's office and nearly ran right into him as I pushed past the door.

"Lyssa," he said, touching my shoulder to steady me and then nodding to acknowledge Hatter, who'd come in right behind me. With the sleeves of his white button-up pulled straight over his muscular forearms and his dark curls slicked back from his face more forcefully than usual, he looked like he meant business about whatever he was preparing to do.

He gave my shoulder a light caress before letting me go. "I was about to summon another meeting. You can come with me."

"No," I said, the words spilling out in a rush. "We don't need a meeting. There's only one thing to do that makes any sense."

"All right," Theo said, calmly enough, taking a step back to give us room to really come in. "And what's that?"

I sucked in a breath. "Smith turning himself in didn't stop the Queen's plan. She's obviously going to keep grabbing random people until she's convinced she's gotten all of the Spades, or at least most of you. And maybe me too." That last bit made my throat constrict. I forced my voice out. "Sacrificing someone else isn't going to help, and you said yourself that you're not in a position to take her on head-to-head yet. Hatter got a lead—we know where my grand-aunt went exploring outside the city. I'm going to track down those artifacts, and then we'll stop the Queen from killing anyone else."

I couldn't see another head waved on a pike. I couldn't watch her slaughter Wonderland's citizens to prove her warped and vicious point. Not when there was a chance the tools to defeat her were right here, waiting to be uncovered.

Theo's gaze snapped to Hatter. "You found out something about Alicia's travels?"

Hatter's mouth twisted. He hadn't been quite as committed to this plan as I was. I got the sense he'd come to the Tower with me at least as much to keep an eye on me as to provide support.

"Carpenter said the last time she came to Wonderland, she went out to the Checkerboard Plains," he said. "I've got no reason to doubt him—he said she asked him to help her get on the train. That's all he knew, though. It's a still a lot of terrain to cover, without a very clear idea what we're looking for."

"But there's got to be something important out there," I put in. "Either she found the ring there, or something to do with the ring… Whatever she found, it made her feel like too much was riding on her—that's why she ran back home and never came back."

I wouldn't falter like that. If my childhood had taught me anything, it was how to stand steady even while everything around me was falling apart. And this was about saving dozens, maybe hundreds, of lives.

"The Checkerboard Plains would make sense," Theo said. "It's a confusing place, often difficult to keep your sense of direction—ideal for hiding things the Queen would hope no one ever discovered."

"Ideal for us ending up lost and without anything more than we started with," Hatter said, but he didn't sound too set in his pessimism. He *had* come with me rather than trying to argue me out of my plan.

"We have to try," I said. "If there's something in the Checkerboard Plains that the Queen is afraid of, we *need* it. Once we're out there, maybe I'll be able to figure out more as we go—maybe I can connect the dots from things Aunt Alicia said that I didn't realize the full meaning of at the time. It's not as if I can head home and look for more clues there instead."

Even as I laid out my case, my heart thumped faster. I didn't actually like the idea of rushing out onto unfamiliar terrain—terrain Theo had just admitted was difficult and confusing—with only that vague plan. This was Wonderland. Almost *anything* could be waiting for us out there.

But *because* this was Wonderland, I also had people here on my side. Knowing that helped balance out my uncertainties.

As if he'd read my mind, Theo's next words were, "You can't go on your own. I'll go with you—the legends I've heard may help guide us too. And we might need more help than that. I'll gather a small team, assemble a few devices that may be useful along the way, and we'll set off."

I exhaled in relief. "All right. Good. We should leave as soon as possible, right? How long do we have before the Queen fills her dungeon if she keeps taking more people each day?"

Theo frowned. "I don't know its exact capacity—and she may decide 'full' is a subjective term. I wouldn't count on more than a week."

Seven days to save Wonderland. Great. But it was a heck of a lot better than no chance at all. "Is there anything I should pack to bring along?" I asked. "I don't know what to expect out there."

"We can pack together," Hatter said. "I'm coming."

I glanced at him, startled. He crossed his arms over his chest in a defiant pose that I guessed was aimed at Theo, because a faint smile crossed his lips when he met my eyes. "I'm not sticking around here while you do all the work."

He turned to Theo. "And we'll bring Doria too. The way things are going, it'll likely be safer out on the Checkerboard Plains than it will be here in the city the next few days. The Knave already dislikes me. I wouldn't put it past him to 'randomly' choose her for the dungeon next."

If he'd expected an argument from the White Knight, he didn't get one. Theo just smiled in return.

"It's settled, then. Meet the rest of us on the road at the Plains-ward end of town as soon as you're ready."

The road Hatter, Doria, and I took out of the city didn't look quite as pristine as the one that went by the pond and the mushroom farm. By the time we reached the last few buildings, the orange paint on the cobblestones was worn down and dull. I sidestepped a couple of gaps where old stones had been dislodged and not yet replaced.

"I thought you said people walked everywhere in Wonderland," I said to Hatter. "Now there's a train?"

"The train only circles through the Checkerboard Plains," Hatter said. "Not many have any reason to go out that way these days. Some Clubbers used to take day trips for a little novel excitement, but the dip where the tracks veer closest to the city is still an hour's hike from here. Even those who could be bothered to make the trip got bored after we found ourselves stuck in that one day."

"*I've* never been out there before," Doria said. "Dad wouldn't let me."

Hatter gave her a narrow look. "You get into enough trouble in the city. Anyway, I'm taking you now, aren't I?"

"True, true. I shouldn't complain." She grinned at me. "And I'm getting to go as part of a special secret quest."

Her voice lowered. "Do you really think we're going to find some kind of weapon out there that'll take down the Queen?"

I wished I could answer that question a little more confidently. "I hope so," I said. "If it's out there, I'll do whatever I can to find it."

That reply seemed to satisfy her more than it satisfied me. She bounded on ahead, faster when a group of four figures came into view under the shade of a tree with leaves so vibrant they might as well have been carved out of jade.

"Chess!" I said, a smile springing to my face despite my nerves at the sight of the brawny guy. Theo hadn't said who he wanted to bring for this mission-of-sorts, but I couldn't have asked for any additional company I'd have wanted more.

Chess gave me a broad smile in return. "I wouldn't miss an adventure like this for anything, lovely."

Doria had planted herself between our two other comrades: the redheaded twins. "You guys are coming too? This is going to be amazing!"

"It's still a covert operation," Theo said, his eyes amused but his tone serious. "Let's move out before our gathering can draw any attention. Just a group of friends off to have a mid-day picnic." His eyebrow quirked upward.

I did actually have food packed in the canvas bag that I'd slung over my shoulders like a knapsack. Hatter had bundled up bread and cheese and meat—and of course a few scones—in sheets of waxy paper he'd told me would keep them cool and fresh. I was going to assume he knew what he was talking about, or all of Wonderland would have died from food poisoning by now. He obviously hadn't thought it was likely we'd come across any restaurants or grocery stores out on these plains.

Other than that and a couple changes of clothes, I hadn't brought much. The ruby ring weighed against my breastbone as we set off along the road. It was the most important thing I carried.

"How often does the train come by the city?" I asked. "And how big are the Checkerboard Plains anyway?"

"The squares are always shifting," Theo said. "It could take anywhere from hours to a day to circumnavigate the entire area. But the train has a habit of arriving when passengers are waiting to board."

That made about as much sense as anything in Wonderland did.

After a while, we veered off the main road onto a narrower dirt one that wound through a stretch of scattered trees. Theo motioned us deeper into the sparse woods to avoid a stand of enormous flowers like the ones I'd chatted with before near the pond. The fewer witnesses, the better.

We came out onto a flat stretch of land with shimmering neon-green grass. A dark haze hung over the landscape in the distance like a thundershower, which maybe explained the ozone-y scent that laced the crisp breeze. And just a short walk ahead of us curved an arc of train tracks, gleaming with a coppery tint over black mica-laced pebbles.

There was no sign of anything like a platform or a station. I squinted along the line of the tracks. "Where does it stop?"

Chess chuckled. "It doesn't. Ever. If you want to ride the Plains train, you'd better be ready to hop right on."

Oh. This was going to be... interesting.

One of the twins pointed to a streak of violet smoke that was streaming across the sky in the distance. "Looks like it's on its way."

I adjusted the straps of my bag on my shoulders, making sure my cargo was secure. Doria bobbed eagerly on her feet as she peered off in the direction the train was arriving from. The other twin pulled a dumpling out of his vest pocket and ate it in a few quick bites.

The rumble of an engine and the rattle of wheels moving over the tracks reached my ears. A dark brown shape came into view, speeding toward us. The engine looked as if it'd been carved out of mahogany and then polished. The cars behind it, all four of them, were made out of the same material, I realized as it barrelled toward us.

It was coming awfully fast. A nervous shiver ran over my arms. The most dangerous part of this journey might be setting off on the journey in the first place.

"Get ready," Theo said. "Dee and Dum, you can handle yourselves—and make sure you catch up Doria along the way. Hatter, you're the fastest. You and I can make our way on first, and then—"

"Look what we have here," a sharp hiss of a voice interrupted.

The seven of us spun around. My heart lurched against my ribs.

The Knave of Hearts, with his blunt shark-like face and heart-shaped helm, was emerging from the forest with three of the Queen's guards behind him. All of them carried swords or daggers. My arm twinged in memory of a blade like that slicing through my flesh.

The Knave sneered at us, revealing several jagged teeth. "I heard Hatter was interested in the Checkerboard Plains. And how much company you've brought with you!"

Hatter muttered a curse in which I thought I caught the name "Carpenter." His former friend must have reported their conversation to the palace. I braced myself, not sure what to do. I wasn't equipped to fight, but there wasn't anywhere to run to.

At least we could be glad the Knave hadn't anticipated running into a group this large, or he might have brought even more guards with him.

"I wasn't aware it was a crime to take a ride on a train," Theo said, stepping forward with an air of total authority. "Or were you simply meaning to see us off?"

The Knave waggled his sword at Theo. "I knew I'd catch you at something eventually, Inventor. You think we can't suss out there's treason afoot?" His gaze shifted to me, chilling my skin. "And who is this? Not a face I recognize. She wouldn't be an Otherlander, would she? The one the Queen has expressly demanded be turned over to her care?"

A whistle shrieked, almost right behind me. I flinched.

The train roared toward us, and Theo shouted over its racket.

"Dee, Dum, Chess!"

The three of them sprang forward without a second's hesitation. Chess blinked out of view and back into it right behind one of the guards, knocking the blade from his hand with a powerful blow. Dee lunged for another and hurled him with his elastic arms, sending the man tumbling head over heels into the forest. Dum aimed a kick at the third soldier that propelled him up into the branches of a tree.

Hatter tugged me toward the train, waving to Doria too. "I'll get you on," he said, and dashed ahead, down the length of the train.

Apparently he was as quick on his feet as he was with his hands. In a few swift strides, he'd reached the car second from the end, which had an open walkway along its side. He caught a hold of a rung, swung himself up, and leaned over the railing with his arms outstretched.

The Knave was letting out a furious shout behind me, and someone else yelped in pain, but I couldn't risk looking back. Doria reached Hatter first as the train propelled him past us. He grasped her hand and heaved her onto the walkway beside him. I threw myself forward just in time to snatch hold of his reaching fingers.

My grasp wasn't solid. Hatter yanked me up, but my feet only landed on the walkway's edge. I teetered for an instant, and then a hook snagged the railing beside me.

Theo had tossed an odd jointed rope at the train. At a jerk of his arms, it contracted, launching him toward the train with the same elastic spring as Dee's arms. He caught me against his body just before I might have fallen. His momentum carried both of us into safety. With his arm around me, he looked back toward the fight.

The twins were already hurtling toward us. Dum bounced into the air on his flexible legs and landed at Hatter's other side. Dee flipped over and pushed off his arms with a similar effect. He soared right over the railing.

Chess was still flickering in and out of sight. He ducked under the sweep of the Knave's sword and dodged the jab of a knee.

"Chess!" Theo hollered. The train was rushing onward. We were leaving him behind. The other soldiers were scrambling back to help their commander.

Chess glanced back at us with a wild grin. He vanished and reappeared just long enough to slam his fist into the Knave's face. The Knave stumbled backward, and Chess slipped away into the air.

When he popped into view a second later, he was sprinting after the train. He was already a full car-length behind, and the gap was growing with each thud of my pulse.

Theo whipped out the rope he'd used to pull himself on, but the end pattered to the ground just out of Chess's reach. Shit. My hands clenched around the railing, and suddenly the jolting of the walkway beneath my feet and the thick smell of polished wood and metal flooded my senses. I clenched harder.

Just slow down. Just for a second. Please, slow down.

Heat flared beneath my shirt. The ring felt as if it were

burning my skin. I winced, but I held on—and by some miracle, the engine eased off. The rumble faded.

Chess closed the distance between him and the final car in the space of a breath. He sprang onto the back with a whoop of victory.

The Knave and his men were charging after him. I jerked my hands from the railing, shattering the pressure that had been building inside me. The train lurched forward at its previous speed. And I realized everyone around me was staring at me. Well, at my chest.

I glanced down in time to see a faint reddish light glowing through the fabric of my dress. In a blink, it had dulled, at the same time as the ring had stopped burning. I let out a shaky breath.

Chess strolled out of the car behind us onto the walkway. "That was a bigger trick than I expected you could pull off, Inventor," he said with his unshakeable grin.

"I can't take any credit," Theo said, his gaze still fixed on me. "It was all Lyssa."

CHAPTER EIGHT

Lyssa

"Dee!" Doria said as we filed off the walkway onto the much less precarious floor inside the train car. "One of them got you."

A thin gash ran across the one twin's bicep just below the short sleeve of his shirt. He shrugged with an easy smile. "Just a nick. Nothing to worry about."

"It's still bleeding," Dum muttered, checking his brother's arm. "Good thing the White Knight asked me to bring the rest of that salve I picked up."

"It's totally fine," Dee said, but Dum ignored him. He produced a tube from his pack and dabbed the cut with the same green-and-white gel Theo had used on my wound. So he'd been the one to find that for me—on Theo's request.

And now I knew how to tell the twins apart even

when they weren't using their super-powered limbs. Dee was the friendly one, and Dum was the standoffish one.

The other guys had started to amble through the train car. High-backed seats lined both sides of the space, wide enough to seat two or maybe three very skinny people, although no one was sitting in any of them right now. They were made of the same mahogany as the outside of the train had appeared to be, with padding that looked like moss in both color and texture. The smell of wood polish tickled my nose. The rattling of the rails beneath us sounded ominous in the quiet.

"Is it just us?" I asked. "There won't be any other passengers?"

"No one in the caboose," Chess reported.

"We might as well check the other two cars," Theo said. "But few have much use for the Plains train these days."

That fit what Hatter had said about it. We ventured across the short bridge of wooden slats between our car and the next, passed through another space identical to the one we'd left, and then moved on to the one right behind the engine. I picked up a lacy pink scarf that had been left behind on one of the seats. From before the Queen had trapped time, I had to guess, or it would have vanished back to its original place with the passing of the day. Did the original owner even remember she'd lost it?

Something Theo had said came back to me, about the train arriving when passengers were waiting. "Will the Knave be able to catch up with us?" I asked. "Is there some kind of magic that'll let him hop on this train before we've come all the way around?"

"I don't think he can contrive to end up on this one," Theo said. "But there may be echoes of this train running along the same track—and the palace has other resources for traveling. We'll need to stay on guard. I don't think he's likely to give up the chase."

All at once, the sunlight that had been shining through the windows blinked out, leaving us in darkness. Lights crackled on overhead along the length of the ceiling. Beyond the windows, I couldn't make out anything but black.

"What the hell was that?" I said.

Chess dropped onto one of the seats and stretched out his legs. "We've passed into a new square. They switch between night and day all the way across the plains—like a checkerboard. The way we name things here may not always sound sensible, but there's still plenty of sense to the names."

We were going to keep jumping from light to dark and back again, then? That should be... interesting. I slid onto the seat across from him and peered outside. It was hard to make out anything even up close with the inner lights reflecting off the glass. How was I supposed to tell whether any location out there looked promising?

Well, I guessed Aunt Alicia would have had the exact same problem when she'd come out here, and she'd found the ring anyway.

Dum frowned and leaned his arm against the back of a nearby seat. "Are we going to talk about the way the

Otherlander messed with the train? It doesn't normally slow down like that." His eyes settled on me warily.

Oh, right. I guessed I couldn't blame him for wanting answers even if I didn't have any.

"I don't know what I did," I said. "I just wanted it to slow down enough for Chess to catch up, and it... did. It felt like this ring might have helped." I pulled the ruby ring from under my shirt to show him and anyone else who hadn't seen it before. "This ring is the whole reason we're out here—I think my grand-aunt, Alicia, found it out here, and maybe something else. It's obviously got some magic of its own."

"A magic I highly appreciate," Chess said, beaming at me.

"That's so cool!" Doria took the seat beside me. "Can I give it a try?"

"Doria," Hatter said with a warning note.

She rolled her eyes at him. "I won't do anything crazy."

"I think it's better if we don't experiment with the train's speeds any more than we already have, unless it seems necessary," Theo said, gently but firmly. "Especially when we don't know how close the Knave and his men may be at our heels."

"I don't have any idea how it works anyway," I told Doria when she crinkled her face with disappointment. "It might not have done anything if I hadn't been so worried."

"Still pretty amazing," she said.

Hatter opened up his bag. "Why don't we have lunch

while we wait for the next daylight square? The way things are going, we may not get many good chances to refresh ourselves."

He passed me and Doria sandwiches he'd put together, and the others dug into their own supplies. My stomach churned around the bites of fresh bread, cheese, and ham.

What if I couldn't figure out where we should go from here even when we were in daylight again? I'd dragged six people off on this uncertain mission, and now we had the most vicious of the Queen's guards after us too.

Chess nudged my calf lightly with his foot. "Cheer up, lovely. Focus on the fun parts of the adventure, and the rest can be an afterthought."

I didn't think my brain was programmed to work like that, but I shot him a small smile anyway.

Not long after I'd finished my sandwich, the view outside the window snapped into full daylight just as quickly as it had turned to night. My chest loosened a little as I studied the landscape outside the window. The "square" we were traveling through was all grassy hills, each with a single tree at their peak. Weird. Beyond the hills lay another dark haze I realized must be a patch of night.

The train jostled us as the tracks veered up one of those slopes, and then I could see across what might have been the entire Checkerboard Plains, all laid out in squares of light and dark. Some of the bright squares held thick forests, some massive lakes, others fields as flat as a pancake. Far off in the distance, several squares away, I spotted a taller hill that curved over on itself like a wave frozen just before it crashed.

The moment my gaze caught on it, my pulse stuttered. There was something so familiar about that odd image…

Aunt Alicia's pictures. She'd hung her framed sketches all around her house. I hadn't known what to make of that shape when I'd noticed it before, but I could picture the delicate charcoal lines where that drawing was mounted in the upstairs hall.

Only the angle had been a little different, hadn't it? As if she were remembering looking up at it from much closer.

"That hill," I said, pointing so energetically that my finger tapped the window. "Is there something special about it?"

Theo leaned over to consider it. "Not that I'm aware of. Why?"

"Aunt Alicia drew it. I saw it in one of her pictures in the house. I think she must have gone all the way out there before, or at least gotten pretty close. And it must have stuck in her memory." Because something important had happened out there? My heartbeat had evened out, but it was still thumping along faster than before with a quiver of hope. "We have to go there. Will the train take us that far?"

"It'll loop around the plains. I'd imagine we can get off fairly close to that spot. It'll just take some waiting." Theo smiled at me, but I thought his shoulders had tensed a little. Was he worried that I was wrong—that I really was leading them on a pointless mission?

The train rumbled across the countryside. We passed through another stretch of night, but this time I could make out stars glittering in the indigo sky overhead. A few of them swayed back and forth as if in some sort of dance. I felt a little proud of myself that I didn't even stare. It'd take more Wonderland weirdness than that to catch me off guard now.

We emerged from the darkness into a sunlit stretch of tall waving grass. The train's rattling intensified as the tracks led it over a bridge across a wide river lined with cattails that... looked like they might be actual cats' tails, striped or spotted fur and all. Okay, I might have stared a little at those. Then my gaze traveled along the rippling blue water to the hump of an island barely visible near the night haze of the next square.

A sudden burst of heat against my chest made me bite my lip. The ring was burning against my skin again. I tore my gaze away from the island, and the sensation faded. The second I looked toward it again, a fresh spot of heat seared my skin.

I'd been sure the wave-like hill was important, but how could I argue with the ring's reaction? The train was already whirring off the bridge and away. If we were going to investigate, we had to go *now*.

"There's something by that river," I said quickly, pushing out of my seat. "We have to get off."

Chess leapt to his feet immediately. On the other side of the aisle, the twins glanced at Theo. When he motioned them up, we all hustled to the car's door. This quest might have been my idea, but some of our companions still saw their White Knight as the leader. That was fine by me. I knew I wasn't exactly an expert on anything Wonderland.

"No hesitating; just jump!" Chess said, and did exactly that an instant later. Doria sprang after him. I took a deep breath and threw myself toward the tall grass.

My momentum slowed as I left the train behind, as if my body were moving from one plane of reality to another. I landed amid the grass with only a faint jolt through my knees. Four more thumps followed me.

"Where to from here, lovely?" Chess asked.

I motioned toward the far end of the square. "There was an island in the middle of the river, pretty far down. The ring reacted when I was looking at it, so I think that's where we need to go."

We fell into step in a loose procession, walking to the bank of the river and then along it. The ground turned moist and sticky beneath our feet, and the cattails at the edge of the water whispered against each other's fur. Within a few minutes, I was wishing I'd brought boots as well as my sneakers.

"Still finding the adventure fun?" Hatter asked Chess from where the two of them had ended up side by side just behind me.

"It's certainly a place full of fascinating sounds," Chess said brightly, with a squelch of his foot into a patch of mud.

The humid air was congealing against my skin. I

rubbed the dampness from my arms. "I really hope this ring knows what it's talking about," I said. "This isn't—"

I set my foot down in a shallow silty dip in front of me, and the ground gave way completely.

My body plunged into thick cool muck. I snapped my mouth shut a second before the oozing dirt could have filled it. Then my head was under too, a slimy pressure against my face, my feet still sinking down and down as if I'd fallen into an endless sinkhole. Which maybe I had, it occurred to me with a spark of panic. Or maybe there was something worse than mud waiting for me down here. This was Wonderland, after all.

My arms had shot up as the ground had swallowed me. I groped at the mud around me, searching for something to hold on to, to pull me back up. A prickling burn spread through my lungs as they begged for air.

It might not matter how deep this hole was or what else lurked in it. I might be dead before I had to find out.

My arms flailed again—and my hand connected with something firm. Fingers closed around my palm. I gripped on as tightly as I could, and my rescuer heaved me upward with a sharp yank. My body traveled up through the wet earth with much more resistance than it'd plummeted. But at least I was going up now.

I swept my other hand through the muck and managed to grab hold of my rescuer's wrist. With another lurch, my head broke through the surface of the sinkhole. I spat and sputtered, clutching Hatter's muddy sleeve for dear life.

He was totally drenched in mud, from his spiky blond

hair to his dress shoes. Only his hat, which appeared to have fallen to the side as he'd dived after me, remained untouched. As he hauled me the rest of the way out, Chess shifted to the side, his own arms tacky with dirt up to his elbows. The imprint of his fingers remained around Hatter's ankles.

They'd both dived after me, one and then the other. The swift and the strong. A good thing, too, or Hatter and I would both have been lost.

"Are you all right?" Theo said, hovering over us. His expression was taut with concern.

I spat out a little more mud. Hatter produced a handkerchief from his pocket and wiped his face on one side of it, leaving it nearly as muddy as the rest of him. He offered the untouched side to me. I took it gratefully, swiping at the worst of the grit. The mud had saturated my clothes—my hair felt leaden with it—ugh.

But it was hard to mind that too much when a minute ago I hadn't been sure I'd survive to see this minute.

"I'm okay," I said with a shaky breath, and then my arms threw themselves around Hatter of their own accord. I hugged him tight, not really caring that the collar of his jacket was getting my face muddier again.

"I suppose we'd better steer clear of the clear spots," he said in a dry voice, but he hugged me to him just as tightly.

I let go of him to grab Chess in a similar embrace. Chess chuckled and pressed a kiss to my forehead despite my current dirt-infused state. "No more taking side adventures without inviting us along first," he teased.

"Sounds good to me," I muttered.

Theo touched his hand to my head as if he needed that contact to be sure I really was all right. Then he strode ahead, giving the silty dip a wide berth.

"I'll take lead from here on," he said. "And everyone, hold on to this. I intend to make it back to the city with exactly the same number of people we started with."

He passed the end of his stretchy rope to me as I scrambled to my feet, and I passed it back down the line, keeping one hand loosely around it. Walking along in a rope chain felt very kindergarten, but I'd take that over drowning in mud any day, thank you.

My drenched clothes shifted against my body as I started walking. So gross. At least the mud shouldn't have had much time to seep into my bag. And maybe I could clean off my current outfit—and my hair—when we had to swim to the island.

By the time the river widened, the mud caked on me had dried into a crust that cracked and flaked off in bits of dust with every step. At least the sun baking down on us had warmed me up.

We treaded carefully through the thick grass right up to the bank. The cattails had thinned. We had a clear view of the island, floating there like a massive treed barge. It had to be twenty feet across and at least ten times as long.

The ruby ring burned beneath my shirt as if to say, "Good job; here we are!" I stepped forward to dip my foot into the water, deciding I'd rather walk in squishy shoes than take off my sneakers and expose my bare feet to whatever was down there, but Theo held out his arm to block me.

"It's surrounded by razorweed," he said, pointing. When I squinted, I made out dark sinuous lines wriggling just beneath the surface of the water all along the island's rocky shoreline.

"Razorweed?" I asked. Just from the name, I was going to assume that wasn't good.

"It can slice straight through bone," Dum said with a shudder. "I've never seen it myself before, but I know a man who lost all the fingers on one hand to a clump of it."

"Okay," I said. "So swimming isn't a great idea. How do we get over there? Whatever we're looking for is definitely on that island." According to the ring scalding my breastbone, anyway.

Dee cocked his head. "It's not that big a leap," he said. "I can toss you all over easily enough, then stand guard here. I don't know how you'll get back, though."

A smile crossed Theo's face for the first time since we'd set out. "I can handle things from there."

Dee planted himself on the edge of the river and intertwined his fingers to turn his joined arms into a sort of slingshot. "Shout if you see hide or hair of *anyone*," Dum told him, and his brother nodded before launching him into the air. Dum soared in a neat arc and landed at the foot of the island's nearest tree.

One by one, Dee propelled the rest of us over. I had to swallow a yelp as I careened through the air, but I managed to brace myself for a good landing, and Theo caught my arm before I could even wobble.

Closer to the island's edge, a faint sound reached my ears from the water, like hundreds of teeth gnashing. It rose and fell in time with the slithering of the razorweed. I shuddered and turned to peer between the trees.

Nothing stood out, but the ring blazed against my skin even hotter. Restraining a wince and watching the ground carefully, I set off into the pocket of forest.

Tall spindly shrubs had sprouted up around the trees. I brushed past one, and its round leaves twitched toward me, all of them opening to reveal human-looking eyes. Dozens of eyes, staring at me. A thinner leaf parted with the swipe of a tongue.

I nearly bit my own tongue. Holy shit, that was disturbing.

"They won't hurt you," Theo said. "I'd imagine they function like a scarecrow—designed to make you think twice about continuing."

Yeah, I could see how that could work. Even Doria looked a bit green around the gills taking in those plants.

I pushed on, clambering over a fallen log and dodging another sinkhole dip. A few steps later, I emerged in the midst of a thick ring of those staring shrubs. They surrounded a pool of water that was only seven or eight feet across but so deep I couldn't make out the bottom.

I had just enough time to register that, and then the staring shrubs started to shriek.

All around the pool, they leaned their unblinking eyes

toward me and vibrated their leafy mouths with a sound that perforated eardrums. I clapped my hands over my ears, my nerves scattering. But while I stood there frozen, the shrubs didn't move, didn't do anything other than stare and shriek.

Like scarecrows, like Theo had said. Trying to frighten me off by giving the impression they were a threat when really there was nothing they could do.

The ring lay against my chest like a molten ball. This was where I was meant to be. I scanned the water for any sign of razorweed and stepped into the shallows by the edge.

The water swirled around my legs, cool but not unpleasantly so. Theo, Chess, and Hatter moved to follow me. Chess made a face as he sank in up to his knees. "By the lands, I do hate getting wet."

The comment struck me as so fitting for a man who could turn into a cat that the tension inside me cracked with a laugh. "Really?" I said. "How strange."

He grinned at me sharply as if he thought I might need reminding that his secret was meant to stay secret.

Hatter shook his head at both of us. "I should be the one complaining. I've got the nicest clothes here, and they're getting ruined twice over." He pulled his hat more securely down on his head.

"Wash them off, then," I said. A tugging sensation ran through my chest as I stared into the pond's depths. "I think I need to go down again. At least the coming back up should be easier here."

"Are you sure you want to be the one to do this?" Theo asked.

My gut clenched, but I nodded. I wasn't sure whatever lay down there would release itself to anyone without the ring, and the thought of handing the ring over made every particle in my body balk.

It was mine. It had lit up for *me*.

Theo didn't argue. "Then, in case the coming back up isn't so easy…" He handed one end of his rope to me. "Tie it around your waist. I'll hold onto the other end. Give it a hard tug if you need help swimming back up."

"Thank you." I tied the jointed rope and tested it to make sure it was secure. Then, dragging in enough air to fill my lungs, I jumped from the shallows into the dark center of the pool.

The water coursed over my dress and hair as I plunged down. When I slowed, I jerked my head and shoulders downward, pulling myself deeper with my arms. There was nothing around me but a haze of murky water, the debris so thick I couldn't see more than a foot in any direction.

Where was the bottom? I kicked and swept my arms again and again, my lungs starting to ache with fresh strain. Then my reaching fingers grazed a powdery surface.

I dragged my hands across the floor of the pond, and my other hand snagged on a hard edge. Even in the cool water, the ruby flared hot where it was floating beneath my shirt. A ruddy light glanced off the murk.

I curled my fingers around the edge of the object and yanked. Whatever it was held and then popped free. Wrapping my arms around the thing I'd retrieved, I righted myself and pushed off the bottom back toward the surface.

The guys were waiting to tug me back into shallower ground. I gasped, refilling my lungs, and held up the thing I'd unearthed to see it.

My lips parted. The shrubs around the pool kept up their shrieking, but I could barely hear it, and not just because my ears were full of water.

I was holding a piece of armor, like a fancy version of a chainmail vest. Strands of a shimmering dark gray metal wove together to form a garment that would have covered me from shoulders to stomach. They bent beneath my testing fingers, but those pliant fibers felt as hard as steel at the same time.

A crescent of rubies glinted across the chest, just above the swell that would accommodate my breasts. This was armor meant specifically for a *woman*.

"Wow," I said, but even as the word slipped out, my awe started to dim.

I'd found one of the artifacts the ruby responded to. It was beautiful and impressively made. But a piece of armor wasn't going to defeat a tyrant queen.

CHAPTER NINE

Chess

One of the upsides of traveling through wilderness with the Inventor was getting to sleep in a tent that was really more like a tiny cabin. Somehow our White Knight had been carrying the entire structure I'd just woken up in folded inside his pack along with food and other supplies. The twins had each carried one as well.

The panes of wood-like material that made up the walls were thick enough that no light penetrated them, not that there was much light out there anyway in this square of night. Only the crackle of a fire and the sizzle of what smelled like sausages told me and my stomach that it was morning.

One of the *downsides* of this trip was the variety of terrain we'd already had to deal with, and how much of it was wet. I really shouldn't have complained about stepping into the pool to my thighs. We'd had to outright swim across the awful river to get back to Dee, after the White Knight had cut away a swath of razorweed to clear a safe path with a whirling blade he'd also constructed himself.

I had the urge to shake myself just thinking about it, even though I was perfectly dry beneath my blanket. Perfectly dry and much hungrier than I was still sleepy. I kicked off the blanket and emerged from the cabin-tent-whatever I'd shared with the Hatter.

Lyssa was just emerging from the "girls" cabin where she and Doria had slept. The others were already sitting around the firepit we'd made by the light of the moon, the shining orb which appeared to have slid to one side of the sky and was now yoyoing its way back to the other.

Lyssa's hair shone like moonlight come to earth. When she'd rubbed the rest of the mud out of her pale waves during our swim, the dirt had taken most of the dye with it. She'd have to cover her head when we returned to the city, but I couldn't say I was sorry to see it back to its normal state. It was best when people looked like themselves.

Dum was the one cooking the sausages. Hatter was cutting a few apples into slices with swift flicks of a paring knife. "I'm sure your skills are up to more than that," I said with a grin as I sat down beside him. "Trim out a rosette or a bird like you adorn your many hats."

"If we were going to wear them rather than eat them, maybe I would," Hatter retorted.

Theo passed around halves of rolls toasted over fire,

and then Dum the sausages and Hatter the apples. It was as satisfying a breakfast as I'd ever been able to count on. As I licked the mingled grease and apple tartness from my fingers, Lyssa shifted forward on the rock she was using as a seat.

"What do you think is our best route from here?" she asked. Her gaze traveled around the whole circle, but it stopped on the White Knight. He had shown he knew more about this place than the rest of us did. "We could keep walking across the Plains to head directly to that hill I saw, or we could go back to the train and keep going around."

"The Knave might have caught whatever train comes by next," Dum said. "Soon as we left the first one, we gave up the lead."

"But he doesn't know that," Dee said. He chuckled. "Let him chase all around the tracks thinking he's just behind us."

The White Knight slid the frying pan—which also folded, somehow or other—into one of the packs. "Dum raises a valid concern. It will take longer to reach the other end of the Plains on foot, but there's no way for the Knave or his guards to determine where or even if we got off the train. The question is whether we're safer facing him or dealing with the potential dangers the Checkerboard might present."

"Sinkholes and some weeds?" Doria said. "We handled those. I want to see what else this place can throw at us. I vote for walking."

"Of course you do," Hatter said, but he didn't look

upset about it. I imagined he'd prefer to keep his daughter as far away from the Knave as possible, no matter what the rest of the Plains might have in store. He sighed and leaned back on his hands. "I'd say we walk too. We'll have more control over our route, more flexibility about how we deal with any problems we run into. Unless you know of some danger up ahead that we wouldn't want to face, White Knight?"

The last question came with a bit of bite, the way Hatter often talked to the leader of the Spades these days. Which side of him was more the real Hatter? This one who prickled at the White Knight's presence or the one who'd used to laugh with him and egg him on when I'd first stumbled into their rebellion?

"Nothing I'm aware of," the White Knight said. "But we should still stay on guard. Wonderland may be stretching itself a bit after so long in stasis."

"I'm happy to go by whatever way will take us to the place we're wanting to go," I said.

Lyssa smiled at me with an amused glint in her eye. "As long as it's over dry land?"

I grinned back. "I'll brave the watery depths again for you, lovely. I just can't say I'll like it."

When we set off, Lyssa had pulled her woven vest of armor over the bodice of her dress. The dusky gray metal gleamed almost as much as the embedded rubies did. She made a face when she saw me looking.

"I know I look a little ridiculous. It's just easier to wear it than to carry it."

"Not ridiculous at all," I said. "If we come across

something that wants to stab you rather than drown you, I expect we'll all be glad you've got it on, too."

We didn't come across any trials of either sort as we marched across the moonlight terrain and passed into the next stretch of daylight. A few of the squares were willing to give us some peace. It wasn't the most pleasant going, though. The sun over this square had scorched the sky and the ground dry. Cracked earth gave off puffs of dust under our feet—and sometimes where we didn't step too. Sweat trickled down my back.

We walked at a diagonal to get us back in the row where Lyssa had spotted her special hill, which meant crossing that square took even longer. I think we were all ready to be done with the place by the time we reached the corner where two edges of cool dark haze touched just before another square of daylight. We gulped down a hasty lunch and walked on.

Vines slithered and bats flapped through the jungle beyond. After a few hours' hike, we emerged from at the top of a hill overlooking a wide plain flecked with wildflowers—and a small town.

The White Knight motioned for us to stop where we could stay hidden from view in the shade of a stand of trees. People swarmed around the scattered buildings, far more than could possibly have lived in that place. The sun caught on brilliant glints on their chests and the bright colors of their elegant clothes. Diamonds, I realized. Yes, there were the hunched beetle-like forms of the palace's silver air trolleys parked in a row beyond the buildings.

"What are they all doing there?" Lyssa asked.

As I squinted, two figures broke from the cluster of buildings onto the open plain, both of them wearing scarlet short pants and nothing else. Ah. Unicorn shook his sparkling mane, his glittering horn streaked red and his hooved hands raised to fight. Across from him, Lion let out a roar that shook the air all the way to where we were watching. His teeth flashed, and he lunged forward with a swipe of his massive paw. His claws raked a fresh gash across Unicorn's arm. His own shoulder was seeping blood where the horn had pierced it.

"The Lion and the Unicorn went fighting through the town," I murmured, and turned to Lyssa. "It's one of the many palace spectacles: pitting Lion and Unicorn against each other. The Diamonds never get enough of watching them fight. They must have decided the resumption of Time was as good a time as any for a temporary change in scenery."

"They do this all the time?" Lyssa said. "Don't the two of them mind all the fighting?"

"I suspect they got tired of it a long while ago," Hatter said. "But what the Queen says will be, will be as she said."

I couldn't have put it better myself.

Unicorn landed a punch with one of his hooves that made Lyssa wince. Lion reeled backward. Before the equine figure could even lower his horn, the feline one had sprung up again. He hurtled at Unicorn with another roar, and Unicorn didn't sidestep fast enough. Lion knocked him to the ground. They sprawled, the tawny man pinning the sparkly one beneath his paws.

Lion snapped out a command with a jerk of one hand. I didn't need to be able to hear his voice to know what he'd asked for. My body stiffened as a giddy lady among the Diamonds presented him with the victor's knife. He raised it triumphantly.

I should have looked away, but what can I say? I was stubborn as a cat. My limbs stayed tensed, a metallic flavor creeping through my mouth, as Lion lowered the blade to Unicorn's throat and sliced across it.

Not deep enough to kill. Just enough to mark him with that streak of blood that sprang up in an instant. A jabbing sensation shot through my ribs. Then I yanked my gaze away.

"But if he dies," Lyssa was saying.

"It's only a superficial wound," Theo said with a note of disgust. "A symbolic gesture, though a painful one. They'll seal it up with salve after they've all celebrated the victory."

"I expect Unicorn is used to it by now," I made myself say, my voice steady even if it felt detached from the rest of me. "He's the loser more often than not."

The crowd of Diamonds was milling out of the town around the two fighters, one still prone on the ground, the other standing with paws raised in triumph. Blood had spilled all down Unicorn's pale neck, but at least the knife was out of view.

"Let's leave them to their bloody fun," I said. "We've got better sport ahead of us, don't you think?"

No one seemed inclined to argue. We skirted the edge of the night-bound square until we'd come down the side of the hill. Then we ventured on toward Lyssa's cliff through a shallow grassy valley.

I strolled along at the back of the bunch, drinking in the bright floral air. Other than our company on the other side of the hill, this was my favorite square yet.

Lyssa drifted back to join me. She walked alongside me for a few minutes simply taking in the scenery. Then she said, quietly, "Are you all right?"

I hadn't hidden my reaction as well as I'd hoped. The lingering effects had all vanished now. I could give her a perfectly genuine grin and roll my answer lightly off my tongue.

"The people of the palace are like the food they serve there—so rich they give you indigestion. Nothing a brisk walk and a sweet breeze couldn't cure."

Lyssa nodded even though the slant of her mouth suggested she didn't totally accept my answer. She was getting keen, our Otherlander. I admired that canniness even as I wished she didn't notice quite so much about me.

"You Wonderlanders have quite the violent streak, huh?" she said. "Or maybe just the Hearts and the Diamonds do?"

"I can see how you might draw that conclusion," I said. "And I won't claim it's a false one. Are people in the Otherland so different?"

She grimaced. "Maybe not. Fair point. I guess everything else in this place is so different it's hard not to think the people should be too."

She paused, with a silence that tasted of words on the

verge of being spoken. Her steps slowed to let the others gain more ground on us. I eased up on my pace to match hers. A flicker of pleasure passed through my chest at the thought that out of everyone here, she was taking me into her confidence. That she wanted to hear my thoughts on serious matters despite the fact that I so often turned them into a joke.

"Chess," she said finally, her voice low. "Are you *sure* the Spades didn't kill the prince? Maybe just one or two of them off on their own, without Theo's permission? The way they did it—Doria told me they cut off his head, like the Queen does to everyone else… If that's even true."

"It is," I said with a twist of my stomach. "I saw it myself." More years ago than I'd bothered to keep track, but the memory still rose up vividly behind my eyes. All that blood splashed across the gleaming marble floor. Prince Jack's head lying in the midst of it, golden curls stained red so they almost matched his mother's hair, face bruised and battered as if his killer had played a game of kickball with it.

The Queen had barely had time to scream. Barely time to cast about to find the rest of him. It'd been just a few minutes before midnight when I'd darted over to investigate the commotion. With a tick of the clocks and a jolt, we'd all ended up back where we'd started—and the Queen's youngest son had been wiped from this world.

I willed the images away. "All I can tell you with certainty is that I've never heard so much as a murmur suggesting anyone with the Spades knows more about the murder than I do," I said. "And the way it was done—it wasn't set up like an act of rebellion. They pretended they were trying to *steal* something from the palace—that broken vase—as if killing him were an accident, which is ridiculous anyway because it's not as if anyone could have stolen anything for more than a day before it hopped back home. Or a matter of minutes, in this case. It was nearly midnight."

"Maybe they didn't *want* the Queen to think it had anything to do with the rebellion," Lyssa suggested.

"That's possible," I said. "But I wasn't part of the Spades back then, and even I knew she'd blame them no matter what the evidence showed. I've often wondered if it wasn't carried out by a Diamond."

Lyssa's eyebrows shot up. "Why would a Diamond kill him?"

"Oh, the Diamonds have large appetites, and for many things other than food," I said. "Power, for example. If one of them saw a clear enough opening to grasping the crown, they'd take it like that." I snapped my fingers. "I could see them thinking the murder would destabilize the Queen's rule. She did dote on Prince Jack. Before he came, many said she couldn't have another child, you know— her others were all grown by the time he was born. Losing him definitely broke something in her. But possibly not the way they hoped."

Lyssa made a humming sound. She studied the grass for a moment before saying, hesitantly, "You were there, even though it was almost midnight. Did you stay out at the palace all the way into the night very often?"

"At least as often as I didn't," I said glibly.

She glanced up, turning that pensive gaze on me, as if she were trying to read answers to questions she couldn't quite bring herself to ask out loud. I smiled and picked up my pace to catch up with the others. "Let's not get left behind."

If she ever got around to asking those questions, I hoped she made sure she truly wanted the answers.

CHAPTER TEN

Lyssa

It was amazing how easily I could tell apart the twins now that I'd matched personalities to names. In the moonless, starless square of night we'd been trekking across for a couple hours at least, Dum was obviously the one who'd pulled a lantern out of his pack to help light the way, and Dee was the one making goofy shadow shapes in front of that lantern as they walked.

Theo had kept his place in the lead with a lantern of his own. We'd had to edge across a narrow bridge that connected two sides of a chasm that dropped so far down the lantern-light didn't reach the bottom. After that, we'd needed to circle around a bunch of thorny tumbleweeds that gouged their way across the rocky terrain in an endless ring. At the moment, the walking was pretty easy, comparatively speaking. Especially when I could make out the glow of the next daylight square getting brighter up ahead.

"And then I flung it so hard I'll bet they never found it again," Dee said with a laugh, finishing his recollection of a mission he and his brother had been part of, with shadowy animation to illustrate.

"How long have you two been with the Spades?" I asked. They looked younger than the other guys—I'd have guessed college freshmen age—but Hatter had told me that people in Wonderland didn't age much once they reached adulthood, and then only in fits and starts. You couldn't really judge just by looking.

"Since we were kids, pretty much," Dee said cheerfully. "Our talents showed up young."

"The White Knight didn't have us running missions," Dum put in. "He protected us."

"Yep. Because if the Queen got wind of those talents, we'd have been assigned to the Hearts' Guard in a snap." Dee raised his feet high as if imitating the springy steps his twin could make, his shadow-legs stretching into the distance. "Mom went to the White Knight, and he helped us keep the secret. Started teaching us all the stealthy Spades stuff at the same time."

Dum frowned as if he didn't like his brother telling me so much about their situation. I still got the impression he didn't like me all that much for whatever reason. "Although some of us remember those lessons better than others," he said.

Dee waved him off and shot a smile at me. "Dum

thinks it's his job to worry about both of us. *I'm* actually the older twin, you know. Ten whole minutes."

I wasn't sure what Dum would have been worried about. When Dee had gone on the mission into the palace grounds with us a few days ago, he'd taken it seriously enough, as far as I could tell. Chess was proof that you could be a joker around here but still get the job done without losing your head.

"Well, thank you for coming along to help with this —" I started, and a burbling moan echoed through the air.

My mouth snapped shut, all the hairs on my arms standing on end. Our whole procession jerked to a stop, even Dee's eyes widening.

I'd heard that noise before. Hatter had called it a—

"Jabberwock," Chess said behind me in a deadpan voice. "Oh, how very delightful."

Another wavering groan rippled over us. Dum turned toward Theo. "Should we put out the lamps?"

"What direction is it coming from?" Hatter asked, his head swiveling.

The ground shook with a scrabble of claws that was *definitely* just ahead of us. The next moan sounded more like a roar. Theo spun around, his lantern swinging so the light swayed over us. "Run! Back to the spike-wheels."

I guessed those thorny tumbleweeds might give us some cover. We all dashed back the way we'd come, Hatter waving us on with his hand hooked around Doria's elbow, Chess touching my back to urge me faster.

Jaws snapped behind us with an unnerving rasp of

scraping teeth. Somehow I didn't think my fancy metal vest was going to do much to protect me if that thing decided to chomp on me. Why couldn't it have been a full body suit of armor?

The monster's moan warbled over us so close it rustled my hair, with a wash of hot breath that stunk like raw meat drenched in vinegar. I coughed and pushed my legs faster. The jostling lantern light caught on the prickly edge of one of the tumbleweeds just ahead—and then on four figures charging toward us.

The Knave and his guards. They must have been tracking us, nearly caught up with us. My heart stuttered at the glimpse I got of that gray sharkish face, yellowed by the lantern's glow.

My feet stumbled over a ridge in the rocky ground, and Chess yanked me to the side, out of reach of one of the guards' swords. Hatter and Doria had veered off in the opposite direction.

The Knave slashed at Dum, who sprang out of the way a second too late. Blood welled along a thin line on his forearm as his lantern slipped from his grasp. It rolled across the ground, the light wheeling like the tumbleweeds did, and a massive form barreled into our midst.

The jabberwock looked like the deformed offspring of a dragon and a macaw. Red and gold feathers shuddered all over its bulky body. Its long sinuous neck reverberated with one of its burbling moans. Even the ends of its wings had glinting talons, but I was more nervous about the claws that cut into the stone beneath each splayed toe on its wide feet.

Theo jumped in front of me with a flash of his lantern. The jabberwock's rectangular jaw detached from the rest of its snout to yawn open, revealing rows of jagged teeth like broken glass. Its head shot down, and it clamped those jaws shut around the torso of one of the guards.

The guy barely had time to gasp in pain before his voice cut off completely with a crunch of bones. My stomach churned. The jabberwock shook the now-limp body from side to side like a puppy with a toy and then hurled it off into the darkness.

We scrambled backward as it lunged at another of the guards, its nearest target. The man threw himself out of the way, but the creature veered to follow him at the last second. Its claws plunged into his chest with a gush of blood.

Oh, fuck. How the hell were we going to fight off that? I wasn't sure even an avalanche of thorny tumbleweeds would slow it down.

The jabberwock raked its claws through the guard's abdomen, scattering his innards across the ground. As if bored with its catch, it swung around—toward Hatter and Doria.

Every nerve in my body screamed in protest, and the ruby ring turned hot against my chest. The rubies on my vest gleamed with a faint glow. A tingling sensation ran through me, like the sense of certainty and power I'd felt in that brief moment when I'd slowed the train.

No. This monster would not kill my lovers, my friends, my allies. *No*.

Without thinking, I stepped toward it. "Lyssa!" Theo said, grabbing my arm, but I pushed him back.

"Jabberwock!" I called. My voice rang through the scattered light. "*Stop*."

Hatter had produced one of his hatpins that he usually put to work opening locks, holding it like a narrow dagger in front of him, his other arm extended protectively in front of his daughter. His face tightened and paled even more than it already had when the jabberwock paused. The creature's head swiveled around toward me.

Blood dribbled over the jabberwock's feathered jaw and streaked the ground beneath its feet. Its narrow eyes burned with a violet glow. My pulse thudded hard, but I took another step toward it and another, holding out my hand. The ring flared hotter; the rubies glowed brighter. The sense of sureness flooded me, taking the edge off my fear.

"Jabberwock," I said in a quieter voice. "Stand down. We're not your enemy."

The creature turned its whole body toward me with a swish of its tail. Its head dipped down toward my hand, but so slowly I didn't flinch. Theo had come up beside me. From the corner of my eye, I saw him stiffen. Chess sucked in a startled breath. Across from us, Hatter simply stared.

The jabberwock bumped its snout against my fingers. A whiff of that sour meaty smell wafted over me.

Swallowing hard, I gave the beast a light scratch just above its nostrils like I might have with a horse. Never mind that this thing was twice as tall as the biggest horse I'd ever seen and outfitted with much sharper appendages. It had responded to something—to the ring? To the vest? To both in combination?—and that was all that mattered.

"Thank you," I said. "Now you go, and leave us—"

A figure barreled out of the darkness, sword raised over his blunt head. I yelped, and the jabberwock wrenched away just in time to prevent the Knave from delivering a killing blow. As it was, his blade cut through the creature's neck with a spray of orange-gold blood.

The jabberwock shrieked and whipped toward its attacker. Its legs wobbled under it. The Knave might kill it after all.

A lump of guilt clogged my throat despite the monster's carnage. It was my fault; he never would have gotten that strike in if I hadn't lulled it. But Theo was yanking me away, and I had to follow him. If the jabberwock won its duel with Knave, I wasn't so sure I could calm the beast again if it turned on us afterward.

And if the Knave won, we definitely didn't want to stick around for him to turn his sword on us.

Footsteps pounded around me. It was hard to make out much except a shaky view of the landscape just ahead as Theo's lantern jostled in his grasp. "Do we have everyone?" I asked, taking a quick glance around. There was Hatter and Doria. Chess was still right behind me.

"Pulling up the rear!" Dee called, with a flash of the

lantern he must have scooped up, and I could tell from his buoyant tone that his twin was with him.

All we had to do was put enough distance between us and the two vicious creatures behind us to make sure the victor of the battle didn't find us. Easy peasy. Ha.

The muscles in my calves ached from the mad dash toward the tumbleweeds and now this new marathon. The uneven rocky ground stung the soles of my feet through my sneakers. I pushed myself faster anyway. The glimmer of the next daylight square came into view up ahead, expanding and brightening as we raced toward it.

A groan burbled up in the distance, trailing off with a painful gurgling. A shiver ran through me. I was pretty sure I knew who'd won the fight.

We burst from the darkness and nearly tumbled right over the jagged edge of a gully. Theo caught my hand and Chess my waist as we teetered on the crumbling rock.

A forest covered the landscape all around us, but the trees were so narrow and pointed they only provided streaks of shade from the sun glaring overhead. To our right, the woods stretched out over what appeared to be reasonably flat ground, the vegetation more sparse there. To our left, it dropped away steeply into a valley clotted with those narrow trees and other vibrant greenery.

My head reeled with the abrupt transition from darkness to light, open plain to forestland. The smell of blood lingered in my nose—had it gotten onto my clothes? My gut lurched at the thought. Images of the bodies the jabberwock had mangled darted through my memory.

But I couldn't say it was necessarily a more brutal monster than the Knave who was still on our trail.

"We can move faster on even terrain," Theo said, easing back from the gully.

As my gaze traveled down into the valley, the ring under my shirt heated with fresh energy. I inhaled deeply. Dry piney air filled my lungs.

I could do this. I could keep going.

"I think there's something down there," I said. "Another artifact, maybe. And it'll be harder for the Knave to spot us in the denser forest, won't it?"

I glanced around at my companions. They all hesitated, the three guys I knew best looking back at me with expressions that appeared a little dazed. Theo recovered himself first.

"If you feel there's something down there, then down we'll go. Quickly, everyone."

We hustled along the edge of the gully to a rough path that allowed us to scramble and skid through the brush rather than tumbling right down. After the first several feet, as the trees closed in more densely overhead, the slope evened out a little. We hiked on, needing to hold onto the branches around us less tightly than before. A drone of insect life hummed around us. The sun continued to glint between the tall peaks of the trees.

"There," I said, wiping sweat from my brow. "This isn't so bad."

"What the heck did you do back there?" Doria burst out. "You walked right up to the jabberwock—and it let you *pet* it."

"It was pretty fucking incredible," Dee said.

Oh. Right. *That* was probably why the guys had been looking at me so strangely.

I rubbed my mouth. "I don't know," I said. "It was like with the train. I just... felt I should do it, and the ruby got hot, and so far following it has worked out. There wasn't any other way I could have stopped it from charging at you two." My gaze slid from Doria to Hatter.

"I've never seen anything like it," he said, his tone dry but his eyes warm. "I think you might be able to challenge Chess for the title of maddest one here."

Chess harrumphed. "No one is ever going to top me for madness," he said breezily. He brushed his hand over my hair, and his voice softened. "It was quite a sight."

"Another testament to the ruby's power," Theo said.

Dum let out a sharp breath. "If only it worked on the Knave—or the Queen—too."

I touched the vest where the ring was tucked behind it. "Yeah, I definitely didn't get any impression I could tame *him*."

"Maybe the artifact we unearth down here will lend a hand with that conundrum," Chess said.

"If nothing else, I'm glad to get a breather after all that," I said, skirting a rock that jutted into our path.

And then a giant gnat dive-bombed at my face.

CHAPTER ELEVEN

Lyssa

I ducked down, jerking my arms up to protect my head. The rubies on my vest glowed with a tingling heat, but if it was supposed to protect me, it wasn't covering the currently important parts. The gnat's hooked forelegs rasped across my wrist, scraping raw lines into my skin.

I barely had time to register the pain. As the gnat—which was big enough to take on a mid-sized owl—whirred through the air and whipped back around toward us, more massive insects careened out of the foliage. I spotted a few more gnats, creatures with glossy wooden bodies and horse-like heads that I guessed were the Wonderland version of horseflies, dragonflies longer and thicker around than my arm with prickly wings like holly leaves, and butterflies flapping fluffy bread slices on their backs and baring vampiric fangs.

"You're fucking kidding me," Hatter muttered.

I grabbed a fallen branch from the ground and smacked it into a horsefly that was careening toward me. The impact sent it spinning away, but two dragonflies zipped in to take its place, their wings clicking like knives.

Chess leapt up, batting bugs out of the air like a cat swatting at moths. Theo produced a baton that reminded me of the ones I'd seen some of the Queen's guards carrying before, except his gave off an electric sizzle of sparks when it collided with one of the fanged butterflies. The twins spun around, Dee punching and Dum kicking with their elastic limbs. Doria took her cue from me and grabbed a stick of her own. She snapped off the end to form a jagged point.

"Come on," Hatter said, waving us after him as he scrambled nimbly on down the slope. I skidded over the pebbled ground after him. The others followed in an avalanche of feet and rattling stones.

More bugs shrieked through the air. A gnat slammed right into Hatter's bowler hat. He groped after it, but it went spinning off between the trees and disappeared amid the brush. The next dragonfly tried to take his scalp clean off. Doria leapt in with her branch, and Hatter pushed on with a grimace.

"There's a cave up ahead," he said. "We can hope those things won't follow us in there."

We clambered after him down the last steep incline to the bottom of the valley. A leap over a trickle of a stream brought us to the narrow mouth of the cave Hatter had spotted, its outer walls patchy with glowing yellow moss.

He leapt in, and the rest of us hurried after him into the cool shadows.

Hatter stopped several paces down the cave, where the passage opened a little wider. Water dripped from the ceiling onto the spikes of his bare hair. He swiped his hand over his head, still grimacing, and peered past us to the entrance.

The bugs hadn't followed. I exhaled in relief. When I peered into the cave's depths beyond Hatter, I couldn't make out anything but darkness, but my ruby flared with renewed heat.

"I think this is where the ring wanted us to go," I said. "I'm thinking a lantern or two would be nice?"

The White Knight fished his back out of his bag and passed it to Dum. Theo kept his electric baton in hand as we eased deeper into the cave. Hatter paused and hopped a gap that had opened in the floor ahead of us. He held out his hand to help me make the same jump.

As we walked on, he reached up instinctively as if to straighten the hat that was no longer there. His fingers curled around the air, and he yanked them back to his side. Going without something on his head clearly irked him.

A low rumbling carried from the darkness ahead. We all froze, our taste for caution finely honed after what we'd been through over the last two days.

The sound didn't get any louder, though. There was a pulsing rhythm to it, like some kind of heavy machinery. The ruby's heat seared through my skin.

I headed toward the sound, ignoring the fresh drips of

water off the ceiling and the slick texture of the rock against my fingers when I brushed the wall for balance, but still moving carefully. Dum caught up with the lantern just as the source of the rumbling appeared at the edge of its light.

The floor opened up again in front of us, but not in a chasm like before. This was a pit. And it literally *opened*—and closed, and opened, and closed, the rocky edges knocking against each other in a rough approximation of smacking lips. The floor of the cave seemed to be chewing on something very enthusiastically.

I eased closer. Theo stayed right beside me as the ground beneath our feet quivered. The lantern light fell into the pit, and my breath caught.

At the bottom of the pit, maybe seven or eight feet below us, a sword gleamed. Its grip was wrapped with some sort of pale cloth, but the pommel and the guard had a golden glint, and a large ruby shone at the top of the hilt. I wasn't exactly an expert on olden-time weaponry—okay, or any weaponry—but I didn't need to be to know it was gorgeous. And the sizzling energy of the ruby beneath my shirt insisted it was also *mine*.

As long as that freaking pit mouth didn't chew me up the second I tried to grab it.

I circled the pit, absorbing the rhythm of the chomping rocks and the shape of the sword beneath them.

"If I had something to hook it and pull it up…" Theo said. "The rope I brought wasn't made for this."

"There are swords back in the city," Hatter said. "You don't have to risk your life for one."

I shook my head. "The Queen is scared of *this* sword. She tried to make sure no one ever retrieved it. That means we need it." A sword would get us a lot farther in a battle than the armored vest would.

Hatter shrugged off his suit jacket. "Then I'll go for it," he said, rolling up his sleeves. "I'm the fastest here."

"I could hop down and spring right back up," Dum put in.

"I could hold the rocks open as well as I can," Chess offered.

That suggestion made me think of the sound of crunching bones. The rock was too relentless. And the same sort of prickling was creeping over me as with the jabberwock, as with the train.

"I think I have to do it," I said. "I have the ruby. It might not... *let* anyone else take it. But that also means..."

I breathed in and out, focusing even more intently on the rhythm. My hand came up to the center of my chest over the ring, willing more of its powerful heat through my body. That was magic. While I had it, I had magic too.

"We can do the same thing we did with the pool yesterday," I said, motioning to Theo. "Tie your rope around my waist. I'll jump down and lie down flat under the rocks while I grab the sword. The second they open again, you haul me back up as quickly as you can."

"Lyssa." Theo touched my cheek, turning my gaze

toward him. "Are you sure you want to do this?" he asked, his dark eyes holding mine.

"Wouldn't you, if you thought you had the best chance?" I said.

His jaw tightened for a second, but all he said was, "I would."

"Then there you go. Get out the rope."

I stood braced at the lip of the pit for a few seconds after he'd secured the knot. Then I jumped.

My body tucked itself into a crouch instinctively. The second my feet hit the rocky base, I sprawled forward, my hand shooting out to clutch the sword's hilt. The rocks chomped over me even closer than I'd bargained for, catching a bit of my hair and yanking. But the rest of my body stayed uncrushed. The rocks jolted open, and the rope jerked my body upward with a massive heave.

I swung around to push my feet off the pit's wall and bounded back out. As I landed, a laugh tumbled out of me. My fingers clutched tight around the sword. I held it up toward the cave's ceiling, unable to stop myself from grinning like a maniac.

"The sword of the blood-marked ruby. The Queen of Hearts had better watch out."

"You mean you're actually going *hunting*?" Doria said, looking from one twin to the other. "Do you even know what you're doing?"

Dee grinned. "Our mom sometimes gets paranoid

about what the butcher shop offers. She taught us a few tricks. It'd be nice to have something extra for dinner to celebrate, don't you think? Why don't you come with us?"

Doria glanced over at Hatter where he was standing with the rest of us contemplating the site we'd picked to spend the night. The hilltop gave us a vantage point all around the square in the starlight from the clear sky. With at least a couple of us standing guard at any given point in the night, the Knave wouldn't have a chance to sneak up on us.

Hatter made a shooing motion at his daughter. "Stay close to them. They've proven they can take care of themselves; I'd imagine they can handle you too." He shot the twins a look that said they'd better or there'd be hell to pay.

Dee saluted him, and they set off down the hill.

Theo grabbed a couple things from his bag. "Chess, why don't you come with me to make sure there's nothing else in the area we need to be worried about. I have a couple deterrents I'd like to set down too. If there's one jabberwock on the prowl, there could be others." He turned to Hatter and me. "Can you two get the cabins set up? Holler if you need anything. This might take some time, but we won't go *too* far."

"Cabin assembly it is," Hatter said with a waggle of his nimble fingers. "Come on, looking-glass girl."

I stripped off the metal vest, which was starting to weigh heavy on my shoulders, set it next to the sword by my bag, and got to work.

The assembly of the tiny but sturdy cabins Theo had

brought for us to sleep in happened about three quarters through Hatter's efforts rather than mine. In my defense, it was hard to keep up with him. His deft hands bent the folded structures into shape and snapped this piece and that into place as if he'd spent most of his life making temporary homes and not hats.

I managed to do most of the work on one, though. I stepped back to study it in the amber light of the lantern the others had left behind for us, making sure the roof was straight where it slanted around the height of my shoulders. When I decided it was level enough and glanced toward Hatter, he was watching me, an awed warmth in his gaze.

"What?" I said, abruptly self-conscious.

He shook himself out of his apparent reverie. "Sorry. I was just remembering that moment when you had the jabberwock bowing to you." He let out a rough chuckle. "That was something special all right, even if it was mad."

My cheeks heated. "The ring is special," I said, and grabbed a couple of the blankets and the lantern. "I couldn't have talked it down without that."

Hatter made a dismissive sound as he ducked after me into the first cabin. He spread a blanket at one end while I took care of the other. The spongy floor wasn't as comfortable as a mattress, but it offset the hardness of the actual ground we'd had to sleep on just fine.

"I happen to be pretty familiar with people and their accessories," he said, sitting back on the blanket. "I should know the impact has a lot more to do with how the person wears the item than how the item wears the person."

My gaze leapt to the uneven spikes of his dark blond hair, still uncovered. "Or how the person doesn't wear it? I guess you didn't pack another hat."

Hatter winced. "No. I suppose I'll just have to hope everyone can remember my name without one until I get back."

He said it like he was joking, but I could read genuine discomfort in his expression despite the softness of the lantern's glow. I scooted closer so I could ruffle those spikes. He caught my wrist when my fingers had already grazed his hair. A different sort of heat washed over me, kneeling that close to him, his fingers encircling my arm, his hair unexpectedly silky beneath my own fingertips. I could almost hear Melody egging me on: *Go get him, girl.*

"I didn't expect you to have to sacrifice so much, coming out here with me," I said, half teasing, half serious. "I'm sad that it came to this."

"I suppose I'll survive somehow," Hatter replied. "Better my hat than my head."

His grip on my wrist loosened, and my hand came to rest not-entirely-by-accident on his thigh. It was a little hard to think, but part of me felt the need to be completely serious for a moment.

"Really," I said, looking into his green eyes. "You didn't have to come with me at all. You weren't even sure the artifacts existed. I wouldn't have blamed you if you'd stayed back in the city, and I hope the trip hasn't been too horrifying."

A smile twitched at his lips. "Lyssa," he said, "loss of hat, sinkholes, blood-thirsty monsters, and all, there's nowhere I'd rather have been. What we're doing here is worth some unpleasantness." He paused. "*You're* worth going through some unpleasantness for."

"Oh," I said, a giddy flutter rising in my chest. "Well. I'm sorry about your hatlessness anyway."

His smile curved higher, the corners of his eyes crinkling. "You could always distract me from the agony of the loss."

I couldn't help grinning in return. "And how would you suggest I do that?"

He didn't bother to answer, just lowered his mouth to mine.

If Theo kissed like he was taking command, then Hatter kissed like he was dedicating himself to the cause. His breath mingled hot with mine, and his fingers eased up my side, trailing tingles of warmth in their wake. I leaned into him, my hand sliding behind his neck and then pushing at his suit jacket. He shed it as easily as he had when he'd been volunteering to dive into that chomping pit to retrieve my sword.

His body felt even hotter with only the thin layer of his dress shirt in the way. He kissed me harder as I traced my fingers over the muscles of his shoulders and down his chest. Then he palmed my breast with a quick swivel of motion that raised my nipple to a point with a spark of sensation. I gasped into his mouth.

Hatter tugged the wide neckline of the dress down over my shoulder and dislodged my bra at the same time.

His hand slid under the fabric to cup me skin to skin. With one flick of his skilful thumb, my whole body was quivering with desire.

"Perhaps best if we merely rearrange clothes rather than removing them," he murmured. "Seeing as our situation here may turn out to be precarious." He hesitated, his hand stilling. "Unless—if this isn't how—if you'd rather wait—"

For what? A bed we might never actually make it back to if this adventure took a turn for the even worse—a bed where we'd been just as easily interrupted anyway? The others were out around the camp keeping an eye on things, and it'd sounded like they'd be gone a while. And right now I wanted this man with all the determination and tenderness he was capable of more than I'd ever wanted anyone.

"Fuck no," I said.

Hatter beamed at me, so brilliant in his delight that I had to catch the knot of his tie and pull him into another kiss.

He tipped me over on the blanket, one of his knees settling between my legs. As we kissed and caressed, my hands yanking his shirt from his slacks and traveling up over the bare skin beneath, I couldn't help arching toward him. My core ached for attention. My thigh brushed the bulge beneath his fly, and his breath stuttered before he re-captured my mouth.

That contact appeared to be all the cue he'd needed. Hatter reached down to draw the skirt of my dress up, his fingers tracing an electric path across my skin to the hem of my panties. His thumb grazed over the fabric in a teasing circle and then pressed down right on the spot where I needed it most.

My hips bucked up with the bolt of pleasure. I sucked back a cry. If Theo and Chess were close enough to pick up a holler, I didn't want to test the limits of their hearing.

I felt more than saw Hatter's smile. He worked my panties down just a couple inches and cupped me completely, his mouth marking a scorching path across my jaw and down the side of my neck at the same time. Another gasp escaped me as he dipped two fingers into the slick needy center of me. With a few swift strokes, he found the perfect point of pleasure. I bit my lip against a moan, bucking into his touch.

There are many uses a nimble set of fingers can be put to, he'd told me once. No fucking kidding.

I reached for his slacks, but Hatter nudged my hand to the side. "Not yet," he said by my ear, his voice rough but steady. "I want to watch you find your bliss, and then I want to hear you, and then I want to feel you."

My mind was already too hazed with the bliss he was generating to totally make sense of that, but as his fingers pulsed inside me and his thumb whirled over my clit, I was in full agreement with whatever he wanted to do with me.

His mouth came back to mine, our tongues twining together until my breath broke into panting. Hatter gazed at my face with so much hunger that his expression as much as the deft twist of his fingers tipped me over the edge. My eyes rolled back with the wave of pleasure that radiated through me. In an instant, my limbs turned into ecstatic jelly.

"Beautiful," Hatter said in a ragged voice that turned me on even more. He brushed his lips against mine once more and dipped his head to my chest. As he caught one nipple in his mouth through the dress's delicate fabric, a fresh knot of need formed down below, as quickly as the last one had shattered.

He worked over one breast and then the other until I was whimpering, my fingers tangled in his hair. Tugging my dress higher, he eased his way down. His lips grazed my sternum, my belly, the dip just beneath. Then he swept his tongue across my clit, and a fresh rush of pleasure raced through me.

All I could do was clutch on to his hair, trying not to pull too hard, as his mouth provoked a whole new range of sensations from my sex. Lips and tongue and teeth as skillful as his fingers had been, and oh God that surge of bliss was building all over again, so swiftly I could hardly breathe.

He'd said he wanted to hear me. I let more of the whimpers I'd been trying to contain slip out, followed by a moan as he gently nipped my clit. "Hatter," I mumbled. "So fucking good." And then something inarticulate that hopefully got the idea across all the same as his tongue curved right up into my slit. My body shuddered with the force of my second orgasm.

I still hadn't gotten what I wanted most, though. Hatter raised his body so he could kiss my collarbone, my neck, before making his way back to my mouth, and I found the wherewithal through my jellified state to grasp the zipper of his slacks. This time he didn't stop me. My fingers grazed his straining erection through the silky material of his boxers—question finally answered!—and he groaned with a shaky inhalation.

Together, we tugged his slacks down, and he yanked my panties completely off. I raised my hips, and he bowed his head over me as he slid inside. I was so wet and ready his cock practically glided through me, hard and hot and exactly what I'd been waiting for.

The deeper sense of bodily connection brought a rush of emotion into my chest. I hugged him tightly where I'd slipped my arms back up under his shirt and lifted my head. Hatter met me for the kiss I'd been seeking, drawing it out as he started to move inside me.

After all that build-up, I'd expected our final coming together to be frantic. Hatter rocked into me, sinking a little deeper still with each pump of his hips, intense but deliberately drawing every ounce of pleasure he could out of our joining. It was the most delicious torture. My body quivered with the heady sensation expanding from my core. I wanted him to hurry up already, and I wanted this never to end.

I raised my legs to brace against his thighs, letting him plunge so far his body brushed my clit. I gasped, and the control Hatter had been holding onto broke. He thrust into me harder, faster. "Lyssa," he muttered into my hair, gripping my hip and urging me higher to meet him. "Fuck. You drive me mad, but in the best possible way."

A giggle slipped out of me. "You make me pretty

bonkers too," I managed to say before I was whimpering again, rocking into his thrusts, chasing one more ecstatic release. His cock pressed against that sweet spot inside me as it filled me in a way his fingers hadn't managed. The bliss of it swelled from my core through my entire body. Then it hit me like a tidal wave, crashing through my body.

I clenched around him, and Hatter made a strangled sound of pleasure. His hips jerked faster. As I clung to him, he came in a searing liquid gush inside me.

We stayed like that for a moment, him braced over me, our bodies joined, both our chests heaving. Then he eased himself down beside me, rolling me to face him. With his hand on my cheek, he kissed me as thoroughly as he'd just made love to me.

"We should probably finish getting the camp set up," he said under his breath when he drew back. "But... maybe not quite yet?"

"Definitely not quite yet." I squirmed closer to him and tucked my head against his chest. The citrusy smoky smell of him filled my nose, and a pang formed in my chest.

All of this was only temporary, only until I could find my way back to the Otherland. I didn't belong here in Wonderland. I didn't *want* to abandon my life back home. But in that moment all I wanted was to pretend this brief bliss could last forever.

CHAPTER TWELVE

Theo

Lyssa was already starting to bloom into her role. I could see it in her posture, in the ease with which she pulled the woven metal vest back on after she'd eaten a brief breakfast. She didn't even know what she was meant for yet, and still she was moving toward it at full speed.

The observation sat strangely in my stomach, admiration and irritation mingling together. The former she'd earned; the latter had nothing, really, to do with her. Maybe when we were back in the city, where I had my office and my materials at my fingertips, all my people to call on, it would fade completely.

I certainly hoped so. It didn't befit the man I was meant to be at all.

The twins shuffled around the fire pit, dousing the flames and packing up the few dishes we'd used. Hatter and Doria were folding up the cabins. Chess stood poised at the edge of the hilltop, gazing toward the square of daylight we'd recently left as he kept watch for the enemy who might emerge at any moment.

I stood up and turned toward Lyssa. "I think we've found enough. With the Knave potentially so close at our heels, we should head back to the city now."

We'd have to deal with the Knave and his remaining guard along the way, if the jabberwock hadn't fatally wounded them in the skirmish. We couldn't let him go back and inform the Queen of the company Lyssa had been keeping. But I didn't think that idea would go over well with our Otherlander. Better for her conscience that I arranged it more as if by chance than as a straightforward plan to end a man's life.

Perhaps I could send the twins off on a little side mission when we had a better idea of the commander of the guards' location. He hadn't appeared overnight. I wasn't going to assume anything from that fact, though. He might have only temporarily lost our trail, or he might be hanging back on purpose, wary of our now much greater numbers, waiting for an ideal opportunity to achieve an advantage.

Lyssa frowned, blinking at my suggestion. "Head back? But there's got to be at least one more thing. Mirabel said, 'The sword, the scepter, and the shield.' I guess this must be the 'shield'." She tapped the vest. "So the scepter is still out there. *Something* is at that hill Aunt Alicia drew. I'm sure of it. What if we need it if we're going to stop the Queen?"

That something was what had sent her grand-aunt running, no doubt. I wasn't sure Lyssa finding it would do more good than harm. And the thought of the Knave getting his hands—or his sword—on her made every part of me tense.

I tipped my head toward the sword she'd leaned against her bag. "I expect a sword will be a lot more useful for that purpose," I said honestly.

"We don't know what magic the scepter might have in it, though. We're already out here. The hill can't be that much farther."

True. I didn't think it would take us more than the day to reach the spot we'd seen from afar. Nevertheless…

"We've already escaped death by a hair multiple times since we arrived here," I said. "Sometimes only through luck. I'd rather we return in one piece with what we've gotten so far than die trying for more. You've done enough, Lyssa. You've done more than most people would have believed was possible."

I let all the warmth I felt for her flow into my voice, but the praise didn't soften her expression the way I'd managed in times past. She'd believed in me above anyone else in Wonderland back then.

She was learning to believe in herself here in our land. I wished I could have been nothing but pleased to see it.

"It doesn't feel like enough," she said, and hesitated. Her jaw set. "If anyone wants to head back now, that's all right. I don't want anyone risking their lives just because I said so. But I'm going to that hill. If there's something there, I'm going to find it."

More protests swelled in my throat. My concern about the dangers ahead was perfectly real. And also, she wasn't ready for the full truth of these artifacts yet. I needed more time to ease her into it. But I couldn't tell her that.

What else could I say that she would listen to? I could push on the idea of the Queen beginning her executions, but I'd told Lyssa before we should have at least a week.

The longer we argued without my convincing her, the more my authority diminished in the eyes of everyone watching us. My whole body balked at the thought of backing down, but looking at the determination in her face, I suspected that was the stronger move.

I certainly wasn't leaving her to fend for herself against whatever other horrors the Checkerboard Plains might offer up.

I let out a chuckle, forcing my lips to form a wry smile that I hoped didn't betray the tension inside me. "I should know better than to underestimate you," I said, as if it were only her willingness I'd been concerned about. "If you're ready to adventure onward, then let's see where the Plains take us next."

No one else offered any argument. Doria scooped up one of the lanterns and set off in the lead as soon as we'd packed up. Hatter hurried after her with a wary scan over the landscape. Chess grabbed the other lantern and meandered a little apart from our procession to cast the light over a wider span. Lyssa jogged to catch up with Hatter and his daughter, the ruby-set sword swaying awkwardly in her grasp.

Anyone who knew anything about sword fighting

could have seen that Lyssa knew nothing at all. When we'd been making our way through the gully yesterday, she'd tried wedging the weapon into her bag for a while, but the hilt had kept banging into her back, so she'd switched to carrying it by hand. The way she was holding it, an opponent could have knocked it out of her fingers in an instant. And that was when she hadn't switched it to her weaker hand to rest her arm.

When we were back at the city and I could unearth a sword of my own, I'd have to give her a few lessons. It should actually be rather invigorating, in more than one way, watching her take to the weapon. The ten years of training under my belt might as well have some additional use.

My imagination drifted for a moment to the way I might set one hand on her hip and stand against her from behind as I guided her arm, feeling every motion of her muscles tensing and relaxing. At the thump of a stone Dum kicked, I jerked my mind back to the present.

My gaze lifted to Lyssa automatically. My feelings for her were all tangled through the rest of me, too thoroughly to be easily picked apart. By the will of the lands, I wouldn't need to.

"Any idea what specific dangers we might be up against today, White Knight?" Dum asked where he'd fallen into step beside me.

"Of course you'd ask about that and not what wonders we might see," Dee teased at my other side. "It's been a wild ride, that's for sure."

"Thank you for coming along for it," I said. The twins

had proven themselves dependable in their different ways as they'd matured, but I hadn't been able to warn them of all the risks we'd face on this particular journey. If I'd known the Knave would wind up chasing us, or that we'd find ourselves walking clear across the Plains…

No, they probably still would have come. I'd earned that loyalty, and they gave it happily. As if I would have turned away their pleading mother and let the Queen's recruiter notice their fledgling abilities. With their rebellious spirits, they'd have been lucky to make it a year before they were sent off to the Oyster Cove to have their heads regrown like dim automations.

They'd always balanced each other out, Dum holding Dee back when his eagerness got away from him, Dee helping Dum loosen up. That was the kind of teamwork you couldn't manufacture.

"You asked, we came," Dum said, as if it really were that simple to him. He shrugged. "It hasn't been *that* bad on the whole." He paused and glanced sideways at me. "Are you sure continuing on was the right idea?"

That argument had sown doubt in the wrong places. I gave a light laugh. "I simply thought it was a good moment to test our Otherlander's resolve for going forward," I said, in a low voice so Lyssa wouldn't overhear. "If she wasn't completely dedicated to continuing, she could falter and get the rest of us into trouble."

"No need to worry about that one wavering, from what I can see," Dee said. "She's got the guts it takes to run with the Spades, no question." He sucked a breath through his teeth with a soft whistle. "Can you imagine how much these artifacts will freak out the Queen? We'll turn the tables on her for sure. I can't wait."

Dum shot him a skeptical look. "I don't think it's going to be *that* easy, even with a pretty sword and all. And the Otherlander…" He studied Lyssa's back. "She's held her own. No one could argue that. But she's shifting things too. She still might get us into a lot of trouble, and does she really know what she's in for then?"

She didn't. Which was exactly why we couldn't drop a huge burden on her head without proper preparation.

"Can she even fight with that thing?" he added, nodding to the sword.

"We can always pass the ring and all on to someone who's a better fighter, right?" Dee said. "Her aunt or whoever might have found it, but it belongs to Wonderland."

It did, and it also belonged to her. The weight of the falsehoods I was juggling pressed down on me for a moment. I squared my shoulders. "Always a possibility," I said. "We'll see how we can best position ourselves and the things we've found once we return to the city."

That answer appeared to satisfy the twins for now. As we walked on through the hazy darkness, the weight sank down to my gut.

How many doubts would they have if they realized how much of the truth I'd held back from them? Was there some way I could make it seem as if I'd only just discovered the full story too?

But then, there were other, deeper lies I'd been telling

for much longer, lies I couldn't avoid taking responsibility for when the time came.

No point in building a solution until you see what the problem is, the old White Knight, my mentor, used to say. He might have had some odd ideas about some things, but he'd been wise about that.

I strode on faster. The sooner we made it to Lyssa's hill, the sooner I could be back on familiar ground.

A long hike later, we reached the next daylight square. We stepped out into dry heat beneath a clear sun-soaked sky. Sand shifted beneath our feet. Cacti dotted the desert that sprawled out ahead of us. As we paused to take in the landscape, several of the prickly green forms adjusted their positions, twisting one way, turning an arm up or down. Lyssa stiffened for a second.

There didn't appear to be anything especially threatening about the vegetation. I motioned the others onward, stepping up to the front of the procession.

The sand hissed, and a serpentine body arced up into view, purple spines jutting along its sinewy back. Lyssa let out a squeak, and it dove deeper. In a second, it had vanished.

"Scrapeworm," I told our Otherlander. "It won't hurt you as long as you don't eat it. Highly poisonous."

She sputtered a laugh. "I don't think there's much chance I'll do that."

The sand dragged at our shoes as we marched on. It felt pleasant enough, soft and smooth, but walking over it was twice the strain solid ground was. We weren't going to make great time through this square—but detouring would take even longer.

I focused on finding a rhythm. I'd just settled into one when a skittering noise brought my gaze to the right.

A pack of birds trotted toward us down a dune flecked with gravel. They looked for all the world like overblown basketballs decked out in fluffy blue feathers, tiny heads posed tight against their rounded bodies, each nearly as tall as my waist. My spine went rigid. Jubjub birds.

"Oh my God," Lyssa said. "Those are actually really *cute*. That's a nice change of pace from disturbing and bloodthirsty."

"Ah," I said, and that was all I managed to get out before the couple dozen birds broke into a full-out charge.

The Jubjub birds' heads shot out from their bodies on spindly necks, pulling out the long piercing beaks that had been hidden in their feathers too. Beaks hard and sharp enough to puncture steel. Human flesh was a piece of cake. And unfortunately they did enjoy fresh meat when they could get it.

Hatter whipped out one of his hatpins, and Chess raised his fists. Lyssa swung her sword in front of her, her arms wobbling, and something inside me twisted.

I couldn't stand to see her try to take those things on and lose. I wasn't sure I could stand it if she saved the day all over again either.

"Lyssa!" I said before I could second-guess the impulse. I held out my hand. "The sword. Now!"

I still knew how to make a command. Lyssa startled, but

she heaved the sword toward me, aiming the hilt toward my reach. As she ducked back behind the others, I snatched the sword out of the air. In one swift motion, I sprang forward and sliced the blade through the pack of Jubjub birds.

With that one slash, three of their heads burst off their bodies, their fluffy forms collapsing. I gave a shout, stomped my foot, and ran at them with another swipe to cut through a couple more.

The one thing you need to know about Jubjub birds, if you're going to know anything, is they're cowards at heart. The spray of a few of their companions' blood and my yell sent the others scattering. The pack raced back over the hill they'd attempted to ambush us from, leaving a rain of frightened feathers in their wake.

Dee started to clap as I lowered the sword. "Nice one, boss!"

I started to smile, but my sense of accomplishment faded behind a prickle of shame when I remembered why I'd asked for the sword in the first place.

Maybe there hadn't been time to talk Lyssa through what she needed to do. Maybe it'd made the most sense for me to step in. But I could admit that hadn't been the only reason I'd done it.

That didn't matter as long as no one but me ever knew it.

CHAPTER THIRTEEN

Lyssa

Theo adjusted his grip on the sword, looking every inch the warrior even in his white button-up and gray slacks. It was easier to admire the strength in his form, the speed with which he'd dispatched those freaky killer birds, now that said freaky killer birds weren't stampeding toward us. I'd started to freeze up, and he'd been there, ready to tackle anything in the blink of an eye.

Should I have gone along with his suggestion this morning that we head back to the city immediately? It hadn't *felt* right, and my feelings had seemed to guide me pretty well over the last few days, but I hadn't enjoyed arguing with him. He'd guided me awfully well since I'd arrived in Wonderland too.

But it hadn't been personal. I had more of a connection to the artifacts than he did, thanks to Aunt

Alicia's ring—I understood the power coursing through those rubies better than he could. And he must have recognized that, because I hadn't needed to say that much before he'd agreed.

He'd trusted my judgment. That memory made me almost as tingly as watching the flex of his muscles as he lowered the sword.

Theo started to turn toward us, and the ruby flashed red. His fingers jerked apart, dropping the sword as if it had burned him. It thumped on the ground. Theo smacked his hand against his side. From the flinch of pain through his expression, it really had hurt him.

"Are you okay?" I said with a hitch of concern in my chest, stepping toward him.

He waved me off with his other hand as he lowered the possibly wounded one to his side. He kept it angled toward him so I couldn't see the skin on the inside.

"The grip heated up all of a sudden," he said in an even tone. "Took me by surprise. Those rubies do pack a lot of kick, don't they?" He shook his head ruefully.

He bent as if to pick the sword up, and I leapt forward first. I was the one who'd started us on this quest—if it was going to burn anyone, it should be me.

"Thank you," I said. "I revise my earlier statement about those bird-things. Definitely not cute. Definitely not a change of pace."

Theo's chuckle didn't sound particularly strained. But as he let me take the sword, he motioned Dum over. The solemn twin passed him the tube of salve without any spoken request.

I curled my fingers gingerly around the sword's grip. The cloth that bound it felt warm, but not unpleasantly so. Of course, the ruby had gone dull too. I'd felt how searing the ring could become.

It had never physically burned me, though. Did the sword not like to be used for killing monsters? I wasn't sure it would be much use to us then. It would figure if a weapon worked that way in Wonderland.

"Onward?" I said, with a tentative look Theo's way.

"Onward," he said with an easy smile. Maybe it hadn't even hurt him, only startled him. He might have wanted the salve for a blow one of the birds had struck during the fray.

I held the sword a little tighter as we walked on, scanning any slopes we passed for hints of blue feathers. The cacti kept up their periodic vogueing, but no more killer birds appeared. We even passed a pool of faintly sweet water where everyone refilled their canteens. I gulped a little extra with my hand to counter the dryness in the air.

The dark haze of the next night square ahead of us shifted in rippling patterns as we approached. I understood why the second we crossed the threshold. Wind whipped through the darkness, yanking at my hair and swatting my face. The lanterns tossed in the guys' hands.

I braced the sword against my vest so the wind couldn't catch it. How far were we going to have to walk through this?

We formed a tight line, Theo at the head with one

lantern and Dum at the back with the other, huddling against the wind as we walked. If Hatter hadn't lost his hat yesterday, I doubted he'd have been able to hang onto it through this place. My gaze settled on the back of his head, the tufts of his hair blown even spikier than usual, with a flutter in my stomach that was both affection and heat in memory of our little interlude yesterday.

The wind fell back, even though it still howled all around us. Had we entered a sort of eye in the storm? Doria eased up beside me as we hurried on through the dark. Maybe she'd noticed my fond glance a moment ago, because she cocked her head and spoke just loud enough for me to hear her over the bluster around us.

"So… you and Pops are having kind of a thing, huh?"

I nearly swallowed my tongue. "Um…"

"It's okay. That's why I'm asking. *He'd* have a conniption before he told me anything like that. But I think it's kind of cool. You're cool." She smirked. "You got him to stop being such a spoilsport all the time."

"I mean, it's not—" I hesitated. It was hard to say whatever I had with Hatter wasn't serious, especially after our intense encounter yesterday. Especially with the way my heart lifted just looking at the back of his freaking head. I groped for the right words. "I'll be going back to the Otherland when we can find another mirror that'll open up the way there. Hopefully after you all take down the Queen of Hearts, but… I'm going back."

Doria shrugged. She'd grown up in Wonderland with all those laissez-faire ideas about relationships and intimacy, after all. I guessed I shouldn't be expecting her to react like the teenage daughter of a guy back home might.

"Most people here don't stick together very long anyway," she said. "Dad says my birth parents were unusual that way. They had something really special." The corner of her mouth turned up as her gaze traveled to one of the twins—Dee, I thought, from his relaxed expression. "Maybe I'm weird, but I hope I get to have that too someday."

It looked like I wasn't the only one crushing hard. Did Hatter know his daughter was swooning over one of the guys here?

Probably better if he didn't. I didn't know how Wonderlanders felt about age differences, but Dee didn't seem like the type to take advantage where he shouldn't anyway.

"You know," I said, "back in the Otherland, wanting that wouldn't be weird at all. Never settling down is weird to us."

"Hmm. Maybe I should visit sometime."

She laughed, and the sound was caught by the wind as it roared up around us again. Goodbye, eye of the storm. I ducked my head against it, shielding my watering eyes with my arm, and we trudged on without trying to talk any more.

Between the sandy landscape before and the windblown one after, my legs were throbbing by the time the edge of daylight crept into view ahead of us. My knuckles ached where my fingers were clamped tight around the sword's hilt. I pushed myself faster anyway, just wanting to be out of this blistering gale already.

The second we stepped out into the gentle sunlight, my spirits leapt. We'd finally reached the hill I'd spotted from a distance. It looked even more like a wave up close, arcing up over the landscape with its narrow peak pointing almost straight down. All that lay between us and it was a stretch of field scattered with several trees hunched in a similar shape and strands of long grass that also bent over on themselves, as if the whole environment were echoing the hill.

As I gazed at our surroundings, taking a moment to catch my breath, a faint clattering broke through the peaceful murmur of the breeze. The Plains train with its mahogany engine and cars whirred into view at the far end of the square, beyond the hill but near enough that I couldn't imagine it was more than a couple hours' walk farther. A grin sprang across my face.

"We're right by the other end of the loop," I said. "We can check out the hill and then hop back on right away." Maybe we could make it back to the city before even one more day had passed.

"Let's get to it, then," Dee said, bounding forward. I hustled after him with a skip of my pulse. What had been so important here that this specific place had stuck in Aunt Alicia's mind—that she'd drawn it and kept that drawing even long after she'd left Wonderland behind?

We were several steps into the tall grass when the blades around me whipped upward. With an unsettling hiss, they split apart into flayed strands that shot toward my legs, my waist, and my arms.

A squeak of protest slipped from my lips. My sword hand slashed out instinctively. The shining blade sliced through the flayed blades of grass with a snickering sound, but more were already launching themselves at me.

Several strands snagged around my ankle. One licked over my wrist just before I chopped it down, scraping across my skin with a sandpaper texture that left a raw trail in its wake.

Someone swore behind me. I swung the sword again, hacking this way and that, managing to free my ankle. I dodged out of the way of another spray of strands and chopped right through them. The grass all around me lay cut and limp.

The others were still struggling against the grassy bindings. Theo was slicing his way free with a little knife that was making slower work than my sword had, but the others hadn't been carrying any blades they could quickly reach. I hurried to Doria, severing the strands that had yanked her wrists together and then those that were tangled around her legs from thighs to feet. She darted away from that spot with a sputter of relief, and I turned to the guys.

Hatter had fared the best with his full suit. The grass hadn't managed to scratch him up at all. When I'd hacked him free, he produced a hatpin from inside his suit and set to work piercing and ripping the strands that had wound around Dum while I slashed the ones holding Dee. The cheerful twin had managed to snap the strands around his wrists with his flexible arms, but they held him tight around his waist and knees, and the ones he'd broken had left tracks across his bare forearms.

By the time I'd finished with him, Theo was just hewing away the last few bits of grass twined around his ankles. Where the hell was Chess? My heart lurched as I scanned the field. Had he been whisked away somehow in the chaos?

My gaze caught on a heap of grass that appeared to have formed a sort of funnel farther across the field. It twitched slightly as if moved by some presence inside it. An invisible presence.

"Chess?" I said, moved toward it. He might have slipped out of sight to avoid any additional dangers that came at us, but I didn't know why he was staying so still and quiet now. A nervous prickle ran down my back.

He didn't answer. I stopped in front of the heap of grass, more obviously shaped around a brawny torso and legs now, and tentatively reached toward the air above it. My fingers collided with the warm fabric of Chess's shirt over his chest. It rose and fell with a shallow shaky breath.

Had the grass done something else to him while it held him—poisoned him or put him into some kind of fugue state? My pulse thumping harder, I slid my hand up to cup his jaw.

"Chess," I said softly, trying to keep the panic out of my voice. "I need you to make yourself visible again so I can cut the grass off you. I don't want to cut *you* by accident. Can you do that?"

He gave a twitch of a nod. Then he shimmered into

view, all of him at once, no floating grin. Because he wasn't grinning at all. His mouth was set in a tight line, his forehead damp with sweat and a glassy look in his eyes.

The grass must have poisoned him or made him sick somehow. Gritting my teeth, I chopped at the strands that held his wrists and then his waist and his legs. When he was free, he stumbled forward, and the edges of him wavered as if he were going to vanish on us again.

"Hey," I said, catching his elbow. "Stay with us. Stay with me." I turned to look toward the others. "Do you have any idea what's wrong? Is there something we can give him?"

Theo shook his head, looking genuinely confused. Hatter's eyes had darkened with what looked like understanding.

"I think he'll recover now that you've gotten him out," he said. "Give him a minute."

What did he know about Chess that I didn't? I turned back to the other man. A bit more color was starting to return to Chess's face, but he still looked sick. My stomach knotted.

On an impulse, I eased closer to him and wrapped my arms right around him. "I've got you," I murmured into his shirt.

Chess's hand came up to rest on the back of my head. After a second, a chuckle escaped him—a little weak, but much closer to his usual self. "So you do, lovely," he said in a light tone. "We did get ourselves into quite a tangle for a moment there, didn't we?"

I looked up at him, not releasing my embrace. "Are you okay?" I asked. "You seemed really... out of it for a minute there." And all the minutes he'd stood there silent while I was helping the others.

"Oh, I go out and in and all around," he said with a wave of his hand. His grin came back, solid as ever. He tucked his arm around my shoulders and turned me toward the hill. "We've almost reached your destination. Let us go and see where it gets us, hmm?"

I didn't totally believe his nonchalant demeanor. Something had really shaken him up. But he obviously didn't want to tell me about it, at least not right now, here, with the others.

The knot inside me expanded to encompass my entire stomach. The men around me put forward a tough front in their various ways, but none of them were invincible. I had the feeling they were putting on that front for *me*, so I wouldn't feel guilty about dragging them on this quest— so I didn't think I needed to worry about them. But they'd been here for me so much. I wanted to be strong for them when they needed it, if they'd let me.

I bobbed up on my toes to brush a quick kiss to Chess's cheek. "If you want to talk about it with me later, whenever, you can," I murmured for just him to hear. "I want you to know that."

He dipped his head to kiss my temple in return. "Sentiment appreciated, but there's nothing to talk about," he said. His hand closed around mine, with a gentle squeeze that felt like a thank you in itself.

That answer didn't really satisfy me, but we did have

the end of our quest right in front of us. Keeping my fingers twined with his, I strode forward.

The bowing grass at the edge of the ring I'd cleared hissed as I approached. I waved the sword at it, and to my relief the strands stilled. I'd shown them there was a force to be reckoned with around here.

All seven of us stayed close together as we waded through the subdued field, me staying in the lead this time, sword ready. Nothing jumped at us or grabbed us the rest of the way to the hill. As we came up on the immense shadow beneath the curve of the wave, I made out the raggedly arched entrance to a cave at the base of the hill beneath.

We'd just reached the edge of the shadow when a slim figure stepped out of the cave. I stopped in my tracks, raising the sword higher defensively.

The man gazed at us with a joyful light filling his wizened face. He swiped a hand over his wisps of white hair in an effort that didn't do much to smooth it down and stepped forward with a clink of his plated armor, tarnished metal dappled with patches of worn red paint. With a grand sweep of his arm, he dropped into a bow on his knee in front of me. His voice creaked out of him like a wind-swayed branch.

"It is an honor to finally greet you, your Majesty."

CHAPTER FOURTEEN

Lyssa

Your Majesty?

I let the sword drop to my side. "Er," I said to the old dude in the armor, who was still crouched in his very committed bow. "There's been some mistake. I don't think any of us here is a majesty of anything. I'm definitely not."

He looked up at me with an expression that was both awed and amused. "You wear the armor of the blood-marked ruby. You carry the sword. I assume you have the ring on you somewhere, for it will have led you to them. You are of the line of Alice, are you not?"

"Well, yeah," I said. "If you mean the Alices who came here from the Otherland. Our family isn't royal."

His pale blue eyes twinkled. "Not in the Otherland, it isn't. Here in Wonderland, you are our rightful ruler. The

Red Queen, come to reclaim her throne from the usurping Hearts."

None of this was making a whole lot of sense to me. If there was a Red Queen who could topple the Queen of Hearts, wouldn't someone have mentioned that before?

Beside me, Chess looked bemused. The shocked confusion on Hatter's face echoed all the emotions rushing through me. I couldn't see the others, but no one had piped up with an, "Oh, right! We forgot to mention that completely vital fact," so I was going to guess this was news to them too.

"I really don't know what you're talking about," I said. "My grand-aunt Alicia left the ring for me. I was using it to help the Spades find the ruby artifacts so they might be able to stop the Queen of Hearts, not so I could turn into some kind of queen."

The man straightened up, his wispy white hair drifting with the cool breeze. "You don't need to turn into a queen," he said. "You already are one. But I know the Hearts family has wiped out every trace they can of their true history. Come here, all of you, and we'll talk." He glanced over my companions. "It's good that you already have allies. Better still that you braved this land's threats to find the sword and the armor. I hope that means you will stay with us where Alicia did not."

He motioned for us to follow him deeper into the shadow of the arced hill. My pulse stuttered as I hurried after him. "Wait, you knew Aunt Alicia?"

"That ring led her to me," he said over his shoulder. "I told her what her true purpose here was, but she didn't want to believe me. Perhaps it is better that the task came down to you, if she wasn't ready to face it."

The words from Aunt Alicia's letter came back to me. *I didn't really know how I fit in there or what my true purpose was. When the pieces all collided, I panicked. I ran away.*

She'd run away from whatever this guy was about to tell us? I swallowed thickly. I'd come into the Checkerboard Plains hoping to find answers, but maybe I was going to get more than I'd bargained for.

Theo's voice carried from behind me, a bit of an edge in his normally smooth baritone. "Who exactly are you, if we can ask that?"

"Ah," the old guy said in his creaky yet resonant voice. "I am the Red Knight, loyal servant to the Red royal family. I have guarded the last of the artifacts until such time as the true rulers of Wonderland could be restored. It has been… a long time."

No kidding. From the looks of him, he might be over a hundred in Otherland years. In Wonderland that could mean way older.

"Do you have a real name?" I asked, thinking of the other man I knew who went by the label Knight. "I mean, one that's not just your role?"

The Red Knight paused at the edge of a firepit ringed with crumbling stumps. "I believe I did," he said, his voice diminishing. "But I can't say I remember what it was. I haven't had much opportunity to introduce myself to anyone out here."

Clearly. I sat down gingerly on one of the stumps near him. The others took seats all around me, Doria sitting on the grass between Hatter and Dee when it turned out there weren't enough stumps. The Red Knight made an apologetic grimace.

Theo was watching him, his gaze considering but his jaw clenched. With the question he'd asked—did he not trust this guy? Had something the Red Knight had said contradicted his understanding of his world?

It was hard to figure what motivation the old man could have had for making this up, though.

"Let me try to tell the story fully," the Red Knight said. "If I ramble some, I apologize in advance. There's much to tell. And if you find yourself confused, do stop me and say so. It's been fifty years since I last needed to explain, and that attempt didn't go particularly well, as I've mentioned."

He shifted forward in his seat with a clink of his armor, the tarnished steel plates covering him from feet to neck with small gaps in between. His gaze skimmed the people I'd brought with me.

"The only Queen you know of is the Queen of Hearts, am I right?" he said. "You believe Wonderland has been ruled by the Hearts for as long as it has been Wonderland."

"Of course," Dum said. "No one's ever talked about any other royal family."

"Because the first Queen of Hearts took the heads of anyone who breathed a word about it," the Red Knight said. "I was there, nearly two centuries ago, when the Hearts family and the followers they'd rallied stormed the palace. We weren't prepared for a sudden assault. It was the middle of the night, and the attackers went straight to the royal chambers—slaughtered the few guards there, the king and the queen and their children in their beds. Claimed the rule as their own, made the property over in their image, smashed or beheaded anything and anyone that might hint at their treachery."

"And Wonderland just *forgot*?" Hatter said.

"I expect some memory of it was carried on for a brief time," the Red Knight said. "But as those who could directly remember the Red Queen and King passed on, there were so few left who'd heard, and the risks for speaking up were so great—and she'd destroyed any proof she could that would prove the story—" He gave us a tight smile. "History is to the victors, is it not?"

"You said the 'first' Queen of Hearts," I said. "Not the same one who's ruling right now?"

He shook his head. "She would be the third, if my understanding is correct. Her mother was a child when the coup took place. From what I hear of her attitudes, I'd imagine *that* experience was passed down: the knowledge that no matter how high you sit, you can always find your neck at the wrong end of an axe in the blink of an eye."

"You haven't connected this story to Lyssa," Theo said quietly. He didn't sound as if he doubted the guy now. "You said the Hearts killed the entire Red family."

"They thought they had." The Red Knight looked down at his hands, his mouth tensing and then releasing. "I had a daughter then," he said. "A year younger than the youngest of the princesses, who'd only just turned sixteen. They didn't look a great deal alike, but their hair was a similar color, and in the night, when the attackers cared more about spilling blood quickly than checking who lay in which bed…"

He let out a ragged breath. "I heard them coming. I understood what I was hearing. I loved my daughter, you understand, but my first duty, the duty I'd sworn to carry out before all else, was to the Red family. Princess Alice had the last bedroom in the row—the most time for me to act. I got her up and had Matilda take her place in bed, and I fled with her, by the best ways I knew."

"Princess Alice," I repeated. My pulse had started to race.

The Red Knight met my eyes. "Yes. But I didn't know where to take her to keep her safe. The murderers realized *I* was gone and took up the search for me. We found ourselves at the edge of a small pond outside the city. The one they call the Pond of Tears now, for all the weeping, even though no one remembers what anyone all that time ago would have been weeping for. Princess Alice looked at her reflection in the water, and she declared it was like a mirror, and that like those other special mirrors, it would carry her to another world where the ones who'd come for her blood couldn't find her."

Chess raised his eyebrows. "And it worked? Lyssa could have gone back through to the Otherland through the pond all this time?"

"No," the Red Knight said. "That is, it did work. She leapt in before I could argue with her, and the water swallowed her up. But as she jumped, she commanded the pond that it should admit no one but her to where it would take her. She didn't want there to be any chance of the villains following her, you understand. Even *I* couldn't, diving in right after her. Although I've come to feel that was for the best—that I've served better on this side of things."

"And you think she made it through to the Otherland," I said. "You think I'm related to her."

"I don't know exactly what transpired on the other side of her slapdash looking-glass. But I know that more than once, young women named Alice or a variation on her name have traveled back through the Pond of Tears as no one else ever has. I know the proof your grand-aunt showed me with the blood-marked ruby. You do have the ring?"

I tugged the chain out from beneath my shirt, cupping the ring in my hand. He motioned for me to take off its protective shell. "Have you pricked your finger on it yet?" he asked.

"Yeah," I said. "It—"

Oh.

"It glowed, yes?" That awed light came back into the Red Knight's face. "Let me see it, if you don't mind?"

My chest tightened, but I touched my thumb to the sharp point in the middle of the ruby anyway. It pinched through my skin. The drop of blood fell, and the ruby shone with that magical light.

"That ring is the marker of the Red royal line," the Red Knight said in a hushed voice. "It will only glow for those who bear royal blood. Not even I…"

He held out his hand to demonstrate. The ruby's glow

had already faded. I let him nick his finger against the stone. Like with Theo, the blood simply seeped away into the stone dully.

Aunt Alicia had talked about the magic that ran through our bloodline. That had to be what she'd meant. I still couldn't wrap my head around it.

"There were ruins—part of a wall—out near the Topsy Turvy Woods," I said. "It had the ruby symbol on it."

The Red Knight nodded. "During the reign of the Reds, the royal family had structures all across Wonderland. The people of Wonderland wandered farther abroad much more often. The Red Queen and King served well, with generosity rather than greed. The Hearts destroyed all of that."

"So, Lyssa is really going to be *queen*?" Doria said, her eyes wide.

I didn't know how to answer that question. To my immense gratitude, Theo patted her shoulder and gave me a reassuring smile. "I think we'd better give our Otherlander some time to process this revelation. *All* of us need to rethink a lot of what we believed."

The intent look he fixed on me felt like an offer of help, if I wanted it. I wasn't sure what he could do to make this situation any less complicated.

The Red Knight stood up. "I should bring you to the last artifact," he said. "I only managed to track down and recover the one of them after the Queen of Hearts hid them away. If I could have gathered all of them for you…"

He sounded heartbroken over his supposed failure. I pushed myself to my feet with a twist of my gut.

"It's fine," I said. "I got the other ones anyway. And that was hard enough with company. I can't imagine doing it alone."

"You'll never be on your own again," the Red Knight said with a determination that sounded almost more ominous than comforting to my ears.

This guy had been waiting almost two hundred years for his new queen to show up. No pressure or anything.

He led me into the cave at the base of the hill. Inside, the rocky floor and walls were smooth and dry, almost pleasant as caves went. I caught glimpses of a few rooms near the entrance, one holding a narrow bed, another with shelves of food.

At the end of the tunnel, the Red Knight ran his hand down the wall and pressed a spot that didn't stand out at all to me. A stone slab slid back, revealing another room.

Mirabel had seen right about the three artifacts. A scepter lay on a small stone platform, most of its length a polished cherry wood, its head a massive glittering ruby encased in a chamber of gold shaped like a crown. More gold shimmered at its base.

I picked it up to test its weight. The scepter wasn't half as heavy as the sword, which was a relief. It'd have been nice if my supposed royal ancestors had thought to include a scabbard or some sort of carrying case for their weaponry.

The ring I'd tucked back under my shirt flushed with

pleased warmth. "What does it do?" I asked, turning the scepter from side to side.

"I have to admit I'm not sure," the Red Knight said, with the same shamed air he'd had when he'd talked about not retrieving the other artifacts. "I saw the Red Queen— my first Red Queen, begging your pardon, your Majesty —command a herd of borogoves with it once. But the royal family didn't use the artifacts often. I hadn't much chance to witness their powers. I'm sure now that they're in your grasp, your instincts will aid you in discovering all they can offer."

Because I was on my own in this. If I believed everything he'd said, I was the only surviving descendant of Wonderland's Red Queen—and as much as I'd have liked to argue his story away, I didn't know how to dismiss the proof of it. The ring. The way the train had slowed for me—the way the jabberwock had gentled.

Hatter had been right. It wasn't just the ring I was wearing. It was because it was me, wearing that ring.

Everything and everyone in Wonderland depended on me.

My lungs constricted for a second, with a flash of memory that shot me back to my eight-year-old self, watching my mother sob and sway over Dad's old clothes. Pushing her toward the door to get to work, grabbing the money she left out before my brother could and buying the cheapest dinner fixings I could find after school, reading the bills, writing checks for Mom to sign, and on and on.

I'd survived that. I'd held my family together and

made it through. But an entire land was a lot more than our tiny family.

I hadn't signed up for this. Not at all.

"I don't know if I can even do this," I said to the Red Knight. "I don't have any idea what it takes to be a queen. I don't have any… training, or whatever queens usually get."

"You'll find your way," the knight said confidently. We stepped back into the cave's main hallway. "It's your heritage. You're meant for this."

I could have had a hundred doctors in my family tree, and I still wouldn't have known how to do a heart transplant just by being "meant for it." Somehow I had the feeling ruling a country was at least as complicated.

And a task that took quite a bit longer. A task that never really ended.

"I have a life back home," I said. God, what would Melody say if I tried to tell her about any of this? Wonderland had been crazy enough before I'd been a supposed *queen*. "I know you think this is what I'm supposed to be doing, but I'd never even heard of Wonderland until a couple weeks ago. I have a family back there, I have friends—"

"They will understand that you must rise to your new role. How could they deny you an honor such as this?"

Well, for starters, if I told them they'd probably deny that I was sane. And that answer ignored how *I* felt about this new role. "That's not really…"

I trailed off. What could I say to him that he'd understand? Even after Aunt Alicia had taken off on him, he still believed in me, in the rightness of me picking up where the queen he'd served had left off, as if it were entirely inevitable.

"Red Knight," I said, still figuring out what I wanted to ask.

A frightened shriek pierced through the air from outside.

CHAPTER FIFTEEN

Hatter

"This is amazing," Doria was saying as she hopped from one stump to another around the shadowed firepit. "We've got the real queen right here with us! Bye-bye, Hearts!"

Dee rubbed his hands together. "Can you imagine the look on their faces when they find out we know their claim on the throne is a bunch of bull? It's going to be epic."

"Completely epic!"

I watched them, wishing I could absorb their enthusiasm. My thoughts were racing around in my head as if they'd been sucked into a whirlpool that had no bottom. My balance felt rather unsteady too. I glanced toward the cave Lyssa had disappeared into with the Red Knight, torn between wanting to see her coming back to us right now and wanting to have the right words to say to her before she did.

I couldn't say I didn't see it. What quality would I want in a queen that Lyssa hadn't proven she possessed in the past several days? Courage, compassion, determination, patience, smarts... The very fact that we'd made it here with the two artifacts no one before her had been able to retrieve showed she was meant for this role. I could picture her so easily standing with chin raised and eyes bright like she had when she'd insisted we set off on this quest, only with a crown resting on her head.

She hadn't come here looking to wear a crown, though. She hadn't meant to stay more than a couple of weeks. She wouldn't be the Lyssa who lingered in my mind even while she was gone if she hadn't cared so deeply for her loved ones in the Otherland.

And perhaps some selfish piece of me was niggling at me about where *I* could possibly fit into the life of a queen, if somehow she stayed.

Chess sidled closer to me, rubbing his hand over his auburn hair. He appeared to have fully recovered from his lapse in that field of vicious grass, but then, I suspected this was the sort of revelation that would shock any other emotion right out of your system. His gaze kept creeping back to the cave entrance too.

"Well, now we know why the Queen of Hearts was so obsessed with the idea that the Otherlanders named Alice were after her throne," I remarked. "Even if she thought the princess was dead, it'd be hard to see that name as a coincidence. Especially when you're a raging lunatic."

"But not a lunatic on that score," Chess said glibly.

"She wasn't being paranoid. They really *were* the echoes of her past come to haunt her."

"Not on purpose," I couldn't help pointing out. I'd thought we were putting a lot on Lyssa just telling her about the Queen and the rebellion against her. This… She'd simply looked stunned as she'd followed the Red Knight to retrieve whatever he'd been keeping in that cave.

Theo's arms were crossed over his chest in a pose that looked uncharacteristically defensive, but when he spoke, his voice was as steady and assured as always. "Accepting this new role is a lot for Lyssa to deal with. We need to rally behind her, show her that she has all our support."

"White Knight?" Dum took a step back from where he'd been gazing across the field beyond the curved hill. "We might need to rally right now, for other reasons."

The ground shuddered as we spun around. A burbling cry carried across the field as not one but two jabberwocks charged across the thick grass toward us. Their eyes blazed with a white-hot fire, and smoke gushed from their maws like a rapid dog's drool. Their huge feathered bodies shook with fury.

We hadn't provoked that fury. The Knave and his remaining guard rushed from the square of night after them, the Knave cracking a whip across one jabberwock's tail and then the other. I didn't know where he'd found the creatures or how he'd gained control, but he was driving them now as surely as the wind in that patch of darkness had driven us.

At the next lash, flames belched from the jabberwocks'

jaws, charring the grass in front of them in an instant. The acrid stink of the smoke clogged my nose. Doria let out a shriek, more terrified than I'd ever heard her. With the thump of racing footsteps and the clank of aged armor, Lyssa and the Red Knight burst from the cave.

My body went rigid. Two monsters—four if you counted the Knave and his man, which I would—were barreling toward every person in this world I still gave a damn about. My daughter, my lover, my friends...

A dizzying surge of emotion crackled through my nerves right into my head, hazing my vision, jolting me into action in a way I hadn't felt since I'd left the Spades, probably not since that last night—

I threw myself away from the memory and out of the shadows under the hill. My fingers closed around the base of one of the hair pins tucked into my jacket and yanked it free. The hard thin length felt good in my hand, but it wasn't going to stop a jabberwock.

My legs carried me on instinct, close enough to one jabberwock to wave the hair pin almost under its snout, leaping out of the way when it snorted another sputter of fire. "Dad!" Doria yelled, but her horrified voice only propelled me onward.

Now the jabberwock was pissed off at me. It thundered after me with a hissing rustle of its wings and another burbling moan. I was counting on the story I'd heard that those wings were only for show, that they couldn't actually hold the creature's massive body up. If that was wrong, well, in a minute I'd be cinders and jabberwock chow.

I veered around the far side of the hill and scrambled up its slope. The jabberwock hurtled after me over the thinner grass. My feet slipped on the steepest section, sending me to my knees. I scrambled up and hurled myself onward as flames singed my heels. Up, up, and then skidding down past the crest of the wave toward the sudden drop…

I almost misjudged my speed and toppled right over myself. At the last second, I tossed myself sideways and managed to grab hold of a ridge of rock protruding through the soil.

The jabberwock was too blinded by rage to notice the hill ended. It careened on over the edge—and plummeted down.

Its wings flapped frantically but barely caught the air. It tumbled head first and hit the ground below with a skull-cracking thump. Its body sprawled, the smoke dissipating around its crumpled snout.

Adrenaline from the dash coursed through me. I heaved myself to my feet. Down below, the others had scattered in the wake of the other jabberwock—and the Knave and his man were taking advantage of the chaos. Doria had ended up at the edge of the hill's shadow, and the guard was racing toward her with sword drawn.

Fuck, no. "Dee!" I shouted with all the air in my lungs. "Catch me."

His redhaired form appeared just beneath me. I sucked in a breath and jumped without a second thought.

We might not have pulled off this specific move in over ten years, but it seemed our bodies hadn't forgotten.

My feet hit his arms in just the right spot, and he catapulted me toward Doria. I braced myself as I landed on the earth and whipped around.

The guard had diverted to another target, but the Knave was lunging at us now, dagger clutched in his hand and a killing glint in his beady eyes. I only had an instant to react. In that instant, my arms shot up. I slammed the hair pin into the vulnerable flesh just above his collarbone.

The Knave still managed to hack at me with his dagger. It raked across my sleeve as I jerked out of the way. Blood welled up through the cut he'd landed, but a lot more blood was bubbling from his throat.

A gurgle escaped his bulging neck. His face turned even grayer. He tried to sputter something over his jagged teeth, but the words didn't come. With a shudder, he slumped at my feet.

"For the honor of the Reds!" the Red Knight was hollering. He stabbed his sword into the guard's gut, and the other man keeled over. Lyssa had leapt in front of the jabberwock. Its head was weaving from side to side, that manic flame still dancing in its eyes, but she'd brought it to a halt.

"Go!" she said, waving a large wand with a ruby at its end. The last artifact, I supposed. "Go back to wherever you came from. We don't want to hurt you, but I can't let you hurt any of us either. Go on!"

I tensed as the jabberwock lurched toward her, but it was only heaving itself into a turn. It wheeled around and loped back across the field.

Dum was lying on the ground, clutching a burnt spot

on his side, but his gaze was clear, his breaths coming steady. From the bruise forming on Theo's jaw, he'd taken a blow or two. Nothing too serious, though.

We were all alive. We'd survived.

Everyone on my side, anyway. My gaze fell to the blood-soaked grass around the Knave's limp body, and my stomach flipped over. The adrenaline high that had carried me through the fight was fading, and queasiness churned beneath it.

"Well, now," Chess said with a grin, clapping me on the shoulder. "There's the Mad Hatter we all loved. I knew you couldn't have lost your grip on insanity completely."

Doria was staring at me. At the bloodstained hair pin still clutched in my hand. I dropped it. I had another one in my jacket.

Resolve formed around my nausea. I hadn't had a real choice. I'd protected her—I'd protected Lyssa, and all the others too. I had to keep doing that until nothing in this land still threatened them.

If someone had to fall, better it was me than them.

Theo had knelt to see to Dum, who was smearing salve on his burnt flesh now. The White Knight straightened up now. He took in our fallen enemies.

"We've bought ourselves a little time," he said. "But there'll be a new Knave risen; there'll be more guards. If we want to make the most of this advantage, we'd better get on that train and back to the city while there's still a chance no one there has put two and two together."

Night had fallen long before we made it back to the city. The clouds congealing in the sky overhead turned the landscape even darker. A faint drizzle came down through the damp air as we waited for Dee to return with the ally the White Knight had sent him to collect.

Doria stepped closer to me, tugging nervously on her dark hair. This was her first rainfall.

The twin came into view with a woman at his side whom I recognized from the recent Spades meetings. She studied our group with curious eyes where we stood amid the trees near the road outside town.

"What's the word since I've been gone?" Theo asked.

The woman's lips pursed. "The Queen has taken more people from the city each day, as she promised. Three yesterday, five today." Her gaze slid to Chess. "The guards are out looking for Cheshire now too."

Theo grimaced. "The Knave sent word back one way or another, then. They'll be waiting to haul all of us in. All right, we'll simply—"

"No," the woman broke in. "It's just Chess. The call went out just this afternoon. They're saying the Duchess made a claim that he's a traitor."

I only caught Chess's brief stiffening because I was already looking at him. A second later, it was gone. "Well," he said, "if it was going to be anyone, it may as well be me, seeing as I'm the only one here who can vanish quite literally."

The drizzle picked up speed, droplets flecking my face. I adjusted my suit jacket. Chess's shoulders hunched slightly under the rain, the only sign that it bothered him.

"You could come back to my place for the night," I said. "I have room. We have the White Knight's alarm system in place. You still get wet even if you're out of sight, don't you?"

Chess shrugged. "Not if I remove myself from the source of the wetness. Offer appreciated but unneeded, Hatter. I think I'll go take a closer lay of the land."

He brushed Lyssa's arm in a farewell gesture and faded away.

"You would not believe what we found out on that trip," Dee started saying to the woman, excitement dancing in his eyes. "The—"

"Dee," Lyssa said quickly. "I think I'd like some more time to figure out how I'm going to handle this situation before we tell anyone else. There'll be a lot of questions… I want to be able to answer them."

Dee glanced at Theo, as if he needed the White Knight's approval to follow Lyssa's request. The request of his probable future *queen*.

And Theo gave it, as if he had that authority. He dipped his head. "We'll meet tomorrow. For now, I'm sure we all need our rest, in proper beds." He turned to Lyssa. "You could stay in the Tower tonight if you'd like."

Lyssa's arms came up to hug herself. "The Knave almost caught me there before," she said. "At Hatter's, I have an easy escape route. I think I'll stick with that for now."

He nodded and leaned in to kiss her, clearly suffering from no doubts himself about how he fit into her life now. In fact, something in his stance gave me the impression he was staking a claim. I swallowed a prickle of jealousy.

"Let's go then," I said. "Before anyone notices us standing around out here."

"Where Lyssa goes, I go too," the Red Knight announced, clicking his visor up. He'd grabbed a helmet to match his worn armor before we'd caught the train. "She is my purpose."

Wonderful. "Fine," I said, waving for him to come along too.

When we reached my building, he eyed the shop and then the main floor of the apartment grimly.

"There's a guest bedroom free on the third floor," I said.

"No," the Red Knight said. "I will stand guard through the night."

"You've got to sleep sometime," Lyssa pointed out. "Theo gave us a device that'll wake us all up if anyone comes up the stairs."

The Red Knight hesitated. "I will rest on the sofa," he said, pointing across the room. "So that I may be the first line of defense for your Majesty if the occasion arises."

Lyssa winced at the "your Majesty." Doria hurried on up to her fourth-floor bedroom ahead of us, but Lyssa paused by the bathroom door. She looked tired, and I didn't think it was just from the long days of travel behind us.

I stopped outside my bedroom door. "Do you want to talk?"

She opened her mouth and closed it again. For a

second, her expression turned so haunted it made my gut clench. She tugged her gaze up to meet mine with a smile that looked forced.

"Does it change a lot, this whole thing about me being queen?" she asked.

Between us? Hearts take me, was that what she was worrying about? The corners of my lips quirked upward. "It hasn't lowered my opinion of you in the slightest, I promise," I said.

Lyssa's smile relaxed a little. She stepped toward me, and I met her for a kiss that sent a thrill through me even though I could tell she wasn't looking for more in this moment. It had been an honor to make this woman tremble with delight little more than a day ago.

She walked up the stairs with more lightness in her steps than before, but my heart still squeezed as I watched her go. I'd helped some, but was it enough? I couldn't shake the sense that I was failing her. Maybe failing her and Doria both. I might have already failed them by stepping back from so much of who I'd been before either of them had really needed me.

No more hanging back. No more shying from danger. From now on, I ran straight toward it.

CHAPTER SIXTEEN

Lyssa

I'd had plenty of restless nights in Wonderland, but none of them half as bad as this one. The rain drummed against the window like the thoughts that wouldn't stop nagging at me even as I buried my face in my pillow. The warm metal of the ring pressed against my breastbone under the blouse I was wearing as a nightshirt.

I was something like the great-great-great-great-great-granddaughter of Wonderland's rightful queen. The land fucking *recognized* me as its ruler, responded to me like it did no one else. There was a man resting downstairs who expected me to challenge the Queen of Hearts and then take back my family's place on the throne. Possibly some of the people who'd been with me for that revelation expected the same thing.

Back home, I couldn't even convince my mom not to

fret about me constantly. How the hell was I going to command an entire country?

Could I just run away from all this like Aunt Alicia had? My stomach knotted at the thought. Ten innocent people were sitting in the Queen's dungeon right now waiting to have their heads chopped off. Hatter, Chess, Theo, and the others could have lost theirs just for helping me in my quest, which they'd done before they'd had a clue I was anything other than a wayward Otherlander. What kind of person would I be if I let them keep suffering when I had the ability to change that?

Also, there was the slight complication of having no available means to get home at the moment.

Stewing over it wasn't making my mind any clearer. If I could just get to sleep, maybe I'd feel less confused in the morning.

I tipped from my front onto my side, and a sharper rapping joined the patter of the rain against the window. My heart stuttered. I jerked upright, my hand shooting toward the ruby-set sword I'd left on top of the covers next to me.

Thunder rumbled, and a flash of lightning caught on auburn hair and high cheekbones as the figure outside leaned close to the glass. It was only Chess.

A short laugh sputtered out of me. I scrambled off the bed and unlatched the window to push it open.

Chess slipped inside, his wet clothes plastered to his brawny form, his darkened hair sending droplets over his pale face. When I grasped his elbow to help him in, the fabric chilled my fingers. A puddle of rainwater formed on the floor beneath him in an instant. He held his body tight, but a shiver he couldn't restrain rippled through him.

"I rethought Hatter's offer," he said, with a click of his teeth as if he'd snapped them shut to stop them from chattering.

"Stay right there," I ordered him. I switched on the bedside lamp and hustled down the hall as quietly as I could. No need to wake up the whole apartment.

I grabbed a couple of towels from the stack in the fourth-floor bathroom and carried them back to the bedroom. Chess tugged one tight around his torso and rubbed the other over his hair. A little color came into his cheeks as he started to warm up.

"You know, there are these things called doors," I said.

He gave me a crooked grin. "I figured it was better to come in the back way rather than set off the White Knight's alarm downstairs and throw you all into a panic."

Okay, he had a point there. "You couldn't find anywhere to get out of the rain?" I asked. He'd never actually mentioned any kind of a home. Where did he usually spend his nights?

Chess shrugged. "Nowhere with company I wanted to keep. I have to admit, rain is not quite as delightful as I recalled. Maybe there's a better sort, but this kind is entirely too wet." He made a face at his still-drenched clothes. Another shiver ran through his body. I touched his hand and winced at how cold his skin felt.

"Come on," I said, deciding this wasn't the time to be worrying about modesty or people getting the wrong idea.

"Take those wet clothes off and get under the covers before you catch hypothermia."

Despite his shivering, Chess raised his eyebrows, mischief glinting in his bright blue eyes. "You're asking me to strip and hop in bed?"

"So you can *warm up*," I said emphatically, although let's be real, my mind had already gone to all sorts of other places.

Chess chuckled to himself, but he complied. He peeled off his shirt and kicked off his sodden shoes. Rather than ogle him as he tugged down his pants, I slipped back into bed to warm up the space beneath the blanket, scooting over to leave room for him. And then, okay, I ogled him a little as he tucked that well-muscled body—still with a pair of boxer-briefs on for a tiny bit of modesty—under the covers next to me.

I let my hand ease over to rest on his bicep, not wanting to assume he'd want more contact than that. Chess had indicated he was attracted to me, but he'd been pretty restrained with any physical overtures so far. Right now he was probably too busy thawing out to be thinking about any more, er, intimate ways of warming up.

"Sorry I woke you," he murmured.

"You didn't," I said. "I hadn't managed to get to sleep yet."

He rolled onto his side to face me. There was still a foot of space between us, but I could feel the spreading warmth of his body gathering in the cocoon under the covers. "Too many thoughts whirling around in that lovely head of yours?"

"It's not every day you find out you're the heir to a long lost royal family."

"Indeed. And being asked to rule over the lot of us —not the most appealing offer I can imagine." He winked.

"That's not really the problem. I wasn't looking to rule over *anyone*." I paused, considering. "It would be the Diamonds too, wouldn't it? Even if a lot of them hate the Queen of Hearts, would they really want some Otherlander taking over the throne?"

"Difficult to determine how those minds work behind the sparkliness," Chess said. "I suppose they'd have to learn to like it."

That didn't sound very promising. My stomach clenched with an ache of uncertainty. "Maybe it's better if I don't think about it anymore for a while. I'm just tying myself in knots without getting anywhere useful."

It occurred to me that I wasn't the only one with a quandary. "Chess, what are you going to do now that the Hearts' Guard will be searching specifically for you? You can't just stay invisible all the time."

"Technically I could," Chess said in his playful way. "It would keep everyone on their toes on a permanent basis."

"Seriously," I said. "Even if we can stop the Queen from taking new prisoners, she'll still want you now that that Duchess woman has accused you."

I'd seen Chess talking to the Duchess once—an elegant young woman covered in gems and layers of silk. She'd come looking for him specifically. He'd said they'd been… friends, or something, when he'd used to visit the palace and hobnob with the Diamonds.

"Do you know why she'd have done that?" I added. "I thought—she knew you before. She thought you'd *help* the Diamonds by giving her information. Why would she suddenly tell everyone you're with the Spades?"

Chess's gaze slid away from me. "She and I had a… rather fraught affiliation. And I believe she has even less grasp on sanity than the rest of us lunatics. Her reasons seem reasonable to her, no doubt."

There had to be more to it than that. "Chess," I prodded.

His mouth tightened as his eyes met mine again. "There's little else I could say that's fit for a queen's ears."

The tension in his expression made the ache in my gut dig deeper. "I'm not a queen right now," I said. "And I don't know if I'm ever going to be one. And… And even if I become one, I'm not going to be like the queen you've got now. I'd still be *me*. I'd want to know what people are really going through, what's upset them, everything. I wouldn't go around using people's vulnerabilities as weapons against them either."

For a long moment, silence hung over us. I dared to raise my hand to stroke the backs of my fingers over his cheek. "I know *something* has been bothering you. The way you froze up when the grass caught you, this thing with the Duchess, secret powers you don't want anyone to know about… If you'd just rather not talk about it, that's fine. But you have to believe me that I *want* to know. I want to know *you*. Okay?"

I meant those words so much my voice thickened with the emotion that had filled my throat. Chess stared at me. Something shifted in his face. Then he took my hand and kissed my knuckles the way he had when he first helped me find my way back home.

"Okay," he said, his own voice rough. "Ask, and I'll tell you."

Now that he'd given me the opening, I wasn't sure where to start. The thought of the Duchess itched at me, but I didn't want to sound like a jealous girlfriend interrogating her guy about every woman he'd interacted with. So I started with, "Why did getting trapped in the grass shake you up so much?"

That couldn't be too intrusive a question, right? Hatter had seemed to have an idea, and he and Chess weren't exactly BFFs.

Chess's raw chuckle told me I'd estimated wrong. "That's the whole story right there," he said.

"All right," I said. "However much you're ready to tell me."

He eased over onto his back again. An uncharacteristic furrow creased his brow as he contemplated the ceiling. Then he started speaking, in a lilting tone that somehow managed to sound flippant and ominous at the same time.

"I told you before that there was a while when I passed time with the Diamonds. I got bored, and they were different, and treading that close to the Queen and her temper was a little thrilling. I thought if things turned dangerous, I could simply vanish. I thought the only thing I had to worry about was keeping my head attached."

I scooted a little closer, tucking my hand loosely around his arm and tipping my head toward his bare shoulder to indicate he had my full attention.

"At first," Chess went on, "I played around with different people there. Mostly women, but occasionally the men too. But pretty soon the Duchess got her eye on me, and I discovered that was something of a thrill too— being chosen, being coveted. And she… was very different. I never knew what to expect. There was always some new element to explore. So we made an arrangement. When I came to the palace, I belonged to her, and we would try everything."

"When you say you 'played' with people…" I said, pretty sure I already knew the answer.

"Indulging ourselves," Chess said. "With food, with leisure, and very frequently with sex. The appetites of the Diamonds aren't so different from those of the Clubbers."

"Except for the Duchess?"

"The Duchess simply…" He sighed. "We experimented with the line between pleasure and pain. It was during the freeze, so nothing was permanent. She would… cut me, or burn me, or whatever else she'd come up with that day, and I ate it up." He wet his lips and glanced at me. "If you'd rather I didn't keep going—"

I brushed a kiss to his shoulder. "I'm listening." Did he think I was going to be horrified by what he'd told me? Even in a world where you *weren't* being driven around the bend living the same day over and over again, S&M

wasn't so weird. Melody had a boyfriend a couple years ago who'd wanted her to put clamps on his nipples and things like that.

For a second I thought Chess was going to stop for his own comfort. He swallowed audibly.

"All in good fun," he said, with a self-deprecating edge. "She liked to up the ante, and she became more and more controlling about the ways I could speak to or even look at anyone else in the palace. I started to develop the sense she saw me as a toy rather than a person. But I was getting off, and that's what we Wonderlanders care about most, isn't it? I thought, if I ever got uncomfortable, I could simply leave…"

A quiver ran through his muscles, but this time it wasn't from the cold. I hugged his arm a little harder to say I was here, I was with him. What could have happened back then to leave this strong, gleeful man so shaken?

A faint rasp came into his voice. "I came one day, and she was in more of a mood than I'd ever seen her. She wanted to tie me up, and she tied me hard. And then she started to cut. Not just a little, here and there, but deep. I told her it was too much, but she just laughed. After a while I couldn't talk at all. I couldn't shift to slip out of the bonds—when pain is rushing through me, I can't focus enough to use my deepest talents."

So he'd been trapped there like he'd been in the grass. My throat constricted.

"She strung me up over her bed, upside down, and carved away at me until I didn't have any idea what anything but pain was," Chess went on. "Breathing, swallowing, it all hurt. She worked me to the limit of where I suppose she assumed I wouldn't die, and after that she left. She left me alone, hanging, bleeding all over her *fucking* white satin sheets…"

The last few words came out in a whisper and a snarl. He hesitated, his chest stuttering as he exhaled.

All of me hurt, hearing him describe what the Duchess had done to him. I reached my arm across his chest tentatively, wanting to embrace him properly, not sure if he'd even want that. He caught me and tugged me to him, and I hugged him hard, tears leaking from behind my closed eyelids.

"I thought I was going to die," he said. "I thought she'd gotten bored with me and wanted me gone. Toward the end, I *wanted* to die… I can take a hint. When I woke up where I always did the next morning, I knew I was never going back. But she came looking for me a few days later, as if it hadn't even occurred to her I'd stay away after that, and I realized she hadn't wanted me dead at all. She'd just wanted to watch me hurt, and she'd want to do it again."

"I'm so sorry," I murmured against his chest.

"Ah, well, some good came out of it. Seeing how mad the Diamonds were getting gave me the guts to start helping the Spades. And it wasn't as if I hadn't set myself up to be used."

"You didn't ask for that," I said fiercely. "No one would have. No way in hell can you say it's your fault."

"If a queen decrees it, I suppose it must be so," Chess

said. He sounded grateful but not convinced. "In any case, that's the rambling answer to your question. Being tangled up like that reminded me of how she tied me that day… I can't always keep my head straight when the memories leap up. It's also why she's probably made this accusation. She doesn't even know I'm with the Spades. She's just peeved she lost her toy, and it's another way for her to try to control me. And what else was there? Oh, the reasons I keep my transformative skill secret."

"It's all right," I said. "You're *allowed* to have some secrets."

He shifted onto his side and cupped my cheek, gazing into my eyes for the first time since he'd started his story. His eyes were bright again. "Are you saying that for my sake or for yours? If it's too much—"

"No," I said quickly. "I'm just worried about you. I didn't mean to stir up a whole bunch of awful memories."

"Of course you didn't. They're only that—memories. My other form… Being able to shift completely from one thing to another is a rare talent even in Wonderland. If the Queen knew, she'd want me not for my head but for her menagerie. I've generally been circumspect. But more so—when I was more reckless, I let the Duchess see—I had the ridiculous idea of impressing her—and for her it turned into a new type of—"

His mouth pressed flat against something more than he wanted to say. "Since then, I don't shift, even on my own, unless I absolutely have to. It brings back the time with her more sharply. I don't want anyone else to get it into their heads that they could use that part of me.

Hatter knows, because I was madder than usual when I found my way to him in the early days, and he helped me arrange that she would forget. So now it's just him and you. Not too shabby."

How exactly had they "arranged" for the Duchess to forget a detail like that? I wanted to ask, but I'd already dragged so much pain out of him. Questions like that could wait.

"Okay," I said. "I'll make sure it stays that way. No one's hearing it from me."

"I know they won't, lovely," he said, a warm smile crossing his face. "And I—" His gaze followed his fingers as they teased over my hair and then down the side of my neck to my shoulder. "I do want you, you know. Very much. But whether you choose to be queen or not, I don't know if I can be all that good for anyone as anything more than the briefest of flings, and you should have more than that."

"Chess."

"It's not just the damage done, you know," he said before I could go on. "Maybe I was already screwed up even before, to let it go on so long, to let it go that far, to have *enjoyed* it until it was almost murder…"

"I don't think that," I said. "It was a screwed-up situation. And you're already more than that. You can make me laugh when I'm terrified, and you've had my back every time I've needed it, even when you had to risk exposing your secret to protect me. I should get to decide what's good for me, shouldn't I?" And God, the brush of his fingertips had felt so good I was already tingling to experience everything else he could offer.

The flash of desire in his eyes turned the tingling into a surge of heat. He leaned in, the tip of his nose grazing mine. His voice dropped even lower.

"I haven't been with anyone on my own since—since then. It's always been with someone else joining in, usually the White Knight... Less pressure when the focus isn't all on my performance. Less intense. I don't know—I don't want to disappoint you."

"I'll take whatever you're ready to give," I said. "And I'll be a lot more disappointed if you *don't* kiss me, as soon as humanly possible."

He gave me a perfect Cheshire grin, and then his mouth captured mine.

Even after that build-up, his kiss was as sweet as the ones before. He tipped his head, teasing my lips apart, and his hand slid down my side to my hip. He left it there, hot as a brand, as we kissed and kissed again, deeper and sweeter until my whole body was trembling giddily with anticipation of what would come next. The tips of his fangs grazed my lip with a sharply thrilling tingle.

I looped my arm around his shoulders, and he rolled us over. The weight of him over me, braced on one elbow as he trailed his fingers up under my nightshirt, and the tangling of our naked legs made me even hungrier than before. I shifted, arching into him, and my back bumped something flat and hard.

The sword. I eased back from Chess and tugged it out

from where it had gotten tangled in the covers. "I think maybe we'd better get this out of the way."

Chess laughed. "Now that's a dangerous bed companion."

"Meant to be dangerous to the wrong sort of person coming knocking at my window," I muttered.

"I'll be glad you don't count me among that number." He took the hilt from me gingerly, and it occurred to me that I'd never seen him handle anything with a blade before. Maybe he had bad associations with cutting instruments after what the Duchess had put him through. But he didn't look particularly discomforted by the sword. He just tipped over on his back so he could drop it over his side of the bed. It hit the floor with a thump.

The covers had fallen partly off him, leaving his sculpted chest on full display in the hazy lamplight. On an impulse, I followed him, slipping my knee across his waist to straddle him. Chess smiled up at me with a sound that was almost a purr as I smoothed my splayed hands over those planes of muscle. The burn between my legs urged me to scoot lower, to fit myself against him in the most tantalizing way, but that momentary thought about the sword held me back.

"Is there anything I should make sure to be careful of?" I asked, forcing my hands to still over his pecs. "Anywhere that being touched bothers you?"

I didn't know how to phrase it better than that, but the shadow that passed through Chess's eyes told me he understood. He clasped his hand over one of mine. "Don't worry yourself about that. I've had practice at tuning out that kind of discomfort."

Because he hadn't been with any partner before me he felt comfortable telling about his past. A much more intense emotion than lust squeezed my heart. I squeezed his fingers in turn. "I don't want you to have to tune any of this out," I said. "I want you to enjoy all of it. It'll be easier for me *not* to worry if I know."

He let out a breath. "It may be best to avoid my neck, and the sides of my ribs, and the backs of my knees."

The words gave me a flash of an image, the picture he'd drawn with his voice of him hanging there bleeding, the places where she'd dug the wounds deepest. I gripped his fingers a little harder, my throat choking up.

Then he was pushing himself upright to catch my lips again, and everything fell away except the tenderness of his kiss and the intoxicatingly rich scent of his skin.

His hand crept up under my nightshirt again, tracing sparks over my skin, so teasingly slow I squirmed on his lap. His palm finally settled over my bare breast. I barely filled his large hand, but Chess didn't give any sign of minding. He flicked his thumb over my nipple, and I whimpered into his mouth.

He raised his head to look over my shoulder. A smile that was more a smirk curved his lips. "We appear to have company."

I glanced over. The bedroom door had opened a few inches; the lamplight caught on Hatter, rumpled and flushed in striped pajamas. He nudged the doorknob farther and then caught it, as if he wasn't sure whether he should be coming or going.

"I heard a thud," he said, and I remembered Chess dropping the sword on the floor. "I thought I'd make sure everything was all right. You had a change of heart about my hospitality?"

He was talking as if he hadn't found us in the middle of anything particularly exciting, but I felt his gaze on us, on me, like a heated caress. It set off a hot flare between my thighs.

"The rain proved too much for me, I'm ashamed to admit," Chess said, equally casual. He paused. "I believe there's plenty of room here, if you'd like to join in. If our Lyssa would like that too." He gave my cheek a gentle nuzzle.

He would like that, wouldn't he? He'd said he could relax more when someone else was involved. Had he known Hatter's bedroom was right under this one—had he let the sword fall loudly on purpose?

I wasn't sure it mattered. The idea of Hatter caressing me with his hands as well as his gaze set off a quiver of desire through my nerves. I'd never been with two guys at the same time, but I didn't have a doubt that with *these* two, it would be fucking spectacular. Or spectacular fucking?

Both—definitely both.

"No objections here," I said, extending my hand toward Hatter.

He hesitated a moment longer. Obviously he hadn't joined in with Chess for similar interludes in the past. The thought that this would be new for him too sparked an excitement that radiated through my core as he stepped inside and shut the door.

Chess raised my nightshirt to yank it right off me. As he tossed it aside, Hatter inhaled sharply. He came up beside the bed and tipped my head toward his for a kiss, hot and determined. Chess bent down to slick his tongue over the peak of my breast. My fingers curled around the silky lapel of Hatter's pajama top, around Chess's hair, pleasure spiking through me.

Chess had loosened up, all right. He fondled one breast with his hand while he worked over the other with his mouth so thoroughly I whimpered and rocked in his chest. Hatter was devouring me with a kiss so hard my lips tingled. He stroked his fingertips up and down my back, and Chess gripped my hip to tug me tighter to him, teasing a fang over my nipple. The feel of his rigid cock pressing against me through two thin layers of fabric made me want to explode right there.

I pulled back just far enough to squirm out of my panties. Hatter's fingers trailed over my legs as he offered his assistance. He kissed my neck, my shoulder, as he traced his hand back up my inner thigh. I fumbled with the buttons on his top, losing track of what I was doing when he swiveled his thumb over my clit. A cry broke from my lips.

Chess gave my nipple one last swipe of his talented tongue and wriggled out of his boxer-briefs. He dipped a finger into my wetness as Hatter continued working his magic just above. I sank lower instinctively. "Chess…"

"Right here," he murmured, and guided the straining head of his cock to my slit. Oh, God, it was as big as the rest of him. A burn of pleasure spread out from my core as I eased down onto him. Chess groaned, pressing his mouth to my throat. Hatter kept teasing my clit, his other hand gliding up to tweak the tip of my breast, his breath shaky against my shoulder blade.

Chess caught my mouth as we slid together all the way to the base of his cock. He tucked his hand around to my ass to adjust my position, stroking into me at an angle that made me shudder with bliss. Then he held still, his fingers reaching farther to lightly probe my other entrance. A different but no less eager tingling sparked at his touch.

"You could have us both," he said in a liquid voice. "Double the enjoyment?"

I'd never "had" any guy that way, but the pleasure rushing through me and the promise in Chess's voice made me want to try. My agreement tumbled out. "Yes. I've never—we'll have to take it slow—"

Chess grinned at my stumbling enthusiasm. His gaze shifted to Hatter. "Do you have suitable oil?"

Hatter let out a rough chuckle, looking gloriously disheveled with his hair wild and his top half unbuttoned, his face even more flushed than before. The silk fabric of his pajamas did nothing to hide the erection tenting the bottoms. "I think— Yes, there should be—"

He vanished out the door, walking swiftly but lightly. We definitely didn't want anyone *else* in the apartment waking up. I slung my arms across Chess's shoulders, careful not to set them too close to his neck, and rocked with him through another kiss. Just that subtle movement and the fullness of him inside me took my breath away.

Remembering the fears he'd expressed earlier, I tipped my cheek next to his and murmured, "This is good. This is really good. You can climb in through my window anytime."

Chess laughed and kissed me again, penetrating me with a deeper thrust that had me seeing stars. Then Hatter was back, dashing to the bed. He opened the little jar he was holding and rubbed a slick substance between his fingers.

"Better to warm it up first, I think," he said in a low voice that turned me on even more.

I thought I was ready, but when his hand slipped over my ass to my opening, my nerves jumped and a gasp spilled out of me.

Hatter definitely wasn't new at *this,* whether he'd tried it as part of a threesome before or not. His deft fingers relaxed me as easily as they seemed to do everything. He traced their slick tips around my entrance until I was pushing back toward him, wanting more. One and then another worked inside me. A pleased hum reverberated through my chest, and Chess groaned as I bobbed against him.

When Hatter asked, "Ready?" with that one word so charged with wanting it nearly melted me, I was aching for it.

"Please," I said, and whimpered at the press of his cock, slick as his fingers had been. The two men held me steady between them as Hatter stretched me, filling me twice as much as before. The heady sensation of having them both inside me made my head spin with bliss.

I gripped Chess's hair, my lips brushing his, panting too hard to properly kiss him. Hatter brushed my hair to the side and nipped the back of my neck. His rough breath seared my skin.

We moved together, Chess's hand on my thigh, Hatter's arm around my waist, their lengths pulsing through me in a building rhythm. The stars I'd seen before spiraled before my eyes. One wave of pleasure and another and another rushed through me.

"Fuck," Hatter muttered against my back, jerking a little harder, a little faster, with a shudder that told me he couldn't hold back any longer. The urgency of his release tipped me over the edge right after him. I bucked against Chess, the stars behind my eyelids bursting into fireworks in time with the crackle of ecstasy that swept me away.

"Oh, Lyssa," Chess said, soft as a sigh. As Hatter withdrew, he plunged up into me, pushing my orgasm higher, farther, until his breath broke with the hitch of his own release.

I sagged onto the bed beside Chess, and Hatter settled in at my other side. Tucked there between the two of them, more sated than I'd ever felt in my life and the afterglow still tingling through me, it was hard to imagine ever wanting anything more than this.

"Mmm," Chess murmured. "Now that is what I call paradise. We could teach the Diamonds a thing or three. Not that we'd want to bother."

He said it so breezily that I couldn't help snickering. But as the pleasure of the encounter waned and all the other worries I'd had crept back in, my mind slipped back to other things he'd said about the Diamonds, before tonight.

"Chess," I said quietly. "You mentioned that you thought the Diamonds were unhappy enough with the Queen that someone there might have murdered the prince. Do you think… Are there any of them who'd help us displace her?" Whatever I decided to do, she wasn't going to back down easily.

Chess cocked his head in contemplation. The corners of his lips curled up, and he brushed a kiss to my cheek. "You know what? There just might be."

CHAPTER SEVENTEEN

Lyssa

"Y ou're sure he'll be there right now?" Theo asked, glancing over at Chess as we ambled along the road through the city, toward the lane that would take us past the pond of tears. The morning sun glinted off the puddles of rainwater left from last night's storm.

"Unicorn was a creature of habit as long as I knew him," Chess replied. He walked with a spring in his step that I liked to think was as much thanks to our amazing night together as the mission ahead of us. "He always took his run before lunch. The field out past the mushroom stands is a good distance out from everyone. He doesn't like to be watched when he gets down on all fours." He waggled his eyebrows.

He'd told me earlier that he'd followed Unicorn once, invisibly, out of curiosity, and that was how he'd discovered this part of his schedule. Which worked out well for us now, because if things hadn't changed, we should find the palace dweller on his own.

Whether he'd be interested in our proposal was another matter. Chess had seemed pretty certain the equine man could be swayed.

Theo was possibly less certain, as Chess must have picked up on too. "You really don't need to accompany us the entire way, White Knight," he said teasingly. "I'd almost think you don't trust me to spin my words well enough."

Theo smiled, but his eyes stayed grim. "It's not so much how well you spin them but how quickly you can cut to the heart of the matter, friend," he said. "You have to admit you do have a tendency toward obfuscation. Besides, with this much riding on the meeting, I'd like to be on hand even if only to lend authority to the offer of alliance."

The Red Knight, who'd been walking a little behind us, let out a doubtful sounding harrumph. "Can't trust any of the palace folk. No loyalty there."

He'd insisted on coming with us—coming with *me*, mainly—but thankfully we'd managed to talk him into gelling down his wayward hair and shedding his tarnished armor for one of Hatter's suits, which fit his height even if it hung a little loose on his skinny frame. So far he hadn't drawn any unusual attention.

Making sure no one noticed *me* was the bigger concern. I'd darkened my hair with a fresh dose of dye powder and pulled it back into a braid so its length wasn't as obvious. Between that and the bright green Wonderlander dress I was wearing, I felt reasonably disguised, but my skin still prickled whenever we passed anyone.

The streets were pretty quiet, though. The Queen had come through with her procession just a couple hours ago, the guards grabbing six more people, and the city's residents seemed to be hanging back behind closed doors as if worried she might make a second sweep.

That thought brought back the doubts that had been dogging me since the Red Knight had first told his story, along with the more specific ones that had risen up this morning.

"Even if he will join us, even if I wanted to try for the throne, are we in any position to do that right away?" I asked quietly, looking to Theo. "No one else in Wonderland knows about the Red royals—do you think they'll believe that story and take our side if I challenge the Queen of Hearts?"

Theo let out a slow breath. "Unfortunately, no," he said. "To both questions. If you can convince Unicorn, he may turn enough of the palace folk to our side to spur on a rebellion that way. If you can demonstrate the powers of the artifacts, we should be able to sway enough Clubbers to overcome the Hearts' Guard without the Diamonds help at all. But both of those scenarios will require time and care. As soon as the Queen catches wind that you truly are aiming to displace, she'll put all her power into destroying you."

In a weird way, his answer was a relief. It took off a bit

of the pressure. If we couldn't try for the throne now, then I didn't have to decide yet.

"Is that what I should ask Unicorn to do first, then? Talk up the cause with the other Diamonds?"

Theo shook his head. "Our first priority has to be getting the prisoners out before she orders their execution. Her dungeon is filling fast. If we lose them, no amount of magic is going to win the city folk over. Unicorn can give us a more in-depth account of the security and perhaps get us access so we can retrieve them."

"Besides, once they're out, it'll be easy to convince more of the Clubbers to join the Spades," Chess said brightly. "Onward toward rebellion."

I tried to ignore the knot in my stomach. "Onward, one step at a time."

That was how I'd approached everything in my life. Get food on the table. Get Mom to work another day. Get this bill paid and then that one.

If you looked too hard at the big picture bearing down on you, it could overwhelm you.

At the edge of the city, just beyond the last of the off-kilter buildings, a woman with wiry gray hair and a slightly stooped back was swaying from side to side as she peered off down the road. She was gripping the shoulders of the boy standing in front of her, who looked to be about ten. His gaze shot toward us at the sound of our feet, and his eyes widened. He shifted backward as if trying to urge her out of view.

Theo frowned. He picked up his pace to pull ahead of us, walking with swift but smooth strides. "What's the matter?" he asked, coming to a stop in front of the pair.

The boy opened and closed his mouth a couple times. "Nothing. Everything's fine."

"We're waiting—" the old woman started, and the boy clenched her hand.

"No, Grandma. We're just—just enjoying the view."

That comment sounded so unlikely that even I knew he had to be lying. Theo's attention shifted to the woman, his expression mild despite the concern in it. "You know me, don't you, Gladey?"

She swayed a little toward him, her eyes twitching before they settled on him. "Inventor," she said. "Why, where are you off to today?"

"To see about solving a problem or two, as I usually am," Theo said. "I'm getting the feeling you might have one."

The boy's eyes had widened even more. "Inventor!" he exclaimed, and bit his lip. "Sorry. I didn't realize…"

"It's all right," Theo said. "I don't believe we've had a chance to meet before. You're Gladey's grandson?"

The boy nodded, suddenly shy. "Winden," he said. "I —I don't know what to do, but I don't think there's any invention that's going to help."

"That's all right." Theo bent forward so their heads were level, as if they were about to conspire. "Sometimes I simply invent plans. What's the trouble here?"

My heart fluttered where the other three of us had hung back. I'd seen Theo leading the Spades as the White Knight, commanding and passionate, but I hadn't had much chance to see him act as Inventor to the Clubbers and other city people. His presence still held its usual air of authority, but softer around the edges, his smile gentle and his stance relaxed, welcoming these people into the opportunity to rely on him.

You couldn't watch and not know how much they mattered to him.

The woman jumped to answer his question. "It's Mallowy," she said. "She's not come back from the mushroom stands yet. I'm going to be here when she comes. I'm going to see her."

"Grandma," the boy said tightly. He looked at Theo and spoke under his breath. "The guards took my mom. Two days ago. Grandma was *there*, but she keeps talking like she thinks she's just got to wait here and Mom will show up. I don't know why. Mom *won't* come, and if the guards see Grandma here acting like this—she was *yelling* for her earlier…"

His voice wobbled. My gut twisted in understanding. If the guards noticed someone standing around talking about wanting to find one of the prisoners, they might see it as an act of defiance. They might take Gladey too.

Theo's jaw tensed. He patted the boy's shoulder, but I could see the pain in his expression. I was feeling it too. We didn't have any real reassurance to offer, any guarantee that the boy's mother would be returned safely. We didn't partly because of my own hesitation.

I braced myself for Theo to glance at me, maybe not even to say anything, but just to catch my gaze and share this moment with me, making sure I knew how much I was needed.

He didn't. He didn't shift his attention off the boy and his grandmother for a second. He simply straightened up and touched Gladey's elbow.

"Gladey," he said kindly, his smile going crooked. "I know where Mallowy is. She's not out at the mushroom stands. You won't find her waiting here. All right?"

"But she must be so lonely, off all on her own," Gladey said. "How will she find her way home?"

"I'm working on a way to bring her back," Theo said firmly. "I promise you, I'll give it everything I have. In the meantime, I know she'll feel so much better if she can be sure you and Winden are at home keeping everything in order for her. Should we go and see if there's anything there I could fix for her before she gets back?"

The old woman lit up, her swaying slowing. "Yes. Yes, there is—that ledge has tipped again. All those years it stayed in place without Time messing with it, and as soon as we're moving again…" She shook her head with a huff.

"Let's get that done right away, then," Theo said. "Let me just give my leave to my friends, and I'll join you."

The boy beamed at him gratefully and clutched his grandmother's hand as she started to shuffle down the road into the city.

Theo came over to us. "It looks like I'm trusting you to pull this off on your own after all," he said to Chess. His gaze slid to me. "You'll be all right, won't you? I'd ask them to wait, but the longer she's out here, the more chance the guards will take offense."

"Of course," I said quickly. "I'm sure we can manage."

He leaned in. "Don't be afraid to show Unicorn how much authority *you* can wield," he said by my ear. He gave me a grateful peck on the lips before pulling away, there and then back to his duty.

An ache of emotion swelled from deep inside me as I watched him go. He took on so much. When did he have time to think about what *he* needed?

I already knew what he'd say to that. He'd say that seeing Wonderland's people safe and free was what he needed more than anything else. And he'd mean it.

He was the one who should be ruling Wonderland, not me. It was an honor that a man like that would even think me capable of it.

I tugged my focus back to the task at hand.

"Come along," Chess said with a careless wave of his hand. "We have time, but not so much we should squander heaps of it."

"I don't recall a Unicorn in my day," the Red Knight muttered as we passed the looming ferns that hid the pond from view.

"From what I heard, here and there, the second Queen of Hearts brought him around to act out that poem with Lion, and the Diamonds simply never tired of it," Chess said. "I've got no idea what he occupied himself with before then. But I'm quite certain *he's* plenty tired of the gig he's got now."

He motioned us off the road into the underbrush

when the giant pink-and-purple mushrooms came into view up ahead. "We don't want any of Caterpillar's harvesters spotting us," he murmured. "Follow me, and keep quiet."

We eased between the fluffy fronds of the ferns, a herbal scent tickling my nose, until Chess decided we'd gone far enough. He led us off into a dense evergreen forest where the golden pinecones squirmed and wriggled across the branches like fat bristling worms. I set my feet carefully, avoiding any stray twigs that might crack, pebbles that might rattle.

We heard Unicorn before we saw him. There was a snort, just like a horse, and then the thump of hooved feet against the ground. We crept closer until we could make out the field between the trees without Unicorn noticing us.

The wide clearing was ringed by trees on all sides, which I guessed was why Unicorn had picked it. The grass grew so short it was barely more than moss, reminding me of astroturf with that vivid green shade. Good for running on, presumably. And that was what the equine figure was doing right now. He'd left all his clothes in a pile near the trees except for a sleeveless undershirt and a pair of gray short-pants similar to the red ones I'd seen him in for his fight with Lion, and he was galloping around the clearing on all fours. Muscles rippled in his shoulders and legs beneath the sheen of the coarse, pearly horsehair that covered his body.

"We'll go together and talk to him as we discussed," Chess whispered to me. He raised an eyebrow at the Red

Knight. "*You* stay right there, unless it looks certain someone needs running through. Someone other than the two of us."

"Well, you don't need to clarify that," the guardian of the Red royal family muttered.

"It protects me more if he doesn't see you," I reminded the Red Knight. "You're the secret advantage I have in my back pocket."

"Yes," he said, drawing himself up with his narrow chin high. "They will never see me coming."

I didn't know about that, but if we could keep him away from his armor, at least no one would *hear* him coming.

Chess shot me an amused grin as we walked together to the edge of the field. My heart started to thud almost as loud as Unicorn's hoof beats when we emerged from the shadows that had hidden us.

Unicorn was just loping around the curve in his makeshift racetrack. He jerked to a halt, yanking himself onto his hind legs in an instant, having to wheel his forelegs—arms?—to keep his balance.

"Unicorn!" Chess called, his grin widening. "No judgment here. That's not my style. You remember me, don't you?"

Unicorn strode a few paces closer, his mouth curling into what looked like the horse version of consternation. "*Chess?*" he said, and stiffened. "You're a Spade. A criminal."

Chess rolled his eyes. "When the laws are mad, aren't you mad to accuse by the laws? You *know* me,

Unicorn. When have I ever worked all that hard at anything?"

Unicorn took another hesitant step forward. "Why are you here?"

"To introduce you to someone I thought you might like to meet," Chess said. "I saw your battle last night. He got you again, didn't he? How would you like to get them all, hmm?"

Unicorn couldn't suppress the spark of interest that lit in his dark eyes. He turned them toward me. "Who are you?"

I started where Chess had told me too. "I heard you might be tired of the role you've been given," I said. "I think you're worthy of so much more than that. And I can give you a straight path there if you help us open up a path in turn."

The glint of hope didn't die, but Unicorn snorted in frustration. "I can't listen to this," he said to Chess. "You know it's a fool's—"

"You *can* listen," Chess said, crossing his arms over his chest. "And believe me, you want to. You haven't let her answer your question yet."

Unicorn paused. I drew in a breath to steady myself.

It would be okay. I wasn't committing to anything other than helping to take down the Queen of Hearts. What I did after—that was still up to me.

"I'm the thing the Queen fears the most," I said, "and the thing she has the most to fear from. I'm of the line of Alice. I'm the Red Queen, and I will see her off my throne."

The words gained resonance as I forced them from my throat. An unexpected conviction gripped me as I held Unicorn's gaze.

A queen's blood ran through my veins, whether I was prepared to follow it or not. And I was sick and tired of seeing Wonderland's people crushed by that horrible woman.

Unicorn blinked slowly. He snorted again, but it sounded more like awe this time.

"Well," he said. "I think I do want to hear more about this."

CHAPTER EIGHTEEN

Chess

Insomuch as I was like a cat, I would be one of those types that prowls around getting into scraps and yowling loud enough to wake the whole street. I would definitely *not* be the type to curl up on a warm lap and spend the rest of the evening there. Which was probably why I had the White Knight's entire luxurious apartment to loll around in, and after a few hours the white walls all over the place were starting to feel like a cage.

Thankfully, my mind was as swift as my patience was short.

"You know," I said where I was sprawled on my back on one of the White Knight's sofas, "we should go to Caterpillar's. It'd be good for Lyssa."

The White Knight glanced up at me through the steam rising off the cup of tea he'd just poured. He'd also been doing quite a lot of poring over the map one of the twins had brought him, though all he'd told me about it was that he wasn't sure yet what it would do for him, if anything at all.

"What makes you say that?" he said in the tone indicating that he was open to suggestion but that I'd better start stringing sense into it quickly.

"She's still nervous about the whole queenly bloodline this and that, isn't she?" I said, stretching out one leg and then the other. "Even with Unicorn pitching in to clear her path to our goals. We'll say it's for her to dance out some tension, get back to the joys of Wonderland, which would be good for her too, but it'll also remind her of all those people she could be saving."

"You're a wanted man," he pointed out.

I shrugged. "In that crowd, with that lighting, no one's likely to notice me—or her. They're even less likely to take a mind to tattle if they do. Caterpillar might be another story, but if he comes out onto the floor, we can always scram."

The White Knight ran his thumb across his square jaw, his dark brown eyes turning thoughtful. "That's true. You do raise a good point, Chess—and paying a visit to the club might help with my own end of our plans as well. Caterpillar must still be sending Rabbit through a looking-glass somewhere to get his Otherland ingredient, or the Clubbers would be getting even more restless than they already are. I'd like to know which one and how they're getting to it."

"Perfect!" I sprang up. "Where has our royal Highness gotten to, anyway?"

"She went up to talk to our White Queen-who-is-not-actually-a-queen," the White Knight said with a quirk of his lips. "They must be getting along well. She's stayed quite a while."

He started to get up too, but I motioned him back. "I'll retrieve her. You finish your tea, your Knightliness."

He chuckled, but he let me go. I hustled through the apartment to the elevator with a grin I couldn't have restrained if I'd wanted to. There were many things I enjoyed doing with our Otherlander, some of them very recently discovered, but dancing was up near the top of the list.

When I reached the White Queen's pastel-filled apartment, Lyssa had already come to the door, the White Queen trailing behind her. Lyssa's face was tight with worry.

"What is it, Chess?" she asked. "Is there more trouble?"

My dear lovely woman. The fact that she reacted to my arrival assuming the worst was exactly why we needed to break the stressful cycle we'd dragged her into.

"Not at all," I said, and held out my hand to her with a mock bow. "I wished to request your company at the Caterpillar's Club. You've had a dreadful stay in Wonderland this time, fleeing for your life and trudging through mud and strangling grasses and the rest. Letting loose might help clear your head. The White Knight will be joining us too, with plans of his own."

Lyssa hesitated, but then a small smile crossed her face. "Maybe that would be a nice change of pace," she said. "If Theo thinks we'll be safe enough. Just for a couple hours—to clear my head, like you said." She turned to the White Queen. "Would you like to come?"

The other woman looked startled by the invitation. She curled a strand of her pale hair around her finger, her mouth working. "No," she said in a distant voice. "I don't do that. But thank you."

"Okay, well, maybe another time then," Lyssa said. She slipped her hand into mine so easily my heart skipped a beat. I twined my fingers with hers, relishing just that simple contact as we went down a floor to collect the White Knight.

She knew everything. All the twisted, painful parts of my past I'd tried to forget—and her desire for me, her *caring* for me, hadn't faltered in the slightest. I still wasn't sure I was whole enough to be everything she needed, but I didn't have to be. She had Hatter and the White Knight too.

I could make her laugh. I could make her gasp with pleasure. If that was enough for her, then it'd be enough for me too.

When the White Knight stepped into the elevator, he slipped his arm around Lyssa's waist. "Did you have a good chat with Mirabel?"

"Well, she didn't tell me anything that I'm sure can help us get the prisoners free," Lyssa said. "But it sounded like the Unicorn is trustworthy. If I got the gist of that part right. And then she showed me her knitting—she offered to make me a dress—and we talked a little about Wonderland in general. I asked her if she wanted to come with us to the club, but I guess she wasn't up for it."

Just for a second, the White Knight looked as startled by the idea as the woman herself had been. "That was kind of you," he said warmly. "It isn't any comment on whether she enjoyed your company, you know. Mirabel never leaves the Tower."

Lyssa blinked at him. "*Never?*"

"Not for as long as I've been here, at least. My people bring by food and whatever else she needs. You've seen her scar…" He motioned to his temple. "Her attacker was never brought to justice. She's afraid if she's discovered, the next attack will be worse."

"That's awful." Lyssa winced in sympathy. "I hope someone does catch him so she can feel safe again."

"We've certainly tried," the White Knight said. "You've seen how easily violence can lurk beneath the surface here."

She nodded with a sharp exhalation. "Oh, we'd better bring the Red Knight along too. He'll freak out if he checks in on me and I'm no longer in the building."

When we'd stopped by there, the White Knight had set up his sort-of counterpart in the third floor apartment that various Spades used from time to time. The Red Knight preferred to keep up his "watch" closer to the ground floor. *First line of defense!* he'd declared, without any explanation of how he expected to determine anyone needed defending, but I thought Lyssa had been glad to take a little break from him shadowing her. He couldn't provide any protection the White Knight couldn't offer tenfold.

True to form, when Lyssa told the Red Knight where we were off to, he blustered about crowds and secure settings. But he was also loyal to the core, so he came along, muttering his continued complaints under his breath.

As we came up to the club, *I* was glad when he came to a halt and remarked, "I feel I can be of most service guarding the outside of the building. Should any threatening figures make an appearance, I will reach you and usher you to safety before they can carry out their evil deeds."

"Perfect," Lyssa said. "But if you change your mind, feel free to come in even if there isn't any evil to warn me about."

As soon as we stepped through the spinning walls onto the vast undulating dance floor, most of the tension that had been gripping me fell away. The thump of the bass oscillated through my bones. Red and orange strobe lights flashed over the mass of dancers, making them look like a churning wave of human flame. No one gave us a second glance.

If the Clubbers had even heard about the Queen's call for me, they didn't give a shit. Keep your head low, dance your heart out, and don't let the darkness touch you—that was the way things worked here. These were my people as much as anyone in Wonderland was.

The Duchess could sic however many guards she

wanted on me. I wasn't letting her own me again. I could
live my life exactly as I had been before.

The White Knight gave Lyssa a quick kiss and turned
to me. "I might need you later," he said, just loud enough
for me to hear despite the music. For my vanishing skills,
no doubt. I tipped my head to him.

My gut pinched at the same time. Finding another
looking-glass meant offering Lyssa a way to her home in
the Otherland. But she'd found out that *this* was her true
home. She'd see that we were better for her than anyone in
that dreary place could be, wouldn't she? Once she was on
the throne, everything in Wonderland could be joyful.

The White Knight moved off through the crowd to
get eyes on Rabbit or Caterpillar. The hulking owner of
the club with his turnip-shaped head and segmented,
quadruple-armed body was nowhere to be seen in the
main room. All the better for us. I grasped Lyssa's hand
tighter and spun her around with me, merging with the
throng.

Lyssa laughed as her body settled into the rhythm. She
let her head fall back and swayed her arms in the air. Her
dress, another of May's old ones I thought, swished
around her thighs. With her hair darkened and pulled
back, she didn't look like quite the free spirit she had
when I'd first brought her here, before she'd had any idea
there *was* anything to this land other than joyful self-
indulgence, but her eyes shone brighter when they met
mine again.

Yes, this had been the right idea, for both of us.

The songs bled from one into the other like they

always did. Lyssa stayed with me, her fingers brushing over my chest as we swayed together, her body easing even closer when I rested my hand on her hip. I leaned in to kiss the crook of her neck, teasing the tips of my sharpest teeth over her skin to make her breath catch. Her fresh scent filled my nose. Hearts take me, how could I want her this much when I'd just had her last night?

I'd been holding back before, afraid to offer what I couldn't really give. But she wanted me as I was. And I wanted her, every night, over and over again.

Maybe I could have her tonight. I had the feeling the White Knight would be game once we were done here. We'd played together enough times that I wouldn't have to think at all when he was the other one there. Just feel and enjoy.

I wasn't sure how many songs we'd danced through when I spotted the White Knight's pale shirt catching the sporadic lights as he made his way over to us. I slowed down, loosening my hold on Lyssa, mentally preparing for whatever mission he might be able to send me off on.

A hand grabbed my sleeve, jerking me toward the edge of the room. "Here he is!" the guy who'd grabbed me shouted, waving his other arm in the air. "Cheshire's here!"

My pulse hiccupped. As I tried to yank my sleeve from the guy's grasp, two of the queen's guards hustled over around the fringes of the crowd. Had they been lurking at the far end of the room the whole time? Or had our supposed guard outside been even more useless than I'd expected?

The man hauled at my arm, and panic shot through me. I kicked him in the side with everything I had. The second his grasp broke, I slipped away into the in-between, where the music was dulled and the edges of every form around me turned stuttered and sharp. Where no one could see me at all.

They could still feel me. A dancer's foot jammed down on my toes; another's elbow caught my ribs, sparking a fresh wave of panic. I threw myself away from them, out of the crowd, past the cursing informant and the guards rushing to meet him. In the gap of open space near the wall, I spun around.

Lyssa had come after me, maybe without any clear idea what was going on. I hadn't even stopped to warn her. A shamed chill trickled through me as I watched her freeze at the sight of the guards. The White Knight caught up with her, grasping her shoulders from behind.

He'd get her out of here. *He'd* protect her, when I'd been the one who brought her here, when I'd been the one the guards were looking for.

The Duchess had won after all, hadn't she?

Even as my throat tightened with that thought, one of the guards whirled around and snapped at a young guy— a boy, really—who'd accidentally bumped into him. The boy paled under the dappling of the lights. He held up his hands.

"I'm sorry, I really didn't mean—"

"You need to learn proper respect for the Hearts' Guard," the other guard bellowed, and whipped out his baton. He smacked it across the boy's skull so hard the kid reeled.

"No!" another voice shouted—a voice I knew so well my heart stopped before my eyes even registered Lyssa shoving the rest of the way forward. She threw herself between the guard and the cringing boy.

They could see she had a queen's blood running through her veins, couldn't they? She stood straight and steady, her chin raised and her eyes lit with determination.

Oh, lands, what did she think she was doing?

I took a step toward her, wanting to intervene, but if I showed myself, even invisibly, I'd only make things worse for both of us. As soon as they knew she had anything to do with me, they'd take her whether they realized she was the Alice their queen was looking for or not.

"Now look here," one of the guards started to growl, raising his baton threateningly.

Lyssa's gaze twitched. A flicker of fear passed through her expression—but only a flicker, and then her jaw set again.

"He didn't do anything," she said, pointing at the boy, who was still clutching the side of his head. "Aren't you supposed to be catching a criminal here? Why are you beating up on some kid instead of doing your job?"

I could have laughed if I hadn't been so terrified for her. She was turning their loyalty back around on them, acting as if she were even more concerned with the Queen's decrees than they were. A perfect gambit.

Perfect enough to work? One of the guards had

stepped back, but the other was still eyeing her, his knuckles white where he was gripping his baton.

Then the White Knight was there, hooking his arm around Lyssa's and giving the guards an apologetic shake of his head.

"My apologies, men of the Hearts," he said in his ever-smooth voice. "I ran into a Dreamer and thought I'd show her the sights, but she hasn't quite figured out the rules of this place yet. I'll see she doesn't interrupt any more of your work."

Lyssa's lips flattened with annoyance, but she was smart enough not to protest in front of the guards. The White Knight ushered her toward the exit.

Where I'd better go too. I hurried after them through the muted space of the in-between, the momentary exhilaration of seeing Lyssa challenge the guards fading as quickly as it had rushed through me. My spirits sank with it.

Queen or not, how could I possibly be worthy of her when my solution to the first sign of trouble was to vanish?

I couldn't blame that on the Duchess, not completely. That was me, through and through.

CHAPTER NINETEEN

Lyssa

Theo led the way back to the Tower through a series of side streets he must have felt were most likely to keep us out of view. I kept waiting, hoping, for Chess to appear out of thin air beside us with his carefree grin. The shining silver spire came into view up ahead, and he still hadn't turned up.

"Do you think Chess is okay?" I asked in the elevator shaft after we'd let the Red Knight off on the third floor.

"If there's anyone who can keep out of sight, it's our Cheshire," Theo said, but I could still see a little strain in his expression. The confrontation in the club had bothered him more than he was trying to let on. The frustration that had been niggling at me since we'd left chomped down harder.

I held my tongue about that for now. "Did you find out anything about Rabbit?"

"If what I saw indicates what it should, then we're not much closer to finding you a route home than we were before," he said. "I believe I saw the mark of the Queen's seal on his hand, which would suggest she's given him permission to travel via her personal looking-glass."

"The one you already knew about," I said, my heart sinking.

"Yes. I'm sorry, Lyssa. I'll test my suspicions as soon as I can."

I wasn't sure how much I'd really believed there might be another mirror, easier to get to. I definitely still wasn't sure what I'd do if we found one.

When we came into his office, Theo headed straight across the room toward the hallway that led to the more private rooms. I stopped in my tracks halfway there. If I was going to say it, I might as well say it now.

"You didn't have to step in, back there in the club," I said. "I was fine."

Theo turned, his shoulders tensing. "You were challenging the Queen's guards. They have the authority to take your head without thinking twice, Lyssa. The less you talk to them, the less you even *look* at them, the better."

I crossed my arms over my chest, fighting the urge to outright hug myself. "I didn't give anything away. I made it sound like I was on the Queen's side. And I stopped them from hurting that... that *kid*. He hardly looked older than Doria."

"He was already apologizing. They wouldn't have taken it too far."

"How far is too far?" I said. "Even if they just bash him around, he isn't going to reset in perfect health overnight like everyone used to, remember?"

The flicker of Theo's eyes suggested maybe he hadn't quite remembered that. He'd been born into the freeze, after the Queen of Hearts had trapped time, he'd told me. Until the last week, he'd never known anything except a world that reset around him with every midnight.

He raked his hand through his chestnut curls. "He'll be a lot worse off if we lose you," he said. "You're the key to bringing her down, whatever you decide to do after that. Wonderland needs you—with your head attached."

"What kind of queen am I going to be if I stand back and watch while a couple of bullies beat up a kid?" I demanded. "If I'm going to make a decision, I have to know—I have to see—I have to at least *try* to stand up for someone. I have to know how much risk I can handle. I have to know if I'm willing to do enough. I sure as hell shouldn't be taking any thrones if I can't handle myself even in a little scene like that. Shouldn't a queen be ready to defend her people?"

For possibly the first time since I'd met him, the confidence in Theo's stance faltered. He stared at me. There was something so fraught in his expression that my stomach knotted.

"I get that you want to protect me," I said. "And I appreciate it. You've done so much for me. I just feel like it's time I start to find my own feet here. I want to do the right thing. Can you understand that?"

His chuckle came out ragged. "I understand. Lyssa, you don't have anything to prove."

I swallowed hard, my arms tightening around my chest. "I do. To myself, to find my limits. And..." I thought of him this morning, the way he'd responded so quickly to the plight of that old woman and her grandson. All the times before that I'd watched him devote himself to the cause of helping Wonderland's people. It wasn't just my hesitation about my supposed role here that had pushed me to act. The ache in my heart propelled the words up my throat.

"I want to prove to you that I'm strong enough to at least see this rebellion through. I—I want to prove that I'm worthy of your respect, as an equal, not some stumbling Otherlander."

"You've already proven all of that," Theo said. "And my opinion shouldn't matter that much anyway."

"It does," I said. His dark brown gaze held mine so intently I couldn't look away. I couldn't stop the words from coming out either, even though my voice dropped to a whisper. "It does because I'm falling in love with you."

His whole face shifted then, with a mix of emotions I couldn't track. Somehow his eyes brightened and darkened in the same moment, relief and hope and horror colliding.

"Lyssa..." He didn't seem to know what to say.

"I don't expect anything because of that," I said quickly. "It is what it is."

Theo was shaking his head. He gripped the edge of the worktable beside him. "That's not why— We haven't had much time to get to know each other. I haven't let you get to know certain sides. There are things about me that, if you knew them... I doubt you'd even like me anymore."

Now it was my turn to stare at him. Was he kidding me? "I'm sure there can't possibly be anything that bad," I said.

He gave me a tight smile. "Oh, there is."

I found the courage to take a step toward him and then another. What painful secrets was he holding in, like Chess had, out of masculine pride or whatever?

"Why don't you tell me then, and see if I think this stuff is really so awful?"

Theo let out a halting laugh. "You know, I thought I was holding back because I was putting Wonderland ahead of everything. But more and more I'm not so certain. I'm starting to think it's actually that I'm more selfish than I'd like to admit, and I haven't convinced myself yet that telling all is worth the risk of losing you."

Something like hope fluttered in my chest. What we'd shared together had meant more than just a little enjoyment to him too, then. God, I didn't even know how much longer I was staying here, but faced with him looking at me with all that conflicted passion, it was hard to think of how anything could be more important.

I walked over until I was close enough to rest my hand on his chest. He gazed down at me. I charted every inch of his face, from those warm eyes to his beautifully crooked nose to the full lips set over that square jaw.

"I don't think you could have done anything I wouldn't understand," I said. "Maybe I haven't known you that long, but I've seen you when lives are on the line, when everything depends on the orders you give or how you act. I *know* you. I know how much you care about people. I know how far you're willing to go for them."

Theo set his hand over mine, letting his head bow until his forehead almost touched mine. "You have no idea how much I'd like to be the man you've seen and nothing more—or less."

"You are that man," I said firmly. "I don't think you're perfect. Everyone makes mistakes. But, hell, I'd bet *no one* could meet whatever standards you're trying to hold yourself to."

"I should be able to. I'm the Inventor, and the White Knight, and— I'm the person all of Wonderland needs to turn to."

"Not on your own," I said. "At least for a little while, they can turn to me too."

Theo made a strangled sound, and then he was sweeping his fingers into my hair and tugging me to him. His mouth claimed mine with a deeper hunger than I'd ever felt from him before, so forceful and potent I lost my breath. He *was* claiming me, in every sense of the word, one hand loosening my braid, the other tracing a heated path down the side of my body, his hot tongue delving into my mouth.

His fingers traveled up over my ass and back beneath my dress, hiking it to my waist. He loosened my bra with a yank. I whimpered into his kiss as he fondled the sensitive curves of my breasts, not rough but raptly, as if he meant to work every ounce of pleasure he could into my body. My tongue tangled with his. I quivered with the swivel of his palm.

Theo devoured me with one more searing kiss. Then he pulled back with a sound in his throat as if the brief loss of contact was painful. He wrenched my dress off and tossed it onto one of the worktables. An instant later, he'd captured my mouth again. Without breaking the kiss, he walked me backward until my shoulders hit the wall. His body pressed against me—his still clothed, mine nearly naked—with so much coiled strength my panties dampened at the sensation.

He dipped lower to chart a path across my throat and collarbone before flicking one of my nipples into his mouth. My fingers dug into his hair as he sucked it hard and teased it with the edges of his teeth. A whimper of need broke from my lips. Without missing a beat, he shifted his attentions to my other breast, his thumb massaging over the one he'd just marked. Every swipe of his fingers and his tongue sent shivers of ecstasy through my chest.

I groaned in protest when he released my tender flesh, but my disappointment only lasted a moment. He trailed kisses down my stomach to my panties and pressed his mouth against my core through the thin fabric. I gasped, my hips bucking. Pleasure coursed through me as he worked me over through that delicate barrier and then wrenched them down to taste me skin to skin.

My knees wobbled. I clung to his head as a moan rippled through me. He sucked on my clit, and I nearly burst apart right there. But God, I wanted more than this.

His urgency was catching. I wanted all of him, and I wanted him now.

"Theo," I gasped out, my grip tightening. I urged him upward, and he came. His mouth caught mine again, tart with my own musky flavor and his rose-raspberry scent. I arched against the bulge of his erection.

"Lyssa," he rasped, tearing his lips from mine for just a few seconds. "I want you to be my queen. I want to worship you on that fucking throne."

My throat swelled with promises I wanted to give when he was driving me this wild but couldn't quite bring myself to say. Theo didn't wait for an answer. He kissed me hard, the solid length of his cock flush against my clit, and I was ready to be worshiped right now, in every way he felt like offering.

I tugged open his slacks. His breath hitched when I curled my fingers around his straining erection.

He hefted me up against the wall and thrust into me in one smooth movement. I cried out as pleasure shot through my core. He held me there, braced between the wall and his weight, his hand clamped on my thigh.

My legs locked behind him. My world narrowed down to the cool surface against my naked back and the scorching-hot man between my thighs, plunging deeper as I bucked my hips to meet him as well as I could. Bliss spiraled through me, faster and sharper each time he drove into me.

"Yes," I mumbled. "Yes." Not to being queen, just to being fucked this hard. I clasped my hands behind Theo's neck. Our kisses had become so sloppy with our ragged breaths that my teeth nicked his lip. He shuddered against me with a groan.

His hand dipped down, and his fingers swiveled against my clit, jerky but sure. The fresh bolt of pleasure sent me careening over the edge. "Oh, fuck. Oh, yes." My head tipped back against the wall, my body shaking in his hold, and my vision whited out in the blaze of bliss.

Theo thrust even harder, and I came apart a second time right on the heels of the first. As my body clenched around him, he came too, the rush of his stuttered breath as hot as the gush of his release inside me.

My legs were still wobbly when he helped me ease them to the ground. He stayed leaning over me, warming me and holding me in place. I grasped the front of his shirt, suddenly unsure what to say. I'd confessed my feelings. He hadn't actually said anything directly about his. I didn't know how much any of this could mean anyway.

Theo made it simple. He tipped his head close by my ear. "Stay the night?" he asked. "I can send one of the twins to let Hatter know you're okay."

I could do that. And maybe the fact that he'd asked was all I needed to know. I smiled and kissed his cheek.

"Yes."

CHAPTER TWENTY

Lyssa

I found the Red Knight sitting with a bemused expression in a boxy armchair in the third floor apartment's living room, watching Dee and Dum play a board game that appeared to involve a lot of cheering and hand-waving. Dee turned one of his waves toward me with a smile. Dum offered me a quick nod.

"I should go by Hatter's and see if Chess has turned up," I said to my recently acquired bodyguard. "And I'm supposed to be meeting Unicorn in a bit. I assumed you'd want to know where I'm going."

"I'll be going where you're going," the Red Knight said with a determined huff, springing to his feet. His gangly body was still pretty limber despite his obvious age.

"Good luck with the horny one!" Dee called after us as we headed to the elevator. Dum snorted at the pun.

Walking down the hall, the Red Knight brushed his hands over his borrowed shirt and trousers. "I would feel more at ease in my customary uniform," he said with a hopeful note in his voice.

"I know," I said. "But no one around here wears armor. If the people here are willing to report Chess, someone's bound to let the guards know if they see you in that get-up. It keeps both of us safer if you blend in."

"That's the only reason I agreed." He tugged at his wispy hair, which was starting to fluff up again, and sighed with a pat of his pocket. "I'm less convinced about trading my sword for this knife. I am trained in the *knightly* arts, not those of pickpockets and scoundrels."

The corners of my mouth twitched with suppressed amusement. "I'm pretty sure honorable people can use knives too. A sword would definitely attract attention. If we plan on getting into a real fight, you can bring it along then."

"And you can bring yours, your Majesty," he said, looking pleased at the thought.

Other than the ruby ring, which I was still wearing on the chain hidden under my shirt, the Red royal artifacts were hidden in a secret compartment Hatter had shown me in the back of my bedroom's wardrobe. I hadn't actually used the sword on anything other than grass so far. The idea of using it on another human being made my stomach twist. I'd do it if I had to, but it wasn't something I'd look forward to.

"Will we be marching on the palace soon?" the Red

Knight asked me as we came to a stop at the elevator door. "It will be a blessing to see you take your rightful place at last."

He never seemed to remember that *I* hadn't been waiting for this moment for hundreds of years—that I hadn't even existed to be anyone's heir until a couple decades ago. What would he do if I left for home instead of claiming the throne after the Queen of Hearts was overthrown? Go back to his hilly home and hope I'd have a daughter or granddaughter who'd be more interested in ruling?

The twist in my gut turned into a pang of guilt when he beamed at me. I paused before stepping into the elevator shaft.

"I don't know," I said. "That's a bigger fight than we were prepared to jump right into. First we have to make sure the prisoners she's been taking get out of there safely. And... you know I've told you I'm not sure I actually want to be queen."

Like before, he brushed off the idea with a guffaw. "Once your place is open to you, you'll feel the rightness of it. You were born for this."

Hadn't Aunt Alicia been born for it too? And the two Alices who'd turned up in Wonderland before her? None of them had ended up on that throne. How could I tell if I was the right one when they hadn't been?

"It just doesn't seem fair that you're spending all your time following me all over the place, ready to protect me, when I'm not even sure what I'm doing," I said. "It's not fair to *you*. Isn't there anything else you want to do now that you're in the city? You should get to have a life that's more than just waiting around for me."

The Red Knight caught my eyes with his pale blue ones. Normally they looked a little foggy, but in that moment they gazed back at me perfectly clearly, with a glint of awareness that made me wonder if he'd been hearing me better than he'd let on.

"My dear Princess Lyssa, soon to be Queen Lyssa," he said. "Your family *is* my life. I went into the service when I was but six, running errands in the palace, and it was my greatest honor to rise to the rank of Knight. For a short time, I was a part of the goodness and grandeur that Wonderland used to be—for all its people. I gave up my daughter so your bloodline could live on. Spending these days with you after spending so many waiting on my own across the Plains is no sacrifice at all."

A lump rose in my throat. "I don't know if I'll be as good or as grand as you hope I'll be."

His wizened face shifted with a soft smile. "It's enough to be here to see you try. I had faith the time would come before my own time ended. My faith was rewarded. That's all I need. There's nothing you could offer me that would make me want to miss one moment toward you finding your place here, however that may come to be."

I didn't know how to argue with that. How could his belief in me feel like a gift and a burden at the same time?

But maybe the trying really was all he needed. I *was* going to try my fucking heart out to make things better here, even if better didn't involve me on any thrones. I couldn't run away and leave these people under the Heart family's thumb, not even if I found a mirror that would take me home with a brush of my fingers.

"Okay then," I said. "Let's see what we can do to bring down a tyrant."

I stayed cautious as we moved through the streets toward Hatter's place. There might not be anything about my looks that should catch anyone's eye, but I didn't want to put myself in view of the guards anyway.

My vigilance turned out to be a good thing, because my gaze snagged on a curved red helm through the window of the hat shop when we were still several feet away. My pulse skittered. I grabbed the Red Knight's wrist and tugged him off to the side, closer to the neighboring building.

There were two figures wearing the red helms and red-and-pink pleated tunics of the Hearts' Guard in Hatter's shop. I didn't dare get close enough to make out more than that. What had they come to badger Hatter about now? Had someone pointed the finger at him like the Duchess had at Chess?

He might need our help. I had to find out what was going on in there. I swallowed past the dryness in my mouth and motioned for the Red Knight to follow me.

We slipped down the alley between a couple shops farther down the street and came around to the back of Hatter's. Like the shop's front door, the back was never locked. I eased it open, freezing at the faint squeak of the hinges. When no one came to investigate, I squeezed inside, the Red Knight right behind me, and padded across the workroom floor as quietly as I could manage.

It looked like Hatter had been working in that room when the guards had arrived. A half-finished sunhat lay on one of the tables, the veil only attached on one side. The door that separated the workroom from the main shop stood halfway open. I nudged the Red Knight to a stop near the table and edged closer on my own, flattening myself against the wall.

From there, I could see the back end of the counter and Hatter standing on the other side of it, but not a whole lot else.

"But you *did* go out to the Checkerboard Plains," one of the guards was saying in a voice with a snarly edge. I caught a glimpse of him as he stalked past Hatter to the other side of the shop: a beefy man with a tiger's head. I'd seen him before, I realized—in the club, a couple weeks ago, when he'd beat up a woman until she'd bled all over the dance floor.

He was wearing a taller helm than the guards usually did. Any of the guards other than— Oh. The idea hit me with cold certainty.

He was the new Knave. And he was following up on his predecessor's line of inquiry.

"I did," Hatter said, his light tenor only a little strained. How long had the Knave been interrogating him? "My daughter had never been out there before, but she's been badgering me for ages. Now that we could spend more than a day taking in the sights, it seemed like an ideal time."

The Knave spun around and paced back out of view. I reached toward the shelves behind me and groped along them until my fingers closed around a pair of fabric shears. Not quite a sword, but they'd do in a pinch. I braced them at my side.

"So you admit you were pleased to see Time freed, then?" the Knave said.

"Not at all," Hatter said. Just the slightest hint of dryness crept into his tone. "I feel for the Queen and the violation of her home. But once it was done, it was done."

"The Knave before me went out to the Plains with the intention of speaking with you," the tiger-man said. "He'd gotten word that you might have other intentions there. Did you not see him?"

"I can't say I did," Hatter said. "And I can't think of what other intentions I might have had. Is there something out there I should be interested in?"

The Knave made a dismissive sound and continued his pacing. "As you can determine from my appointment, he did not return. I think you must have some idea what happened to him."

Hatter spread his hands. "I can make a guess, if you want my opinion. The Checkerboard Plains have gone even wilder than I recalled. Plenty of danger if you venture from the train. I nearly lost my daughter in a sinkhole, and we saw a jabberwock from afar. Any number of things could have befallen the man. I have no intention of returning, you can believe that."

"I see." The Knave stopped with a tap of his heel. "I'd

like to speak with your daughter, then, so I can verify your story."

Hatter tensed, and a movement behind the counter caught my eye. Doria was crouched there in the shadows, out of sight, where Hatter must have told her to stay when they'd realized the Knave was coming in. If the Knave realized Hatter had been hiding her, that was going to look awfully suspicious.

Doria grabbed a dented hat that had been left behind the counter and started to straighten up, maybe thinking she'd use the hat as an excuse for being down there. My grip on the shears tightened.

At the first faint rustle of Doria's dress, Hatter shot forward like he'd been stung. "Come along then," he said, suddenly talking twice as fast. "Although it seems to me she told me that she was—"

A second after he'd passed out of view, there was a squeal and a crash. The guards toppled into my view under the weight of a shelving unit, hats flying everywhere. The Knave gave an angry shout. My heart lurched. What the hell did Hatter think he was doing?

Doria froze, her head just above the level of the counter. Hatter must have made some gesture, because she turned and fled through the workroom. Her panicked gaze met mine with a flash of surprise, but she kept running, her stockinged feet whispering over the floor, out the back the way we'd come in.

As I wavered between following her for my own safety and staying for Hatter's, the Knave heaved the fallen shelving unit to the side with a sharper thump. His sword hissed from its hilt at his side. "You—"

"I'm so sorry!" Hatter said in a quavering voice that hardly sounded like himself. "I was distracted trying to remember, and my hand slipped—those shelves haven't been stable in so long—I really need to get someone in to fix them up. Are you both all right?"

"I will see your daughter *now*," the Knave said, full-out snarling now.

"That's what I was trying to tell you," Hatter babbled. "We could go check for her, but she told me she was going out with friends an hour or so ago, didn't know where they'd end up. That's a teenager for you." He let out a weak laugh. "I understand I've given grave offense. Should we go to see the Queen? I'd be happy to explain to her everything I did to you. Any questions she has, I'll say everything I know."

My chest clenched. He wasn't seriously volunteering to throw himself on the Queen's mercy, was he? Once she had him there in the palace—

I shifted my weight forward, letting the shears drop open so I had a stabbing point if I needed it, but apparently Hatter's reckless gamble had hit the mark after all. The Knave's lips curled in apparent disgust, revealing the gleam of fangs much more vicious than Chess's.

"That won't be necessary," he snapped. "Clean up this mess—and see that your shop's furniture is in order the next time I come by. The Queen has enough to do without bothering with the likes of you. I'll stop in tomorrow to speak with your daughter. Make sure she's here."

He stalked out, kicking aside a couple of the fallen hats as he went. The other guard hustled after him.

Hatter exhaled in a rush.

"Hatter?" I said tentatively.

A moment later, he was yanking open the workroom door. "What are you doing here?" he demanded, in an aggravated tone and with a wary glint in his eyes that felt much more like his usual self.

"What the hell were *you* doing?" I retorted, keeping my voice low. I gave him a little shove. "Are you crazy? You practically attacked the Knave—if he hadn't bought that it was an accident—"

"But he did," Hatter said. "And Doria got out."

"You almost got taken to see the Queen."

"I would have managed that too," he said, the glint in his eyes turning a touch wild. "There's a reason they called me 'Mad' back then, you know. I've been thinking tapping into that side might not be such a bad thing when I have people to protect."

The way he looked at me when he said that last bit made the sharpest bits of emotion melt inside me. "Okay," I said. "If you're sure he's gone, do you want me to help you clean up?"

Hatter glanced over his shoulder and grimaced. "That does look like more than a one-person job. Thank you."

He seemed calm enough as we picked our way among the scattered hats and shattered glass from the shelves, but the tension squeezing my chest didn't loosen. It *had* been kind of mad, what he'd done. Doria had already been thinking up an excuse to use. That might have worked just as well, without potentially pissing the Knave off so much he'd turned his sword on Hatter.

I wasn't sure being Mad was a good thing for protecting *Hatter*.

CHAPTER TWENTY-ONE

Lyssa

"Do you really think coming with me is worth the risk when the Knave was just questioning you?" I murmured as Hatter pushed through the ferns beside me.

"I wasn't going to leave you to meet Unicorn on your own," he said under his breath, and glanced back at the Red Knight, tailing me as always. "Or near enough to being on your own."

Chess had been supposed to come with me, but Hatter hadn't seen Chess since he'd dropped by the apartment briefly last night. At least I knew the guards hadn't caught him then. Where was he now? Why had he taken off like that?

There didn't seem to be much point in searching for someone who could turn invisible. And if we'd missed the arranged meeting with Unicorn, he wasn't likely to trust us to go forward with any kind of plan. It still gnawed at me, though, not knowing where Chess was or how he was coping.

I followed the same path Chess had that first day, skirting the mushroom farm and then slipping through the dense evergreen forest. Near the edge of the treeline, I stopped Hatter with my hand on the sleeve of his jacket. He looked down at me, his green eyes so intent in his handsome face beneath the brim of today's bowler hat that I lost my words for a second.

"I think you should stay here," I said quietly. "It wasn't really a risk for Chess to come with me—he's already been accused. But if Unicorn turns against us after all, it'll be better if he doesn't know who else is involved. Okay? If it sounds like there's any trouble, you can come rushing in and kick as much horsey butt as you want."

Hatter made a disgruntled face at the suggestion, but he sighed rather than arguing. "I can't deny the logic there," he said. "You'll tread carefully with him?"

"I'm pretty sure out of all of you I'm the *most* careful one," I pointed out.

His lips curled upward. "I suppose I can't deny that either. Though you have had your moments. Maybe madness is catching."

I rolled my eyes at him even though I couldn't help smiling back. Hatter dipped his head to kiss me quickly, the heat of his mouth lingering after he'd pulled back. I took a step away from him with an ache in my chest.

God help me, I was falling for all three of them, wasn't

I? Theo and Hatter and Chess. They were all spectacular in their varying ways. Could anyone blame me?

Melody would laugh when I told her. If I got the chance to tell her anything, even a made-up version of what I was going through. If I ever made it back.

That thought sobered me up again. I bobbed my head to Hatter and headed into the field. The Red Knight strode along behind me without comment. I wondered if any of the previous Red Queens had taken multiple partners. Did *that* run through my bloodline too? It didn't seem like the best time to ask.

Unicorn had already arrived. He was strolling around the perimeter of the clearing, his hooved hands tucked behind his back, his equine body fully clothed in a dress shirt, vest, and slacks—yellow, red, and purple, respectively. He stopped and tossed back his sparkling mane at the sight of me.

I hurried over to join him, and he started walking again when I reached him. His restless pace suggested he was still a little nervous of *my* motives too.

"Thank you for coming," I said. "I know it's a lot to ask with the Queen of Hearts as suspicious as she is right now."

Just that acknowledgment brought Unicorn's shoulders down an inch. "It isn't so difficult," he admitted. "I've had a long-standing excuse to come out here and run. It serves just as well for a meeting like this."

"I'm glad to hear that. I want you to know that I realize that even the Diamonds and the other people who stay close to the palace are just trying to survive. I want

everyone in Wonderland to have a better life." Except for
the Duchess. She could go suck rocks.

"You won't find many who'll argue that this is a *good*
life, even if most of them don't have the guts to try to
change it," Unicorn said.

"She took eight people from the city this morning," I
said, resisting the urge to grit my teeth. "Were you able to
find out anything about the timing she's planning for the
executions?"

Unicorn slowed his pace, raising one hoof to scratch
his white cheek. "The palace dungeon is almost full," he
said. "She's already making plans for a spectacle of a trial
—all the top Diamonds as the 'jury,' the prisoners cut
down one by one and displayed in the city." He winced.
"Then she'll send the guards out to call on the city folk to
turn in the Spades among them, so they can be punished
for the deaths they 'caused'."

After seeing dozens of their own killed without any
intervention from the Spades, I wouldn't be surprised if
they did. I wouldn't blame them. We had to save those
people.

"When you say it's almost full," I said, "how much
time do we have?"

"I could see her calling the trial as early as tomorrow,"
Unicorn said.

My heart sank. Tomorrow. Even if we only focused on
saving the prisoners, how the hell were we going to be
ready to orchestrate an escape in just one more day?

"Is there anything you can do to delay that?" I asked.

Unicorn sucked his lower lip under his large teeth. "I

could make some suggestions for the trial, to increase how impressive it is, that would take more time to arrange. But I doubt I could buy you more than another day." He peered down at me with his big eyes, which were an amber-brown like milky tea. "If you're aiming to break those people out, you'll need to make it through all the guards she has in place. It'll take a lot of manpower. They're so afraid of failing her, most will fight to the death."

The image flashed through my mind of all those figures in their pleated uniforms sprawled in pools of blood. Queasiness pooled in my stomach. Even if I fought for the throne, that wasn't how I wanted to start a new reign in Wonderland—with just as much brutality as the Hearts had used. There had to be other ways.

One day, maybe two. How else could we get to the prisoners? I wet my lips, picturing the palace grounds from memory. We'd managed to make it into the palace before, but under the cover of night, and at a time when no one expected an attack. No doubt the Queen would have her security on high alert around this "trial." We'd have trouble making it past the wall.

At least if we only had the garden wall to deal with, not the palace itself, we'd have a better chance. I glanced at Unicorn. "Do you think there's any other way you could influence the way she sets up the trial? Could you convince her to hold it outside in the gardens instead of in the palace?"

A thoughtful gleam came into my co-conspirator's eyes. His mouth formed a horsey smile. "You know, I think I could. Lion and I will be due for another showdown soon. I can suggest that we begin the trial with that, out on the grounds, like a symbol of the Hearts knocking down the Spades. Properly ironic, since I'm more likely to end up playing the loser, but it'll be the Spades who'll win the day. If you can pull this off."

That was the big if. I ignored the comment. It'd seemed best to pretend I was totally confident in my and the Spades' abilities. Our palace-dwelling ally wasn't someone I wanted to be sharing my doubts with.

"Buy us as much time as you can, and arrange the fight," I said. "Are there any other ways you've thought of that you could help us from the inside? We have our plans, but we'll shift them if you can give us better opportunities."

Unicorn cocked his head. "Well," he said, "if we're already outside and dueling, it shouldn't be too hard for me to create a disturbance near one of the gates. Draw the guards away to give you a clearer opening to burst through. Once I know where the trial will be staged, I can tell you which one to aim for."

"Perfect." A little shiver of excitement ran through me. Maybe I didn't know how we were going to displace the Queen of Hearts completely, but I felt so much closer to saving those prisoners. When I told Theo what Unicorn had offered, he'd have more ideas to build on those plans. We could make this happen.

"Is that all for now?" Unicorn asked. "I would like to get in a bit of a run. On my own, if you don't mind." His tone turned a bit haughty, maybe to cover his embarrassment about how he preferred to run, more animal than man.

There was one piece of the larger scheme I'd been wondering about since seeing the new tiger-ish Knave in the old shark-ish one's place. And I didn't know when I'd see Chess next to ask him. He might not even have the most accurate information, since it'd been quite a while since he'd chummed up to the Diamonds.

"Just a couple more questions," I said. "About the Queen and her claim on the throne. The Queen before her, her mother, she isn't around anymore, is she?"

Unicorn shook his head. "Our current Queen ascended on her death. Unfortunately picking up too many of her practices and adding awful new ones of her own."

"There's a King of Hearts too, isn't there? And they have some children—heirs." When the Spades had talked about the murdered prince, they'd called him the Queen's "youngest" son.

Unicorn let out a snort. "The King is good at standing for portraits and saying encouraging words in commanding tones, and not much else. Sometimes I wonder if she's had him beheaded and pearled, he's so dull. And the children... There seems to be more squabbling between her and them and amongst themselves than there is cohesion. I'd imagine you can divide and conquer easily enough once she's out of the picture."

"They don't have any special powers or weapons or whatever I should know about?" If the Queen had found the magic to capture Time, who knew what else we might face?

"Hmm." Unicorn's brow furrowed in an uncannily humanlike way. "I'd say they're all relatively useless. *She* obviously thinks so—that's why she was so set on having another, and why losing the young prince cracked her up. I don't know that she's even thought of who will succeed her, she's been so busy stewing over that loss. Although it is hard to know for certain, given that she keeps at least one of them locked up."

I blinked at him. "Locked *up*? Her own kids?"

He looked abruptly wary again. His feet sidestepped nervously as we continued our amble around the field. "I'm not sure how many even know about the one. I was simply—if she knew I saw—it was an accident, you know."

What, did he think I was going to tattle on him to the Queen?

"Of course it was," I said in the most soothing tone I could manage. "And she won't find out. What did you see?"

His jaw worked for a few seconds as he worked up to the answer, his gaze shifting straight ahead. His voice dropped so that even the Red Knight at his post on the other side of the field wouldn't have been able to hear him.

"There's an inner courtyard, one I shouldn't have been in. It was a long time ago, just before she trapped Time. She came out with a princess I'd never seen before—it must have been a princess, because she called the Queen 'mother.' A young woman, not much older than yourself. It was the strangest thing. The Queen was fretting about her attempts to get with child—all failed so far—and the princess started talking as if the new prince were already born and partly grown. The Queen told her to stop, and then she said something about the palace walls falling, and…"

He trailed off with a sickly expression. A fresh prickling of nausea was filling my own stomach. *Talking as if the new prince were already born.*

"What?" I said. "Then what happened?"

Unicorn ducked his head. "The Queen struck her, right across the head, back-handed with all those heavy rings, so hard the poor thing fell. There was blood everywhere, and… The Queen hustled her right out of the courtyard, and I never heard another thing about it, never saw that princess again. She must still be locked away in the palace somewhere. If the Queen hasn't killed her since."

The nausea twisted up through my chest. I stopped walking. "Where did the Queen hit her? Exactly?"

Unicorn shuddered, but he raised his hooved hand and tapped me gently on my left temple at the edge of my hairline. Right where Mirabel's scar still marked her pale skin.

CHAPTER TWENTY-TWO

Theo

"You were right," Dee announced as he ambled into my office, his red hair looking even more starkly vivid amid the white walls and furnishings.

Normally I enjoyed being right about things, but I had the feeling this was one of those occasions when I'd have been better off wrong. "About what?" I asked, getting up from behind my desk.

"Rabbit and the looking-glass," Dee said. "Caterpillar must have set up an arrangement with the Queen. Our long-eared friend hops his way over to the palace and comes back with the goods."

Damn. That knowledge didn't help us any. The only way home I knew of for Lyssa still lay deep within the palace walls. Even my inventions weren't likely to get us that far, especially now that the Queen would have her guards extra vigilant after our recent break-in.

Even a few days ago, I might have felt a little happy in the midst of my frustration—that I didn't have to face the possibility of Lyssa leaving just yet. Remembering that, my jaw clenched.

She deserved a real choice. She deserved options. Somehow or other, I was going to give her them.

And if she was given the option to leave and she stayed anyway, then we could both be sure she was where she truly wanted to be.

"Thank you for following up on that lead," I said. "Dum is still gathering intel on the shifts in patrol?"

Dee nodded. "You know my brother. Check everything and then double-check just in case. He'll probably be around in a few hours. Did you need me to handle anything else in the meantime, boss?"

"I could use some more singe-powder, if you know where Dum usually picks that up," I said. "And see if you can't track down Chess in the meantime. I'd like to talk to him." And find out why in the lands he seemed to be making his disappearing act a permanent show. Cheshire had always had some odd quirks, but I wouldn't have expected him to pull a fade when we were on a verge of either the greatest crisis or the greatest victory the Spades had ever been a part of.

"Aye, aye!" Dee gave me a cheeky salute and headed out the door.

I'd barely had time to sit down when the elevator's notification system informed me, "Lyssa is arriving alone."

I sprang back up and walked over to the door to meet her. My heart started to thump off-kilter as I waited for my first glimpse of her beautiful face. It'd only been a few hours since I'd last seen her, right before she'd left this morning. I'd spoken to her dozens of times before that over the days before. But one night had shifted the balance entirely.

The way she'd held her ground in the club even when the guards had started to turn on her. The way she'd stood up to them even then. The way she'd talked to me afterward. *Shouldn't a queen be ready to defend her people?*

I wasn't worthy of her, not as I was now. I wasn't sure I was worthy of much in the face of that devotion. She'd proven in one moment that she was braver than I'd been my entire life. How many sacrifices had I stepped back from and let others take on so I could protect my secrets?

And I still hadn't come up with a solution that I could stomach.

Lyssa hurried in the second the elevator door opened, her eyes wide with an anxious glint and her cheeks flushed as if she'd run at least part of the way. My spirits sank. She'd gone to her meeting with Unicorn, and this was how she'd come back?

"What happened?" I said. "Is Unicorn betraying us? Do I need to warn the rest of the Spades?"

Lyssa came to a halt, her hands clenching and releasing at her sides. She dragged in a breath. "No," she said. "It's not Unicorn. But—maybe we do need to warn people. I don't know. I don't know what to think. He told me something— Theo, how long has Mirabel been here in the Tower?"

Tension prickled through my body. "Since the time of the White Knight before me," I said. "He introduced me to her, already set up in her apartment."

"Do you know where she came from? What did she tell you about how she got that scar?"

Fuck. What could Unicorn have revealed to her? But maybe she didn't actually have the full picture, or even the right one.

"All I need to know is that she wasn't treated well there, and she fled after she was attacked," I said. "Why? Did he say something about her?"

Lyssa shook her head. "Not exactly. But he said he stumbled on the Queen of Hearts once, in part of the palace that was supposed to be private, and he saw her talking to a woman who seemed to be her daughter, who was talking as if she could see the future. And the Queen got angry with her and hit her right here—right where Mirabel's scar is." She touched her temple, her eyes going even wider. "She could be the Queen's daughter, a princess of Hearts. Who else could she be? It's too big a coincidence."

Damn Unicorn. I fought to keep my voice steady. "Perhaps it is. Would it matter that much if that's where she came from? She's here, helping us, not the Queen."

"Do you know that for sure?" Lyssa said. "We have no idea—she knew we were going to the Checkerboard Plains, didn't she? She could have been the one who passed on that information, not the guy Hatter went to see. Maybe the Queen bullied her into acting as some kind of spy. Like I said, I don't know. I don't want to think she'd hurt anyone, but why would she keep it a secret otherwise? We have to at least talk to her about it, find out where she stands."

"Lyssa…" Looking at her, I felt my resolve shift. Here was my moment. Did I really want to delay the inevitable when it would mean telling so many more lies to maneuver around this discovery?

No, I didn't. The lies I'd already told were bad enough.

Before I could decide on the right words to proceed with, Lyssa knit her brow. "You don't seem surprised. Did you already know?"

Well, that was as good a starting point as any. "I did," I said in a measured voice. "I'm the only one who does, as was the White Knight before me. We don't talk about it because she came here to find a safe haven away from the palace, away from the Queen. The Queen would have Mirabel killed if she found out where she is. Only a handful of people other than me even see her, speak with her. She wants to see the Queen of Hearts fall as much as any of us do."

"But…" Lyssa set her hand on the edge of one of the worktables as if she needed it to steady herself. "Why haven't we been asking her for more help, then? Not future stuff, but even—details about the palace, the Queen—anyone who's part of the family must know things even people like Unicorn wouldn't."

My throat tried to lock, but I wouldn't let it. "I don't like to remind her about that time because it distresses her," I said. "And we don't need to get that information from her. I know as much as she could ever tell us."

Lyssa blinked at me. "You can't know *everything*, no matter how closely you keep an eye on things or how many people you talk to."

"I don't know everything," I agreed. "But I know more than probably even Mirabel does, since the Queen kept her locked away. I had free run of the palace for the thirteen years I lived there."

Lyssa was smart. She'd heard enough to put the pieces together just from that. She stared at me for a moment, her mouth falling open.

"Theo, you—"

"Mirabel's my sister," I said, to avoid dragging the revelation out any longer. "I was born a prince of Hearts."

For a moment, she just gaped. "Thirteen years… You're *the* prince? The one everyone thinks was murdered?"

My mouth twisted somewhere between a grimace and a smile. "Yes. Do you want—this is a lot to take in. We could go to the other room, sit down—"

"No," Lyssa said with a sharp shake of her head. She let go of the table to stalk a few paces across the room, then spun to face me again. She peered at my face, her brow furrowed, as if she were looking for answers in the shape of my eyes, the line of my jaw. Did she see a family resemblance now? There wasn't much of one, thanks to my efforts at disguise and my having a different father from my older siblings.

"Tell me now," she said. "All of it. I don't understand. Chess said he was *there*, that he saw the prince's head…"

"Was he?" A raw chuckle worked its way up my throat. "All right. From the beginning." I hesitated, caught by the urge for something to lean on myself. It had been so long since I'd really talked to anyone about this.

"I told you before that I was born into the freeze," I said. "That was true. My mother, the Queen—she managed to shield me from the worst aspects of her rule for a little while, but it didn't take long before I realized how cruel and unjust she could be. I started to sneak off the palace grounds to see what people did in the city and noticed how much hardship they were facing at her hand. She wanted me to be her heir, to be ready to take the throne when her days were over, but her ideas about how to reign… I knew I couldn't be that kind of king, and I knew she'd do so much more harm before I had a chance to change anything from the palace."

"So you ran away," Lyssa filled in. "You managed to convince her you'd been murdered."

A jab of guilt ran through my belly. "I wish there'd been a better way, but I could only work with what I had. Maybe there wasn't any way she could have believed I was dead and not blamed the Spades. I went by the executioner's rooms every day for almost a year, waiting for a corpse to turn up that was close enough. By the time a boy did, I had to take the opportunity. I splashed pig's blood around and bashed the face to hide the differences in features…"

Decades ago, that had been now, and I could still

smell the bloody stink of the severed head, still feel its stiffened flesh against my fingers. My stomach turned with the memory.

"I did it late at night," I went on, "so that there wouldn't be time for anyone to notice the head missing from the chambers or any detail that would give away that it wasn't mine before the day reset and the dead disappeared."

"Why didn't *you* reset back to where you were supposed to be?" Lyssa asked.

I smiled stiffly. "The Queen of Hearts has kept many secrets. When she imprisoned Time, she stole a small portion that she tucked away separately for her own use, if she wanted to make a permanent change around the palace. *She* couldn't stand to be stuck, of course. I stole her entire remaining supply when I ran. The vase that was smashed—she kept it in there. I wanted her to think it had been loosed, that it was gone. I used it to escape. I used it to fix myself in this building overnight, once the White Knight had taken me under his wing. I couldn't have managed without it. I thought it was going to be our key to overthrowing her."

"But you didn't use it," Lyssa said, frowning. "When I came—you acted like it was something special that the changes I made and the things I touched stayed that way instead of resetting."

"It was, then. I—I made a miscalculation. I couldn't join the Spades right away. I'd have been recognized. I had to grow older, build my body, change my face... The previous White Knight found me where I was hiding out in the woods. He helped me stay hidden, and he brought supplies like the powder to darken my hair. He broke my nose, as little as he wanted to."

I gestured to my face, the ache of the weeks while that injury had healed coming back to me. "He taught me everything I could have needed to know, and when enough time had passed that we didn't think anyone would notice a resemblance to the supposedly dead prince, he introduced me as his apprentice. He was more a father than my actual father ever was. We were making plans, building our numbers. And then—" My throat constricted.

"And then?" Lyssa prompted quietly.

"A Diamond came, tipsy on something, demanding the Inventor's work," I said, forcing out the rest of the story. "When my mentor told him there wasn't time to finish what he wanted before the day flipped over, he stabbed him and left. I felt his heart stop. He would have disappeared as soon as the clocks hit midnight. I thought there was still a chance, if I could get it beating again—there are ways…"

I'd felt time spilling out around me, fluttering against my skin, as I'd pumped the heels of my hands against the former White Knight's chest, listened for the faintest hint of a pulse, a breath, willing him to come back. That guilt dug so deep I was never going to uproot it.

"I failed," I said simply. "I couldn't revive him. I lost all the time I'd been preserving. I had to work with the same world everyone else did."

"So you took his place, and you kept lying to everyone

about who you were." Lyssa's voice was even, but her stance was rigid. She held her arms tightly across her chest. "How many years has it been? Why haven't you *stopped* her?"

"I've been trying," I said, but that answer sounded weak even to me. "I've worked behind the scenes, and I've kept my true role secret, because I can help more this way, Lyssa. If she found out I was alive, do you think I could fight off the horde of guards she'd send to collect me? I have a lot of faith in my abilities, but I'm still just one man."

"You're her son! Wouldn't she listen to you?"

I laughed sharply. "Not for a second. Why do you think *I* was her heir—the youngest, the baby? All my older brothers and sisters managed to disappoint her somehow or other. She wanted to mold me into an echo of herself. I'd have scars too, you know, if she hadn't been careful, if those wounds hadn't reset. She whipped me to bleeding the few times I let slip something that didn't fit her vision of the king I was supposed to become. If she found out what I've done, she's as likely to take my head in an instant as listen to one word out of my mouth."

"You're scared of her," Lyssa said.

"We're *all* scared of her," I said. "She's a fucking terror. And I've got her blood running through my veins just like you've got the Red Queen's. Simply going back there, getting near the palace with the scent of all those roses—it clouds my head. I did the best I could think to do without compromising everything the Spades have worked for."

I saw my mistake in the flicker of Lyssa's gaze. She

drew back a step. "You lied to *me*, didn't you? Not just about who you are. About who *I* am. You knew your family had no business ruling at all; you knew they slaughtered the Red royal family like the Red Knight said, that the one princess escaped to the Otherland—you knew about the ring and the artifacts—but you pretended you didn't know that part. I asked you so many questions, and you lied to my face like it was nothing."

I held up my hands. "Lyssa, I swear, I had no idea you had any relation to anyone in Wonderland when I first met you. The Queen of Hearts fully believes my great-grandmother wiped out the Reds. She thinks the Alices are some kind of trick played by someone who remembers, but she doesn't believe they're true heirs—and that's what she taught me to believe too. I didn't know what she thought was wrong until I saw that ring light up with your blood."

"You didn't tell me then either. We went all across the Plains, and you didn't say a word! If we hadn't run into the Red Knight, would you *ever* have told me?" The color seeped from Lyssa's face. "You were using me. The whole time, even before you knew. I was a convenient tool to help you get on the throne *you* want."

My heart wrenched. I started to move toward her, but she flinched, and I halted. "No," I said, but I couldn't look away from the accusation in her eyes.

She wasn't entirely right, but she wasn't entirely wrong either.

"I'm sorry," I said, summoning as much as I could of the princely confidence that normally came so naturally.

"I've been fighting for so long to free Wonderland, and I could see how important you were, and I didn't want to jeopardize our progress by scaring you. I didn't want to put *you* in danger by laying all that responsibility on you when you had nowhere else to go. Your grand-aunt found out the truth and immediately fled. I *was* going to tell you —I was going to tell you everything—I was just waiting for the right time—"

"The right time was the first time I asked a question and you lied instead of telling the truth," Lyssa said. Pain vibrated through her voice. "I came back. I've risked my life for this place. Being honest with me was the *least* you could do. Is—Is your name even Theo? It can't be, can it?"

"Theo is the name I picked for myself," I said. "It's been the name I've gone by for more than twice as long as I was anything else. My mother named me Jack."

"Jack of Hearts. That's perfect." Lyssa laughed, but there was no joy in the sound.

"Lyssa—"

"No." She held up her hand to ward me off, backing toward the elevator. "I can't talk to you right now. I can't be around you right now. I don't know if I ever want to see you again."

A cold rush of shame smacked me, but I had to say it anyway. "Please don't tell anyone else what I told you. That's all I ask. It could ruin everything, for all of Wonderland. I've never lied about how much I care about this place or these people." I'd never lied about how much I cared about her, either, but looking at her expression, I didn't think saying that part would go over the way I'd want it to.

Lyssa's mouth tightened. "I won't say anything, for now," she said. "That's the best I can promise."

Then she was gone behind the elevator door, and I was alone again.

CHAPTER TWENTY-THREE

Lyssa

I swung the sword through the air at the angle the Red Knight had shown me, and this time the weight didn't leave all my arm muscles burning. The slice of the shining blade through the air was actually very satisfying. I had plenty of tension to work out.

"Good," the Red Knight said approvingly from where he was standing by the bedroom's wardrobe. "Now try to combine that with the upward thrust I showed you earlier."

An unfortunate choice of words. At the phrase "upward thrust," I was suddenly thinking about Theo—Jack—whatever the hell his name really was—pinning me up against his office wall last night. As furious and confused as I was right now, the memory still set off a flare of heat between my thighs.

I gritted my teeth and swung again, jabbing upward at

the end of the arc. I wasn't exactly imagining running our supposed White Knight through, but the idea that I could do it might have been there in the back of my head.

He'd played me so well, hadn't he? Even yesterday, with his almost-confession, he'd acted like he'd wanted to protect me from what he was—and then he'd gone ahead and fucked me after I'd told him I was falling for him, still holding his secret in. Still pretending he hadn't lied to me over and over. If he'd *really* wanted to come clean, he could have done that then.

Well, whatever. I had two other guys I could count on. Okay, one for sure and the other one AWOL. But there was the Red Knight too. And Doria, slipping into the bedroom now with a curious arch of her eyebrows. And all the Spades who were waiting, ready for action.

It didn't matter who the guy at the top of the Tower was. I could still save Wonderland my way.

As soon as I figured out what way that was.

"Are you waging war on the furniture?" Doria asked, plopping down on the end of the bed.

I had to grin. "Nope. Just trying to get the hang of my royal equipment." I waggled the sword. "All of these things are supposed to have special powers that me being... me should activate. If I can get them to."

"So you can use those powers on the Queen of Hearts?" Doria grinned back fiercely.

"That's the idea, one way or another. It'll help me prove my heritage when we're trying to recruit more people to rise up against her. And I'll take any advantage I can get to help us free the prisoners. A little magical boost could make all the difference when we're so outnumbered. I want to know we've got a real chance."

"I guess it's going to be tough crashing the trial even with a few fancy artifacts, isn't it?" Doria said, her grin faltering.

"The Queen has a lot of guards," I said. "But a smaller group can win against a bigger one if they've got the better strategy." At least, I hoped it could.

"Does that sword do anything yet?"

"Well, I think it'll do a decent job of cutting things." I made a face as I swiveled the blade in a slow circle. "The ruby doesn't seem to want to wake up."

"It's all a matter of attuning your energy," the Red Knight said. "They'll respond to you soon enough. No cause for worry."

Soon enough to stop the Queen from chopping off a few dozen heads? I stabbed the sword toward the desk in the corner, willing all my frustration to the surface, but the blade moved and shone just like any other sword would. The ruby on the hilt gleamed with a tiny spark of inner fire at the same time as a wisp of heat trickled from the ring against my breastbone, but a miniature light display wasn't going to topple the Queen or her guards.

Doria watched me for a few more minutes, her expression pensive. Then she hopped off the bed. "Good luck with that! If you can stop a jabberwock, you can take on the Queen. And we'll give you all the help we can."

After she'd gone out, the Red Knight talked me through a few more moves. I practiced them until the burn in my arms expanded into an ache. The sword remained utterly sword-like. With a groan, I set it down on the bed and picked up the scepter.

It hadn't done anything useful in my hands so far either. I guessed I could hope that holding it up and standing in a queen-like pose would impress all the guards into bowing down in fealty? Somehow I didn't think *that* strategy was going to win the day for us.

Maybe if I was wearing the ring on my finger, where it was presumably meant to be? I took it off its chain and slid it into the ring finger of my right hand, which it fit perfectly. As if I'd been born to wear it. The Red Knight gave me a meaningful look as if to say, "I told you so," but we were past the needing to convince me stage already.

I grasped the scepter's handle and held it up. The ring's ruby gleamed, and so did the larger gem at the top of the rod. I whirled it around a bit, pointed it at a bedpost and then at the window, and sighed when nothing happened other than a flicker of warmth over my hand.

"Often these things come to us in the moment of need," the Red Knight said gently.

"That's not very useful for planning ahead," I muttered.

Because I didn't want to go around slicing open people as I walked by, I put the filigree case back on the ring and strung it on the chain again. After I'd tucked the sword and the scepter away in Hatter's secret compartment, I paused and pulled out the woven metal vest.

That armor would be useful even without special

powers. I should probably get more used to wearing it even in the city. It was flexible and form fitting enough that I could pull a loose blouse over it. Wonderlanders had such odd senses of fashion, I wasn't sure anyone would notice if I seemed a tad bulky.

I tugged the vest on, adjusting it until it lay against my torso comfortably, and then grabbed a blouse that sort of matched the bottom of the dress I already had on. Clashing was all the rage around here anyway.

Hatter appeared in the doorway, knocking his knuckles against the frame to get my attention. "Have you seen Doria?" he asked.

"She came by... it must have been at least an hour ago now," I said. "Just for a bit. Why?"

His mouth slanted with worry. "She didn't tell me she was going out, but she doesn't seem to be in the apartment. Which isn't entirely unusual, but she tends to tell me where she's going unless she knows it's somewhere or to do something I'm not going to like."

And this was not a great time for Doria to be skirting danger too closely. I thought back to our brief conversation, and a chill tickled over my skin. Something about the way she'd said, *We'll give you all the help we can...*

I'd given her the impression any victory we reached would be hard-won. Had she come up with some scheme to try to give us a leg up, without even talking to me or Hatter about it? Shit.

"She seems to like the twins' company a lot," I said.

"Maybe she's gone to hang out with them?" Or get up to some mischief, as the case might be.

Hatter headed back down the hall, adjusting his hat, and I followed him. The Red Knight trailed behind me, of course.

"It's possible," Hatter said. "When you saw the White Knight, he didn't mention anything about a mission before the meeting tonight, did he?"

At the mention of Theo, I stiffened instinctively. "No," I said, in what I thought was a normal voice, but something must have slipped into my tone, because Hatter turned at the top of the stairs to give me a questioning look.

"He didn't say anything about tonight," I added quickly. We hadn't ended up talking about the Spades' plans at all. He didn't know what Unicorn had told me or the suggestions I'd made. Every particle of my body balked at the idea of seeing him again, though.

I'd talked to Hatter about it. We were supposed to meet with as many of the Spades as could make it to discuss strategy later tonight. Probably Theo would show up for that... I just wasn't going to think about it. If anyone asked why I wasn't talking to him directly, he could figure out how to explain it, not me.

I'd said I wasn't going to spill his secret, but that didn't mean I was going to pretend everything was fine.

The street was darkening outside the living area's windows. Hatter peered out into the evening, nervous tension obvious in every twitch of his jaw, every adjustment of his sapphire-blue suit jacket.

"Hatter."

The voice came out of nowhere, and then Chess emerged out of nowhere too, turning visible in the middle of the room. His auburn hair looked scruffier than usual and his face worn as if he hadn't gotten much sleep. My heart panged at the sight.

"I think you should get down to Caterpillar's," he said, looking at Hatter. "A few of the younger Spades, including Doria—you'll have to see it. She's okay, as far as I know, so far, but the Queen is not going to be happy."

Hatter blanched. He dashed for the apartment door.

"I'm coming too," I said, hurried after him. If I'd sounded more hopeful when I'd talked to Doria, maybe she wouldn't have gone off and done... whatever she'd done.

The Red Knight paused just long enough to grab his old sword where Hatter had made him stash it under the sofa. There wasn't time for me to argue with him about it —or to grab my own sword, not that I was going to be much use with it yet. We all hustled down the stairs and through the shop, Chess blinking out of sight as we spilled out onto the street.

Even from this far away, a strange wavering light was visible streaking up toward the darkening sky over to the tops of the buildings between us and the club. Hatter took off at about as brisk a pace as he could walk at without breaking into a run. My heart thudded as I pushed myself to keep up.

Other Wonderlanders closer to the club had clearly caught wind that something was going on. Several people peered from their windows, and a few ducked out onto the street around us. At least that made us stand out a little less.

Hatter stopped at the end of the street so abruptly I had to grip his arm to keep from crashing right into him. Then my gaze caught on the source of the light, and all I could do was stare too.

Someone—the group of Spades that Chess had mentioned, I assumed—had built an effigy I immediately recognized as the ornate gate and wall posts at the main entrance to the palace grounds. It hung from the trees at the edge of the woods beside the club. Flames danced all along the top of the structure, melting the gold-tinted paint on the makeshift bars of the gate and devouring the tops of the stone-like blocks on either side.

Glowing letters across the blocks blazed through the falling dusk. *JOIN US AND WE'LL BURN THE HEARTS DOWN.*

My stomach flipped over. I'd mentioned how outnumbered we were. Doria and her friends had decided to run a little recruitment campaign directed at the Clubbers.

I had no idea if it was going to convince anyone, but it was certainly getting people's attention. A bunch of tonight's early Clubbers had congregated just outside the spinning building to gape at the effigy and its message. The flames flickered, and my gaze caught on a much less welcome sight: the red-and-pink stripes of a palace guard's tunic. Several of them were weaving between the trees beyond the effigy.

If Doria had been here, it looked as though she'd taken off. We stood there at the edge of the street for a few minutes as the flames blazed on. I was about to suggest we head back to the shop and see if Doria had already returned when a shout carried from the woods.

One of the guards strode out, hauling a teenaged boy I'd seen at the Spades meetings by the elbow, baton raised by the cheek he'd already left a red mark across. The flash of panic in my chest eased for just an instant before two more guards hustled out. One of them was dragging Doria by a clump of her dark hair.

"We got a couple of them!" the first guard hollered. "They have spark paste all over their hands."

Doria tried to wrench away from the guard holding her, and he raised his knife to her throat in warning. A wounded sound escaped Hatter's mouth as if he'd been stabbed. Before I could stay anything, he was throwing himself toward them.

If there'd only been one or two, maybe he could have taken them on. But a few more guards were already jogging over to join the three with the captives. Hatter plowed right into the man holding Doria, knocking him to the ground. The next guard grabbed her before she could take a step. Another leapt in and punched Hatter in the face as he spun around. The crack of knuckles to cheekbone propelled me forward.

I didn't know what the hell I was going to do in there, but I wasn't leaving Hatter to fight seven on his own.

The Red Knight charged in with me, letting out a whoop of a battle cry. He slammed his sword right through the gut of one of the guards. I jumped between the one guard and Hatter, and his next punch struck my chest instead of Hatter's head. The impact threw me backward a couple steps, but he'd hit my vest. The guard yanked back his hand, a spasm of pain crossing his face. Then an invisible kick sent him careening toward the growing crowd by the club. Chess had joined us too.

Unfortunately, he wasn't the only one. More guards charged out of the woods and from the other side of the club. My pulse stuttered. I glanced toward the Clubbers, but none of them looked inspired enough by Doria's message to jump in. They just stood there rigid and wide-eyed.

It was their fucking land I was trying to protect. How could they watch and do nothing?

Theo's voice echoed through my head. *We're all scared.*

Hatter hurled himself past me to slam his fist into another guard's jaw. He whipped his hatpin from his jacket. One of the new guards came at me with a baton. I dodged to the side, right into the path of someone else's dagger.

The blade raked across the fabric of my blouse, scraping my vest—and jerked up toward my neck. I tried to fling myself backward out of the way, but hands behind me heaved me forward instead. I gasped, already anticipating the bite of the blade.

"Never!" a creaky voice shouted, and the Red Knight shoved in front of me. His sword clanged against the dagger. He swung it around, his fluffy white hair in disarray and his eyes gleaming defiantly, not quite fast enough to stop the jab of another guard's knife.

A cry of protest ripped from my throat as the guard dug the blade in deep. Red bloomed through the Red Knight's tunic. He staggered to the side.

"I fulfilled my duty to the best of my ability, your—" he rasped out, and the slash of the first guard's dagger cut off his voice and the light from his eyes. He crumpled in a heap on the ground.

My chest constricted. This man had waited so long for me to show up. He'd believed in me so much. And now he'd followed me straight to his death.

The guards didn't offer any time to grieve. They lunged at me and Hatter. Hatter bolted for the one now hauling Doria away, hatpin in his hand. A beefy guy barged into the way, shattering the pin with a smack of his sword. He belted Hatter across the forehead so hard Hatter's hat flew into the air. He skidded backward ten feet across the ground.

They couldn't kill him too. Anguish and desperation seared through me, and the ring beneath my clothes flared. The vest's rubies lit up with a glow that pierced my blouse.

I jerked up my arm to block the blow of a baton, and a wave of energy jolted off me. It slammed into the guards nearby, sending them stumbling backward. What the hell?

I spun and ran to Hatter. Blood was streaking through his spiky hair. I snatched at his shoulder to help him up, but he couldn't seem to lift his head all the way—it kept swaying to the side, his eyes squinting. Oh, fuck, that guard had hit him hard.

And now three more of them were racing toward us, recovered from whatever magic my vest had hit them with. I turned to shield Hatter, willing that magic to activate again, but the rubies' glow had dimmed. The guards didn't even hesitate.

Chess's presence brushed past my side. He hefted Hatter up over what must have been his invisible shoulder and gripped my hand.

"Time to get out of here, lovely," he murmured in a strained voice.

I glanced back toward the Red Knight's fallen body, toward Doria in the guard's grasp—and to the five now rushing toward us. My body protested, but I knew with complete certainty that if we stayed, we were dead meat.

Clamping my jaw against a sob, I spun and fled with Chess.

CHAPTER TWENTY-FOUR

Hatter

I became aware of my surroundings in bits and pieces. First, so loud it drowned out every other sensation for who knew how long, was the blare of pain in my head. It splintered across my scalp and dug through my skull, sparking sharper when someone dabbed a cloth against the wound.

Something was dripping in a halting rhythm, not that far from my ears. A cool earthy smell trickled into my nose. I was lying on a thin padded surface, no weight of a hat on my head. Where was my fucking hat?

Images from before my current situation flashed through my head. The burning replica of the gate. The guards. The guards with their hands clamped around Doria's arms, dragging her off toward the palace, her eyes so round and terrified—

A jolt of horror shot through me. I tried to find my

eyes or my mouth through the pain, but I couldn't quite get enough of a grip on either to open them.

"Are you sure the guards won't find this place?" The haze of pain turned Lyssa's voice fuzzy around the edges. She was the one dabbing at my head. A cool prickling started to seep through the wound, dulling the ache.

"This cellar has been a Spades safe house for as long as I've been around and probably a lot longer before that," Chess said. "If they haven't found it before, I doubt they will now. I'd have hidden out here myself the other night if it hadn't proved leaky."

Her hand stilled against my hair. "I don't know what else to do for him."

"It hasn't been too long. Hatter's a resilient fellow." Chess shifted with a rustle of his clothes. "There are people in the Spades with more medical experience than I can offer. I'll check for guards around here and bring someone who'll be able to help if I can. There are food and blankets down here along with the other supplies. Use whatever you need."

"Chess," Lyssa started, but he must have already slipped away. Her voice fell. Her hand came to rest on my arm with a gentle pressure.

I knew the cellar safe house. Lyssa must have put some of the healing gel on my wound. Its chill had eaten away at the worst of the pain, even if my mind was still muggy. I made another effort to blink, and my eyes popped open.

Relief washed across Lyssa's face where she was sitting next to me. Her hand tightened on my arm. "Hatter, are you all right? How do you feel?"

"I can't say this is the most enjoyable sensation I've ever experienced." My voice came out rusty. I cleared my throat. "What happened? Is Doria—"

The distress that flickered through her features was all the answer I needed. I jerked upright instinctively, and Lyssa let out a noise of protest.

I didn't make it very far anyway. The second my head left the bench I was lying on, dizziness hit me so hard my stomach clenched with nausea. It was either lie back down or vomit and then collapse. I let my head fall.

"I'm sorry," Lyssa said. "You're too hurt to go running off anywhere. There was a really big guard, and he hit you hard. Maybe he's got some kind of special physique like the twins do. Until you woke up, I was worried he'd broken your skull."

Tiny shards of pain were still wriggling around the numbed edges of the wound. "Let's not discount that possibility yet. They took Doria? Someone has to go. She can't— They caught her. The Queen might already have ordered—"

"Stop," Lyssa interrupted, squeezing my arm. Her voice trembled for a second. "We're going to get her back. We're going to save everyone. Chess thinks the Queen will hold onto Doria and the other Spades they caught until she holds her big trial, to add to the spectacle. We've got a little time."

Chess couldn't know that. And even if he was right, my daughter was chained up in the Queen's prison now, not knowing if we'd get to her in time, only knowing I hadn't managed to protect her.

Ignoring common sense, I tried to sit up again. This time Lyssa caught me before my shoulders even left the bench. She bent over me, holding me down gently but firmly. I was going to argue with her when I saw her chin wobble. She clamped her mouth into a firm line, but there was no mistaking the watery gleam in her eyes.

"Please," she said, so raggedly my lungs tightened. "I know you want to help her. I want to too. We *will*. But you can't keep— I think you're taking the whole 'Mad' thing a little too far. Pulling crazy stunts doesn't help her if it gets you killed."

"What else was I supposed to do?" I said. "Watch them cart her off and do nothing?"

"No. But if you'd waited a second, you'd have seen how outnumbered we were at the club. Maybe we could have held back and ambushed the ones that took her on the way back to the palace, once they'd split up more. Maybe Chess could have drawn some of them away with his tricks. I don't know. You didn't give us a chance to figure anything out. You just ran right in there."

"They had my *daughter*," I said, but the truth of her words was already sinking in. I closed my eyes. "Fuck."

"If that's how you were back when you worked with the Spades all the time, I'm surprised you didn't get killed back then," Lyssa remarked.

"I probably wouldn't have done anything quite that suicidal," I admitted. "I didn't have anyone I cared about quite that much. And normally there were more of us, working together. I was a wild card—I could turn the tables in ways the Hearts didn't expect if a mission started to go wrong."

But this hadn't been a mission, and I'd made it go wrong. The pain of that realization stabbed deeper than the wound on my head had.

"Maybe you're a little out of practice after all that time staying out of the rebellion." Lyssa drew in a shaky breath. "I care about you, okay? I *need* you. The guards killed the Red Knight. Chess can't seem to stick around for more than five minutes before he vanishes again, and Theo—" She cut herself off, leaving me wondering what in the lands the White Knight had done to her in the last day. "You've been here for me since the start. Maybe it's a lot to ask, but… I don't think I can do it on my own."

My throat squeezed with emotion. I looked up at her, raising my hand to touch the backs of my fingers to her smooth cheek. "You're not on your own. I'm sorry. I was trying to make up for all that time hanging back, and perhaps I let myself go too far in the opposite direction. Moderation may not be my strong point."

A choked laugh spilled out of her. "I'm not sure it's anyone's strong point around here. You do better than most."

She clasped her hand around mine, looking so damned pleased that I hadn't told her to shove off that I could hardly bear it. She had to at least know why—know that I hadn't thrown myself at the guards' fucking swords without a care what happened to her, just off the high of some adrenaline rush.

She had to know what kind of man she was putting her trust in.

"It was my fault," I said.

Her gaze turned puzzled. She must have been able to tell I wasn't talking about the skirmish tonight. "What was?"

"The night when…" I wet my lips, searching for the best way to explain. My thoughts were still scattered, and other sorts of pain wove through me thinking back to that time. I did the best I could.

"March and I grew up together. Friends for as long as I can remember. We joined the Spades together, and he met May there, and they just clicked in a way people here don't very often. We always ran the same missions together. When I took over the shop, I offered them the upper apartment. They were like family."

"Doria was theirs," Lyssa ventured.

I nodded just enough to accidentally wake up the ache in my head. "They cut back on the missions after she came, and even though I loved her too, I was restless. It wasn't the same going out without them. I found out the Diamonds were planning some stupid celebration one night, and I got it in my head that we'd show them if we ruined it. I convinced March and May that we should go for it, just that once, like old times…"

A sharp ache ran straight down my chest. How could I have let myself think—why hadn't I seen—

Lyssa squeezed my hand in silent encouragement. I girded myself and went on.

"It *was* stupid—on my part too. We weren't

accomplishing anything other than pissing off the palace folk. March slipped on the way back, must have dropped something, I don't even know how, but the guards figured out the two of them were part of it. They came and grabbed them in the middle of the night."

All that anguish on March's narrow face, not for himself but for Doria. The hoarseness of his voice when he'd asked me to look after her. I couldn't draw that picture for Lyssa, not as sharply as it was still stuck in my head.

"It was my bloody idea," I said. "It should have been me. But—I couldn't even stand up for them that much. They'd have taken all our heads, and Doria would have had no one."

For a long moment, Lyssa didn't speak, and I wasn't sure I wanted to look at her. Then she leaned right over on her stool to rest her head on the bench beside mine, her nose brushing my cheek. She didn't let go of my hand.

"That's when you decided the Spades were too dangerous," she said.

"We weren't accomplishing anything in general, really," I said. "Not since the freeze." I paused and managed to gingerly tilt my face so I could meet her eyes. "Not until you turned up, looking-glass girl."

"So, what you're saying is, our current predicament is really all *my* fault."

My lips twitched upward despite myself. "Perhaps a little."

"Well, if you were expecting me to say you should

have gotten yourself killed back then, I'm obviously not going to."

Lyssa eased closer to kiss me, and Hearts take me, the sweetness of her mouth against mine was almost worth the blow to the head. I ran my free hand along her jaw and into her hair. A happy murmur escaped her lips. She deepened the kiss, and I couldn't blame everything about the way my head was spinning on the injury I'd sustained, not anymore.

When our mouths parted, she stayed close enough that our breath mingled between us. "Hatter," she said quietly, "you told me before that monogamy isn't really a common concept here in Wonderland. How about love?"

I swallowed hard, a rush of emotion bubbling up inside me. "It's rare too," I said. "But I think mostly because not many of us want it. March and May had something real. Maybe if we didn't have so much constant threat hanging over us, more people would look for devotion over distraction."

"What have you wanted?"

"Mostly neither, since Doria came along," I said. "I won't lie—I enjoyed plenty of distractions before then. But I can't say I didn't envy what the two of them had. I wouldn't turn it away if I found it." I made myself smile. "And I'd imagine a queen can decide to have whatever she wants."

Lyssa made a dismissive sound. "What about a girl who might not be cut out for being queen at all?"

Did she still doubt her capabilities? I rolled myself

onto my side, scooting backward so I could pull her onto the bench against me, my arm around her back.

"Listen to me," I said, with every ounce of certainty I had in me, "I've never known a woman better for that role than you are. If it's not what you *want*, then you follow the path that's right for you. But don't hesitate for a second if all that's holding you back is fear. You go for that throne, and I'll be right there with you, fighting for you however I can."

Whether there was still room for me in the world she inhabited afterward, I was willing to wait and see.

"Hatter," she said roughly. Then she was kissing me again, and if this was what she needed, if *I* was what she needed, then she could have me any way she wanted.

A throat cleared behind her. We pulled apart as Chess shimmered into view, a little hunched beneath the cellar's low ceiling. He gave me an amused look.

"Glad to see you're on the mend, Hatter."

My face warmed, but it wasn't as if we hadn't shared a much more intimate moment with Lyssa together not long ago. "And I'm glad to see you've managed to stay ahead of the Hearts' Guard."

Lyssa sat up, her fingers still twined with mine. "How does it look out there?"

"The palace has made an official announcement that the prisoners taken tonight will be tried alongside the city folk the Queen has already imprisoned," Chess said, with a tip of his head toward me. "And that trial will take place tomorrow morning. So I feel we should make a hasty journey to the meeting of the Spades. I've determined the safest route."

Lyssa's body had tensed, but her jaw set with determination. She turned back toward me and touched my face.

"We're going to get Doria back," she said. "Whatever I have to do. I promise."

I pushed myself upright, managing to make it into a sitting position without keeling over this time. Only a light prickle of pain crept across my scalp. "*We'll* do whatever we have to do," I said. "But I promise to rein the Mad in."

She gave me a crooked smile. "Keep it in your back pocket. The way things are going, we might need it."

CHAPTER TWENTY-FIVE

Lyssa

My heart sank as I took in the Spades who'd dared to assemble in the dim basement room. We had even fewer than the last meeting I'd attended. Around the low lacquered table, no one bothering to sit on the cushions that served as seats, stood Hatter and Chess, the woman who'd suggested they should hand me over to the Queen, the burly man I'd been sitting next to on those rotating chairs, and maybe a dozen others.

How many of them had the guards arrested after the stunt at the club, and how many were simply too afraid to risk coming now?

Theo hadn't turned up. Neither had the twins. Had *they* been out with Doria, working on her plan? I'd thought they'd had a little more sense than to go that far, but they were her friends, so it was hard to tell.

"Did you hear where the trial is supposed to be happening?" I asked Chess.

He nodded. "Out in the gardens. I noticed a sparkly bit of horsehair snagged on the wall not far from the eastern gate. I'm guessing that was some sort of message from Unicorn?"

"I think we'll have to take it as one," I said. Our ally inside the palace hadn't been able to delay the trial after all, but he had arranged for it to be outside. I hoped that meant he'd talked the Queen into having him and Lion fight first and that he'd be able to disrupt the guards at the gate. We were clearly going to need every advantage we could get.

My fingers itched for something to hold on to. "I should go by Hatter's and get the other artifacts," I said.

"I don't think that's the wisest idea while we want you to stay on the right side of the prison walls," Chess said. "I slipped by there too. There were guards all through the place, one in every room. Even invisible, I couldn't contrive to retrieve anything that's hidden away."

It wasn't as if I'd figured out how to use either of the other artifacts anyway. But they might have kicked in and given us an edge in the moment, like the vest briefly had. I bit my lip.

Just then, Dee and Dum marched into the room. I stiffened in anticipation of Theo's arrival, but no one followed them. They marched to the middle of the room, hopped up on the table, and swiveled to take in the small crowd.

"We bring word from the White Knight," Dum said. "Lyssa will lead our planning to interrupt the executions."

"So you'd better listen to her!" Dee said with a grin. "She's the one who's been talking with our inside man. She'll find the right course of action."

An anxious murmur carried through the room as they hopped down, Dee bobbing his head to me. My stomach knotted. What was Theo thinking? Most of these people barely knew me.

Maybe that was why he was doing it. If I decided to reach for the throne, I'd have to start ruling sometime.

Or maybe he'd just been wary of having to face me after our conversation this morning.

Dum sidled over to me. From his puzzled expression, I suspected he didn't know what to make of his boss's absence either. "He says, anything you can think of that you need that a person could possibly invent, he'll make it happen," he said. "You just need to let us know, and we'll pass on the word."

"He didn't have any ideas of his own?" I asked under my breath.

"I'm sure he has plans," Dum said. "He's always got plans. But he wants to hear yours first."

Great. No pressure.

I sucked in a breath and climbed onto the table myself. The voices of the gathered Spades hushed as I stepped into the middle of the makeshift platform. The expressions aimed at me were mostly confused or skeptical. We were already off to a wonderful start.

I could have announced everything we'd learned on

the Checkerboard Plains. Everything the Red Knight had told us. The memory of his body slumping just a couple hours ago brought bile into my throat.

Your Majesty, he'd always called me. As if I were a queen just by existing. He'd had so much faith that I could find the strength to take on that role, that I was finally the Red Queen he'd waited so long for.

Was I going to tell these people I had some kind of royal magic that would win the day, give them a false confidence I couldn't really back up, and lead them into what would probably be a slaughter? As soon as the Queen of Hearts found out who I really was, she'd have her guards cutting their way through everyone that stood between them and me. It wasn't just about whether I was ready to take on that responsibility. Before I took that step, we all had to be ready for full-out war, and the small group we had here wasn't anything close to an army.

If these were *my* people, if I was going to save them, I had to do it right from the start. Which meant they were going to have to believe in just me, regular Lyssa.

"Here's what we know so far," I said, pitching my voice to carry, willing it not to waver. "The trial will take place tomorrow morning in the palace gardens. First, Unicorn and Lion will be staging one of their usual fights for the spectators. We'll have a chance of entering through the east gate. The prisoners should be out in the gardens too, but we have to assume they'll be restrained somehow. A few of the Spades were taken as well tonight."

"A trial," someone scoffed. "As if there's any question of the outcome."

"I agree," I said. "The Queen is planning on executing them all. It's just a big show to try to turn the rest of Wonderland against the rebellion. Which is why we have to stop her from seeing that plan through."

"I'm all for that," the burly man said. "How do you suggest we do it? For an event like that, she'll have the guards prowling all around the place."

"Honestly," I said, "I'd like to hear what you all would suggest. You've run a lot more missions than I have. What have you found in the past that's worked well when you're dealing with a large number of guards?"

"We don't usually go up against that many if we can help it," a guy near the back said. "The White Knight always says to get out of there fast if the odds turn against us."

Like in the palace, after we'd retrieved the pocket watch where the Queen had trapped Time. When the guards had been breaking down the door, Theo had thrown his devices that had burst into smoke to cover our escape.

Would something like that help us tomorrow? Smoke might confuse the guards and the spectators… but when there were so many of them, I couldn't imagine blanketing the gardens with smoke without getting totally confused ourselves. We still had to make it to the prisoners and get them out.

"I can handle any locks," Hatter said where I'd left him near the end of the table. He had his head cocked a little to the side, probably because his wound was still hurting him. The white patch of the bandage stood out against his dark blond hair. "You won't have to worry about that part."

As if I wasn't going to worry about him running around in the Queen's gardens less than twenty-four hours after one of those guards had nearly put him in a coma.

"Good," I said. "So the main problem is getting to the prisoners and getting them back past the wall."

"Once we're out of the gardens, it won't be too hard to scatter," a woman said. "The Queen won't want to leave herself vulnerable sending too many of the guards after us."

Also good. Unfortunately, it didn't solve the larger problem.

"We've used distractions before," I said. "Can anyone think of something that could draw away most of the guards?"

"From something like this trial she's making such a to-do about?" Dum said doubtfully. He glanced around at the assembled Spades, and I could see him making the same assessment I had.

We were vastly outnumbered, even more than I'd counted on. And the artifacts I'd hoped might make a difference were out of reach thanks to the Queen's guards too.

"At this point, we could probably set fire to the actual palace and most of them would stay with the Queen," someone muttered. "She'd order their heads off if they left."

"What about the mission some of the young ones ran this evening?" the burly guy said. "We might have more support turn up at the wall—that was what they were aiming for, from what I've heard."

"The Clubbers who witnessed the display didn't appear particularly swayed, in my humble opinion," Chess said with an apologetic grimace.

Dee sighed, his normally cheerful expression darkening. "At least they tried. Doria really went big with that display."

His gloom passed over the faces around him, but something in his words made my heart leap.

Went *big*. How big could we go? How big could *I* go?

I had to cover my mouth to contain the slightly hysterical giggle that almost slipped out. Why hadn't I thought about that before? I'd gotten so focused on trying to figure out how to be the queen of Wonderland, how to access the powers of the royal line I'd known nothing about a few days ago, that I'd forgotten who I'd been first.

I was an Otherlander. And Otherlanders could do things Wonderlanders couldn't, as I'd proven when I'd made my dash for the pocket watch.

I could save my people, and I could do it without putting a single one of them at risk. The opposite of what Aunt Alicia had done: I'd run toward the problem and leave everyone else behind where they'd be safe.

That was what they deserved in a queen.

"What are you thinking, lovely?" Chess said, peering up at me with a knowing light in his eyes.

"I know what to do," I said. "I can break the prisoners all free on my own. There are powers I have here as an Otherlander that I can use." It wouldn't have worked when the prisoners were locked away in the dungeons somewhere deep in the palace, but outside in the gardens —it might not even be *hard*. A giddy wave of exhilaration mingled with relief tickled through me.

Hatter was frowning, as if he had anything to complain about after all his mad exploits in the last few days. I swiveled on my feet, taking in the Spades all around me.

"This is the plan," I said. "We'll meet by the road, and you all will wait, hidden, outside the palace walls around the eastern gate. I'll go in alone. You've done so much for this rebellion; I don't want you in any more danger than you need to be. I'll get the prisoners out, and all you'll need to do is help them get away from any guards who pursue them that far. They might need places to hide for a while."

"You're going in alone?" the particularly skeptical woman said. "Are you sure? What's this power you're going to use?"

"You'll see," I said. "I think it's better if as few people as possible know what I'm planning, in case the guards round anyone else up before the trial. I—I'll pass on word to the White Knight, and if he disagrees with my approach, he can direct you differently."

The Spades muttered a little amongst themselves, but they started to disperse. As they moved away from the table, Chess, Hatter, and the twins drew closer.

"What do you need us to tell the White Knight?" Dum asked.

Gears were already spinning in my head. "Chess, the club will still be open, right?"

"It gave every appearance of being so when I moseyed by there," he replied.

Hatter raised his eyebrows at me, and then winced as if the movement had provoked his injury. "*You* need to get off your feet," I told him.

"You're not leaving me behind tomorrow," he said. "Doria's in there. I'm coming."

"You can be right there by the gate waiting for her. All the more reason you'd better rest now." I turned to Dee. "Make sure he gets back to the cellar safe house, will you?"

Hatter grumbled wordlessly, and Dee hesitated, but the more upbeat twin didn't argue. What exactly had Theo said to them about me? As Dee tugged Hatter toward the doorway, I looked at Dum.

"You can tell your boss everything you just heard. He doesn't need to do more than show up to help the prisoners get back to the city either."

Dum crossed his arms over his chest. "I think he's going to want a little more explanation than that."

"Just say I'm taking the opposite tactic to how I handled the pocket watch," I said. "I'll get those people off the palace grounds. He can focus on how to take care of them after."

"You'll be in the cellar tonight if he wants to know more?"

"That's where you'll find me."

He made a face and sauntered off, leaving just me and

Chess. The brawny guy hooked his arm around mine. "I take it we're off to the club?"

"Let's go."

"It's probably best if I'm seen as little as possible at the present moment," Chess said as we headed up to the street.

My heart twinged, but I made myself say, "That's fine. As long as you'll still talk to me."

"I doubt anyone will recognize me from my voice, exquisite as it may be." He chuckled and faded into the air beside me. "Still here."

"Good."

We walked in silence through the dark streets for a few minutes, Chess letting his elbow brush against me here and there to confirm he was still with me. I turned the words I wanted to say over in my head several times before I was sure of them.

"*I* haven't seen much of you since last night," I said. "You were supposed to come see Unicorn with me. I've been worried about you. Where have you been?"

I could almost hear Chess's careless shrug. "Here and there. Did you miss me?"

The question was playful, but it made my throat squeeze.

"Yeah," I said. "I did."

His invisible hand found mine, his thumb stroking over my knuckles. "I'm sorry," he said in a more serious tone. "Last night, it hit me that... that I'm still not totally free, in many senses of that word. I wanted to determine the best route for getting to a place where I am without putting you or anyone else in danger along the way."

I wished I could look into his eyes right now. I glanced up at approximately where his face must have been. "You don't have to protect me like that. I want to help you."

"I know. But I feel this is the sort of quest I must complete on my own." The wry note had come into his voice. He paused as we reached a vacant cross-street and tugged me closer to him. The graze of his lips sent a warm flush through me even though I couldn't see the man in front of me.

"If you go down that street, you'll get to the safe house," Chess said quietly. "I think perhaps you should let me take the route ahead of us on my own too, Lyssa. I can slip into and through the club unseen—you can't. Tell me what you need there, and I'll bring it to you."

He might have a point. This part of the plan didn't require both of us.

"All the mushroom pieces you can get," I said. "Especially the kind that makes you feel larger."

All at once, Chess snapped back into sight. He peered down at me. "You mean the kind that would make *you* become larger."

"Go big?" I said with a tight smile.

He brought his hand to the side of my face, bowing his head over me. "No matter how big you grow, you can still be hurt, you know."

"I know," I said. "But no one else will, and that's what's most important."

CHAPTER TWENTY-SIX

Lyssa

The Queen of Hearts had prepared for the trial as if it were going to be a show at a country fair. From the secret platform among the chittering trees, I could see the stands she'd set up for her "jury" of palace folk, fancier than anything you'd see at a regular fair with the gold railings and red satin ribbons, and the spectator area cordoned off with tasseled ropes. A huge gold throne sat waiting for the Queen's arrival. A glossy podium stood just to the right of it, ready for the supposed witnesses, I guessed. And at the far end of the little meadow between those structures lay a big iron-barred cage.

I'd figured it was wise to keep wearing the armored vest, and the edge of it pressed against my waist where I was sprawled on my belly. I scooted forward. The guards were leading the prisoners out to the cage from the palace now.

My hands clenched as I watched them stumbling along. Doria came in the middle, a bruise blooming purple just below her left eye, and I was abruptly glad that I'd insisted that Hatter stayed on the ground.

The Diamonds started to gather, most of them in the spectator area, but the ones in the fanciest garb settling themselves onto the stands. The Duchess was one of those, primly patting her upswept honey-blond hair. She looked as carefully poised as when Doria and I had spied on her stroll through the city weeks ago.

A fresh rush of anger shot through me with the memory of Chess's story. How she could have tortured *anyone* that way, let alone that sweet, jubilant man…

A few city folk had arrived too—the ones the Queen had under her thumb. Caterpillar's unmistakable jointed body wove through the crowd of spectators. I spotted the long white ears of his lackey, Rabbit, a short distance away.

Trumpets blared. The Queen strolled into view, a blood-red cape draped across her shoulders that would have dragged on the ground if two attendants hadn't been hustling behind her, holding it up. Her massive crown glittered over the whorls of her copper hair. She was smiling the same sharp smile as in the painting I'd seen of her weeks ago, and that eerie gold sheen glinted off her wide-set eyes.

Behind her came a small procession lined by guards on either side. I assumed this was the rest of the Hearts family—the ones who remained in the palace, anyway. The pasty, stoop-shouldered king with his smaller crown followed right behind the Queen's cape, with several men and women I'd have taken to be somewhere in their thirties at his heels. Some had hair matching the queen's coppery shade, some a golden color like Mirabel's. Like the young prince's had been in that painting—like Theo's must be without the dye powder. My throat tightened.

There were no special seats for the rest of the royal family. The Queen sank into her throne, and the rest of the Hearts took spots on the stands at the end closest to her. Everyone, even the princes and princesses, shot wary looks toward their ruler.

We're all scared of her. This was a woman who had kept her own daughter locked away so no one knew the woman existed for decades, who'd hit her hard enough to unmoor her mind even more than it already had been. Who was grinning with a razor edge right now at the prospect of watching dozens of her citizens slaughtered. Nausea pooled in my belly.

The Spades hadn't been wrong about the number of guards. A row of at least fifty of them formed a ring around the section of the garden reserved for the trial, denser by the cage of prisoners. More clustered around each of the gates, including the eastern one I could just make out over the trees to my right.

The Queen clapped her hands, and the chatter that had been flowing through the gathered crowd silenced in an instant. "Where are our champions?" she called, her voice so cutting it carried all the way over the wall to my treetop perch.

"Right here, your Majesty." Unicorn stepped up in front of the throne in the scarlet short pants he'd worn for the previous fight I'd watched. He gave the Queen a quick bow. Lion sauntered over beside him, shaking back the voluminous mass of his mane.

Their duel must be about to start. I'd better get ready. I scrambled down the notches in the tree trunk to rejoin Chess and Hatter.

The other Spades were spread out among the trees. Well, most of the other Spades. When we'd met up, Theo hadn't been among them. Where the hell was he? Even if I didn't want to see him, he was supposed to be here for his people.

I couldn't worry about him right now. "She's there," I said to Hatter immediately. "They haven't beat her up badly or anything like that." But the clock was ticking down on how long Doria would keep her head at all.

My hand dropped to the bag full of mushroom slices hanging from my shoulder. All the growing ones were in there. I'd stuffed the shrinking ones into my pockets.

"I'm going over to the gate," I said. "The fight is about to start. As soon as Unicorn makes his disruption, I'm heading here. You two stay outside the walls with everyone else like we talked about, all right? Just get the prisoners out of here."

"Lyssa," Hatter started with a grimace.

I pointed a finger at him. "You have a head injury." I turned to Chess, whose stance was tense too. "And I don't want to have to worry about accidentally hurting you because I don't see you're there. I can do the inside job on my own. My head will be too far up for them to even think about chopping at it."

Chess grinned at my attempt at a joke, but his voice was tight. "If you need us…"

"I know. I'd better go."

I grasped their arms quickly, bobbing up to give Chess a quick kiss and then Hatter, just enough to leave me a tiny bit warmed as I darted through the trees toward the eastern gate.

The wind whispered through the leaves. I treaded carefully through the brush until I could just make out the gate through the trees. A grunt and a thump of a landed blow reached my ears. The fight had started.

I dug my hand into the bag and pulled out a handful of mushroom slices. My gut clenched, but I forced myself to pop two into my mouth in one go. I had to be ready. I had to be as big as I could make myself if I was going to pull this off alone.

As the tart earthy flavor saturated my mouth, the stretching sensation I'd felt twice before now shuddered through me. My head shot upward, my neck extending, and then my shoulders and chest zoomed after it, the vest expanding around my torso as my body grew.

Wonderlanders only *felt* like their perspective was growing or shrinking when they ate Caterpillar's special mushrooms. It turned out they affected Otherlanders much more literally.

I had to sway to the side as my body loomed up through the trees, my head nearly slamming into a branch. The growth spurt stopped with my head amid the leaves. No, I needed a little more than that.

I gulped down another slice, and my body jerked even taller. A rippling sensation spread through my legs, and I grasped a tree trunk for balance. I topped out with the highest foliage level with my eyes.

Perfect. I could see into the gardens now, but not enough of me was showing for anyone to be likely to notice, especially when they were focused on the fight.

Unicorn and Lion were circling around each other. They'd ended up leaving the meadow of the trial area behind, swiping and dodging on trampled grass closer to the gate. Unicorn must have maneuvered them in that direction.

Lion lashed out with a paw, smacking Unicorn's muzzle with a scrape of his claws. Unicorn shook his head as he yanked himself out of the way. Then he charged, his horn pointed straight at Lion's chest.

Lion started to swerve out of the way, but Unicorn veered with him, driving him toward the gate instead. He dropped to all fours with a sudden burst of speed. Lion wheeled backward, crashing into a guard in his haste to escape that stabbing horn pointed straight at his chest. The other guards by the gate shuffled backward to give them room.

Unicorn hurled himself at Lion, bashing him into the gate with his shoulder. The metal bars clanged, and the door burst open.

Now. I stuffed two more pieces of mushroom into my

mouth, ignoring the twisting of my stomach, and pushed forward through the trees.

My body soared up over the treetops as I charged forward. My lungs strained with the heave of air I drew in, trying to fill them. By the time I reached the gate, the once-immense wall only reached my knees. I could have stepped right over it if I'd wanted to.

Several of the Diamonds shrieked and fled at the sight of me. "Monster!" someone cried out. The Queen, looking so small now down there on her throne—barely as tall as my hand—stared up at me, her face flushing nearly as ruddy as her hair. Her eyes flashed.

"Guards!" she screamed. "Destroy this fiend!"

The guards stumbled into one another, gaping, but some of them had the wherewithal to draw their swords or daggers. I strode past them, careful not to step on anyone while they scurried like mice around my feet.

Vicious mice. Pain pierced through my calf as a guard stabbed his sword into the flesh. Another took a slice at my ankle. I winced and bent down to brush them aside with my hands. More blades nicked my fingers, blood streaking across my skin, but I managed to push them aside to clear my way. How many of them even wanted to be here, and how many had been forced like Dee and Dum might have been if Theo hadn't intervened? They didn't deserve to die for trying to save themselves the only way she'd given them.

I *wouldn't* be a monster. I had to be better than that, better than *her*, right from the start.

"I'm not here to hurt anyone," I said, letting my voice

ring out of my massive lungs. "Not like her." I pointed at the Queen. "I'm here to set right a horrible crime that's been committed by the ones who rule this place. You think you have power? *I* have power. And I can use it well."

More guards were barreling toward me. I grasped the top of the stands with a light shake to displace the members of the "jury" still seated on it, and smacked down the empty structure in the guards' way to slow them down. Then I curled my fingers around the bars at the top of the prisoners' cage.

I hefted it, gently and then with a little more force. I especially didn't want to hurt anyone in there. The cage wouldn't budge from the ground—it'd been fixed there too fast. Okay, carrying it out of the gardens had only been Plan A. I'd known it might not work.

The guards who'd stood around the cage were slashing at my legs. A steady pulsing of pain was spreading through my calves now. Another heaved a spear at my chest, but it clinked off of my hidden armor.

I brushed the guards away as well as I could and reached down to the chain that held the cage door closed. With one quick yank of my giant fingers, it snapped.

"Go!" I said, jerking the cage door open and motioning toward the gate. "You did nothing wrong. The Spades won't allow the Queen to hold you. I stand with them, and I stand against this pathetic excuse for a queen."

The Queen of Hearts let out an ear-splitting screech. When I turned to cover the prisoners in their dash out of the garden, she'd stood up in front of her throne, waving a scepter with a heart-shaped golden tip in every direction. "Where are my guards? Stop her, stop them, or I'll have all your heads!"

Even with an actual giant in their midst, a lot of the guards were still more scared of their queen than of me. Blades flashing, they sprang at me and at the stream of figures hurrying across the grass beneath me. Ignoring the throbbing in my calves and the stinging cuts across my hands, I pushed them aside whenever they got too close to the escaping prisoners. Fat droplets of blood dribbled from my fingers and splashed on the ground.

This pain was just for now. Just for a few minutes, to save all these people's lives, and then I could get out of here too.

The Queen of Hearts let out another screech of fury. I swept aside another wave of guards and swung toward her. The sudden thought struck me that I could crush her with one squeeze of my hand. My stomach listed queasily with the image of mangled flesh and the crunch of bones, but that would end all the terror, wouldn't it? She'd done so much worse to Wonderland's people.

Even as I tried to convince myself, my gaze slid to her scattered children. This woman wasn't the first Queen of Hearts, or even necessarily the worst. There were plenty of daughters waiting to take her place if she fell. Even if I'd been sure I was ready to commit to taking the throne, I didn't have enough allies for me to hold it. I'd just be starting another reign founded on bloodshed—and they'd spill a lot more blood than just mine.

As if she'd read my initial idea in my expression, the Queen hollered at the guards to surround her. A ring of them ten bodies deep closed in around her protectively.

Fine. That meant fewer harassing the prisoners and me.

A little of the tension gripping my chest fell away at the sight of Doria slipping through the gate. I shoved aside the guards who tried to race after the prisoners, watching as the last in that bunch disappeared amid the trees on the other side. Then I straightened up, just for a moment, to scan the grounds and make sure everyone had gotten out.

From my great height, my gaze swept over the entire royal property and across the forests and fields beyond, all the way to the garish buildings of the city at my left and the Checkerboard Plains ahead of me, a great shimmering sea farther to my right. A weird sense of rightness flooded me from head to toe.

This was Wonderland. This was *my* Wonderland, suppressed by a tyrant's rule but vibrant even so. I'd spilled blood on this ground as nearly my entire family had all those generations ago, and now I was back. I was here, where I was meant to be.

A tremor ran through the ground beneath my feet, as if it were responding to my thoughts. Reaching out to me to tell me it was with me, whatever I'd call on it to do. So much of my life I'd struggled just to hold off the chaos around me, and here the world *wanted* to listen to me.

This place belonged to me, or maybe I belonged to it.

Possibly those were the same thing. I *couldn't* go. I couldn't leave Wonderland.

My heart was already in it—in the crazy vegetation and the wild architecture and the bizarre people just trying to be happy. My heart was with Chess and his brilliant grins that could hide so much pain, with Hatter and the fierceness that came from the depths of his caring. Maybe some of it remained with even Theo, with the passionate assurance he'd built on top of his darkest secret.

The certainty radiated through me for one glorious moment, and then my gut lurched.

I doubled over, my vision hazing, my stomach churning as if it meant to toss itself right out of my mouth. My hand clamped over my belly.

Apparently five mushrooms was a little too much for even an Otherlander to handle.

As swords stabbed at my ankles, my gut heaved. A sear of acid raced up my throat. I vomited onto a rose bush, and then wretched again. My legs wobbled, not just with the throb of the wounds but with a pinch of contraction that was an even more unwelcome sensation.

I was shrinking.

CHAPTER TWENTY-SEVEN

Chess

L yssa was something to look at in her regular size. The sight of her striding toward the palace gardens at least ten times taller took my breath away. Across the road from me, Hatter's jaw had dropped.

Her dress rippled around her like an immense tapestry, over the mounds of her breasts like small hills, the curve of her waist I could have tucked myself into. She could have fit me in her hand. She could have crushed my bones with a press of her thumb.

Not that I could imagine her ever so much as considering doing anything that horrifying, which was maybe why the thought could awaken that odd flicker of excitement from the same part of me that had enjoyed playing with matches and knives long ago.

But my mind had other places to be. Even within the numbed space of the in-between, my ears picked up the

Queen of Hearts screaming out commands. The guards were shouting to each other, and other shrieks carried from farther beyond the wall. This would shake the Diamonds up more than they'd ever been shaken before. They'd wanted thrills, hadn't they?

Lyssa let out a little gasp, and my jaw clenched. Those guards would be hacking away at her, no matter how quickly she displaced them. We should be in there, helping her.

But she'd asked us to be here instead.

Lyssa's voice rang out, clearer and sweeter than anything the Queen of Hearts could have produced. Blood streaked across the backs of her hands as she bent down. There was a snapping sound, and a renewed volley of shouts. Then the first of the prisoners, hair bedraggled and clothes spotted with grime, dashed through the gate.

"This way!" one of the Spades near me called, waving the woman off the road into the woods. More figures raced toward us, sped on by panic. Doria dashed straight to Hatter, wrapping her arms around him with a sob. He hugged her tight, relief and regret twisting together in his expression.

"Go on," he said when he let her go, motioning her after the other escapees. "Hide out, and I'll come when everyone here is safe."

One of the twins waved from deeper in the woods. Doria gave her father one more quick hug and then bolted toward Dee.

A few of the guards gave chase through the gate. Lyssa was whirling this way and that behind the wall, but she couldn't catch all of them. I threw myself forward down the slight slope of the road.

An invisible knee to the gut here. An invisible punch to the chin there. Trip this guard, topple that one. They flailed out with their fists and their swords, trying to fend me off, but the blades barely nicked me as I wove and bobbed through the in-between. It almost felt like cheating.

Hatter leapt into the fray alongside me. He jabbed the dagger he'd brought, only slightly thicker than his hatpins, into the gut of a guard who'd snatched one of the prisoners' shirt hems.

The older man wrenched away, and the guard slumped against the wall. Hatter nodded in my general direction as if to say, *We've got this.*

I wasn't so sure we did in our present position. Beyond the gate, a group of stragglers, limping or shuffling as quickly as their aching legs could carry them, were staring around them with faces white with fear as more guards closed in around them. The Queen of Hearts was squawking about something or other again, and blood splattered the grass near her throne. At least some of it was Lyssa's.

I didn't let myself think any more than that. I hurtled through the gate to knock the legs out from under one of the guards lunging at the escapees. Another guard raced toward Lyssa's ankle with a spear. I clocked him across the side of the head and sent him sprawling, scrambling out of the way just in time as Lyssa's large hands scooped another cluster of guards out of the way. They toppled in a heap like toy soldiers. They must have looked like toys to her.

A few dashed off, unwilling to keep up the fight. The Diamonds were fleeing toward the palace too. More guards were heading our way, though, a bunch of them hauling a cannon.

My stomach dropped. I ran over, my feet thumping over the ground, and slammed the lead guard's head against the iron surface. With a shove that strained the muscles in my shoulders, I heaved the cannon's muzzle to the side to collide with the others' guts.

No one was firing heavy artillery at the woman I intended to see become *my* queen. The woman who for all intents and purposes already was.

I spun around and found myself staring into the last face I'd have wanted to see. The Duchess gazed back at the spot where I was standing, not quite able to meet my eyes in my invisible state, but she'd worked out an approximation of where I was standing. She must have seen my ghost-like combat and put the pieces together.

Her face was as pinched and her lips, painted crimson, as pert as ever. Even hustling away from the chaos, her diamond-laced hair hadn't shifted a strand out of place. Despite the shouts and the cries behind us, her mouth curved into a thin but amused smile. "Hello, Cheshire."

The way she said my name made my skin want to crawl off my body. She said it as if she owned it—as if she owned *me*, as if she believed she merely needed to snap her fingers and I'd be at her feet.

She'd almost been right. Because of her accusation, if

I'd been a little slower on *my* feet, I might have ended up in the prison where she could have strolled by and offered her condolences, or maybe a deal to get me out under her conditions.

Every inch of me prickled with the urge to run now. But what I'd told Lyssa last night was true. I wasn't free of my past, not completely, not as long as I had to run or jump because of the hoops this woman set out in front of me.

She'd flayed me nearly inside out, but I'd seen plenty of what lay behind her mask too, hadn't I?

Bracing myself, I strode up to her, letting only my grin flash into view. The Duchess's expression turned as satisfied as the cat who'd gotten the cream. She'd forgotten who the real cat around here was.

I tugged my smile back out of view and stopped beside her, leaning close, crinkling my nose at the bittersweet tang of her favorite perfume. The smell brought back the echo of pain radiating through my ribs, a line of agony across my neck nearly slitting my throat, a searing at the backs of my knees. I squared my shoulders, holding myself steady against the wave of memories.

I was more than those memories. I was more than that creature she'd strung up in her bedroom. And it was time I showed her that.

"Hello, Duchess," I said in a measured, lilting tone. "You've caused me a lot of trouble in the last few days."

She fucking *giggled*. "Poor Chess. And yet you're here. It appears I only told the truth."

"Here's the thing, Duchess," I said, my voice dropping

to a murmur. "You don't know why I'm here. You don't know me at all. But I know *all* about you. So consider this your first and only warning. You don't speak my name, you don't say or so much as *think* about me, from this day forward. There is nothing between us. You do not exist to me, so I cannot exist to you."

"A warning?" she said with an arch of her perfectly shaped eyebrows. "And what will you do if I ignore it?"

I let my grin flash again, wide enough to show my fangs, only just holding myself back from gritting my teeth. "I saw and heard all sorts of things your queen and your fellow Diamonds might be *very* interested to learn. I know more than you could even guess. Haven't you ever noticed your memory turns a bit spotty when you think of certain times with me? I stole some of those moments from you, but I still remember everything."

The Duchess went rigid. I didn't actually know if I'd observed any secrets that could truly damage her standing —or perhaps even end her life—but she'd bragged enough about skirting expectations for me to believe she had some that serious. Most of all, though, she thrived on her sense of control. One jab of uncertainty about what I might know from those blanks where I'd wiped the image of my transformations from her mind, and all her confidence unraveled.

"They wouldn't listen to you," she said tartly, but her haughty mask had cracked.

I slipped around to her other side, as if I were all around her. "I think they would. Especially with the details I could provide. You haven't always been quite careful enough in how you cover your tracks. But please, go ahead and test me. I look forward to seeing the Queen raise *your* head on one of those pikes."

She blanched whiter beneath the sheen of pale peach powder covering her face. I'd said all I needed to. Clamping down my queasiness, I let myself dart away the way my legs had been dying to from the moment I'd seen her.

The ground trembled beneath my feet, and as if in echo, a sense of release shivered through me. I'd faced the Duchess, I'd shown her what I really thought of her, and she'd faltered. I—

Up ahead of me, near the gate, Lyssa's enlarged form knifed over so sharply my heart stopped. Her body heaved. With a strangled sound, she vomited in a shower over a cluster of rose bushes. Another wave followed. After each wretch, her figure contracted, a little more, and a little more.

Fuck. I'd worried that so many mushroom pieces would be too much—none of the Clubbers I'd been around had ever taken more than two in an hour without taking the opposite type to balance out the sensations, and even two was extreme. We had to get Lyssa out of here before the guards removed her in a much more permanent fashion.

I hurtled down the garden paths, vaulted over a low hedge, and crashed through the ring of guards that had started to close around Lyssa. She hunched over, sputtering and shaking, only as tall as I was now. Blood trickled from her fingers as she pawed at her belly.

Hatter must have noticed her distress too. He raced into the midst of the guards, jabbing this one and that with his dagger, darting around Lyssa to push them back as quickly as his swift feet could take him. I leapt in behind him to shove and trip whoever I could. Whirling around, I caught up a short sword a guard dropped after I kicked his wrist. The gleam of the blade nauseated me all over again, but that sensation was nothing compared to my terror for the woman behind me.

"Grab her and break a path to the gate," I said to Hatter. If we could just get past the wall, we'd have the forest to fade into.

He started to push at the growing crowd of guards in that direction, but they just swarmed in closer on the other sides. There were certain limitations to trying to fend off this many packed so tightly together when they couldn't see me. I had surprise, but I couldn't rely on feints or intimidation. My lungs tightened.

I'd stood up to the Duchess. I could stand up to these Queen's-asshole-licking lackeys too. For Lyssa. For our real queen, the one we deserved—all of us, even me.

With a crackle in my ears, I emerged from the in-between, plowing over four guards with one thunderous sweep of my arm. My dagger glinted and my fist flew. For a few heartbeats, the guards fell back, startled and wary. I nudged Lyssa after Hatter, and she managed to stumble onward on legs back to their usual size now. Blood dribbled over the grass in her wake.

Right then, I thought we could do it. The gate was less

than ten feet away. It was crazy, sure, but we were all mad here, and Hatter and I were madder than anyone.

My knuckles connected with a guard's jaw. My dagger sank into another guard's sword arm. We made it another few steps—and then a mass of them pushed in around us too quickly for me to fend them all off.

One guard caught me with an elbow to the back of my head. As I reeled, another kneed me in the back. I spun around, and two clotheslined me in unison, throwing me right off my feet.

A heavy heel jammed me against the ground. A blade slammed straight through my shoulder, attaching me to the earth with a spear of agony. My nerves jumped with the urge to vanish, to contract into my own smaller form, but my body resisted.

I had to focus to find my way there, and the haze of pain clouded my mind too much. Just like it had back then.

I caught a glimpse of Hatter tackled to the ground, of two of the guards wrenching Lyssa's arms behind her back, too forcefully for her to struggle free. The Queen's voice split the air from far closer to us than I'd ever have preferred. Especially considering what she had to say.

"Their heads. All of them. Now!"

The new Knave stepped through the crowd toward Lyssa, drawing his sword with a hiss. I thrashed against the ground despite the fresh flare through my shoulder, and more feet stomped down on me to pin my limbs.

Forceful footsteps thumped across the ground.

Another figure strode through the mob, and for a second, despite my predicament, I found nothing but shock.

Our White Knight was walking up to the Knave, his square jaw lifted, every muscle in his body tensed. Why did his hair look brighter, almost gold? When had he gotten here?

What in the lands was he doing?

His rich baritone reverberated across the gardens as commanding as the Queen's had been, as if he expected even her guards to obey his order.

"Stop."

CHAPTER TWENTY-EIGHT

Lyssa

So much authority rang through Theo's voice that the guards holding me actually hesitated, their grip on me loosening enough to ease the pain of their digging fingers, though not to give me enough room to run.

Where the hell could I have run to anyway? There were more guards everywhere I looked—they'd battered Chess and Hatter to the ground. My stomach was still churning, my throat burning with acid, splinters of pain digging through my legs and my hands from all the cuts that had shrunk with my body but not disappeared.

The Knave raised his sword by my head, and Theo grasped his wrist. The sun gleamed golden on his curly hair, no longer slicked back but allowed to fall loose across his forehead. It wasn't quite as bright as Mirabel's, but close. He must have washed the dye out as well as he could.

An ache squeezed around my heart with a sudden understanding—why he'd have done that, why he'd have held back during the fighting. He'd had his plans. One last gambit, in case mine failed.

"I don't answer to you, Inventor," the Knave sneered, yanking his arm back. "Move aside. Or are you officially throwing your lot in with the Spades?"

"No," Theo said, perfectly calmly, perfectly assured. Like the man I'd thought I was falling in love with. "I'm here to announce that the rebellion is over." He raised his voice. "Anyone calling themselves a Spade should go back to their homes and set aside these futile conflicts. It's finished."

The Queen of Hearts was bustling her way through the crowd of guards, her square jaw jutting out and the eerie sheen in her eyes glowing fiercely. Her vast scarlet skirts flowed around her. "It is not. They must pay for what they've done. You must—"

Theo shook his head as he cut her off. "I've already settled everything that needs settling, Mother."

No. Even though I'd criticized him yesterday, even though I'd told him he'd been wrong to keep so much from me, from everyone, every part of my body protested at the admission in that one word.

I'd wanted him to be honest with us, not with *her*.

Even the Knave faltered at his remark. The Queen stopped dead in her tracks at the edge of the ring of guards. She stared at Theo, her rigidly severe expression shifting just for a second. Then it snapped back into place.

"Mother?" she demanded. "What is the meaning of this?"

Theo gave her a pained smile. "It's me, Mother. It's Jack. I know I don't look exactly the same, but you can see it, can't you?"

Her hand tightened around her scepter, her knuckles blanching. "My son Jack is *dead*. Don't you dare—"

"That's what I needed everyone to think," Theo went on before she could threaten him. It was unsettling how easily *I* could see the similarities now with them standing face to face: the set of their jaws, the confident stance that looked bold on Theo and arrogant on the Queen. The way he could pitch his voice to cut through any others around him.

"What do I need to tell you?" he asked. "How we went through four tutors in a year before you found one who'd teach things right? That my first real lesson was supervising the beheading of the one you liked least? That I once spilled parsnip soup all over your sitting room rug? That the first creature I killed in a hunt was a pheasant I went out and shot with an arrow on my own before presenting it to you?"

The Queen's face had gone as white as her knuckles. Her lips parted and closed and parted again. "It can't be," she said.

Theo was wearing his usual white dress shirt and gray slacks. Without breaking eye contact with his mother, he reached toward his muscled back and drew his forefinger sharply across the linen fabric, first by his waist, then a few inches higher, and then by his shoulders.

"You did it because you wanted me to remember," he said. "Three times. I did remember. This was for bringing scraps from the dinner table to the stable cats. This was for failing to punish the serving girl who brought me the wrong color of wine. And this was for skipping out on a ball to roam in the city instead."

She whipped me to bleeding, he'd told me. She could have without anyone being the wiser. Score him to the bone one night, and the next morning he'd wake up with only the memory of the pain, no evidence of it.

I restrained a shiver. The guards' hands were still clamped around my arms.

"Jack," the Queen said, with so much emotion tangled in that one syllable that I knew he'd convinced her. She gathered herself, needing to maintain her appearance of superiority in front of her guards, I guessed. "You have a lot of explaining to do."

"And I will," Theo said. "The most important part is that you taught me well. I saw that I had to be the prince and the heir that you needed. And that meant ending the one threat that's loomed over our family for so long." He cast his hand toward me. "This is the latest Alice. I deliver her to you."

A sharper chill ran over my skin. He sounded so steady, as if the role he'd taken on really had been one long plan to bring down the Spades and the Red royal line.

"We'll see that she faces the appropriate punishment, but first we must be sure the threat ends with her. I'll bring her to the dungeon while you prepare yourself for the questioning, if it pleases you, Mother."

The Queen's gaze hadn't left her newly recovered son for an instant. When he called her mother, she nodded automatically.

Theo gestured toward Chess and Hatter. "Let them go. Escort them back to their homes. They've all been under her thrall. We must give them the chance to shake off her influence." He grasped my wrist. "Come along now. Don't make your loss any more painful for yourself than it needs to be."

I tried to turn to make sure the guards were really freeing Hatter and Chess, and Theo's fingers clenched tight enough to bruise my skin. A rough pained noise broke from my lips. The Queen smiled as he marched me toward her.

He held up his hand, palm toward her. "I'll need the mark of your seal. Until the guards know me properly again."

Her seal—like she'd given Rabbit, he'd said. The Queen produced a small metal object about the size and shape of a car's cigarette lighter from the folds of her dress. Holding Theo's gaze, she pressed it to his palm. Lines of blood sprang up where the edges cut into his skin, sealing over almost instantly into a stark pink pattern.

"They'll know you properly soon," she said, the shimmer in her eyes almost... joyful. Somehow that was even more unsettling than her rage.

We strode down the path through the garden toward the ruddy walls of the palace, Theo half a step in the lead.

His fingers loosened around my wrist as soon as we'd left the Queen and her guards behind, but he didn't let me go.

I didn't know what to say, what I should do. Should I be trying to escape? Or was this a ruse I'd only survive if I played along? I felt like vomiting all over again, and I didn't think the mushrooms were at all to blame this time.

I'd been angry with him, but I had trouble believing even he could have faked the anguish he'd shown me yesterday over his mother's treatment of Wonderland. If his role as the White Knight had been the real ruse, he'd had plenty of opportunities to hand me over to the palace before now. So I stayed quiet, waiting for his cues. He'd earned that much trust.

Whatever his plan was, I was finding it increasingly difficult to follow. He showed the seal mark to the guards at one of the palace's smaller doors and marched past them. Inside, he led me up a flight of stairs, down a hall, and around a corner to another one. A plush red rug cushioned my feet. The smell of dried roses tinged the air.

Yeah, I was going to go out on a limb here and say this wasn't the way to the dungeons. But where the hell *was* he taking me?

My calves were throbbing again. We finally stopped outside a door with an ornately carved wooden frame, where a squad of guards waited. At the flash of the Queen's seal, they stepped aside. As the door thumped shut behind us, Theo's hand slid farther down, brushing the cuts on my hand. I winced, and his gaze jerked to me. He adjusted his hold in an instant.

"I'm sorry," he said, his voice raw.

Those two words dissolved the last of my doubts. He was still on my side, on the Spades' side, as much as he'd ever been.

He ushered me into a sitting room full of fancy old-fashioned furniture, glinting with gold twined into the fabric and glazed over the wood. Fresh roses sat in a vase on the side table and on the buffet at the other end of the room. The smell of them hung so thickly it smacked me in the face.

Theo pressed on into a vast room with a grand piano and more sofas than I could count. Somehow the rose scent was even thicker there. He coughed and swiped at his mouth. His dark brown eyes were starting to haze.

My heart skipped a beat as I remembered what he'd told me about the roses—that the smell of them clouded his mind. I couldn't lose him, not here, not now. I needed him with me if we were both going to get out of this situation alive.

His steps dragged on the floor. I tossed all my hesitations aside, stepped in front of him, and gripped his shirt to pull him into a kiss.

It was as *with me* as I knew how to accomplish. Let him feel me and not the presence of the roses. Something even clearer, even more potent, that he could train his mind on.

Theo's breath hitched, and then he kissed me back hard, his other hand tucking around my waist and pulling me against him. It only lasted a few seconds, long enough for me to notice that it still felt so fucking good being this close to him, and long enough for my fear to creep back in.

He let me go, his hand coming up to the side of my head, his lips almost brushing my hair. "Thank you, Lyssa."

I swallowed thickly. "I don't understand what's going on. Theo—Jack—"

"It's *Theo*," he said. "I'm not hers. I—I'm going to fix this. I'm going to set things right for Wonderland or die trying. There's been so much pain while I watched and I waited… No more of that. Someone has to stand up to her. It ought to be me."

"You didn't have to do it like this," I said.

He gave me a crooked smile. "She was a hair's breadth from taking your head. We need you alive if things are ever going to be completely right. *I* need you alive. You upended my world, but you saved it—and me—too. It's my turn to save you."

"But how…?"

He eased toward me, and I backed up a step automatically. "I'll do whatever it takes to challenge her, to convince her," he said. "I've already used you too much to fix problems that were my responsibility. You'd try to save us all because that's just who you are, but you've done your part more than anyone should have asked. Now I'll do mine. I swear I'll come for you when it's safe, when I've cleared the way, and you can take the place that's meant for you if you want it."

Another fragment of memory came back to me, from after we'd discovered that the mirror in Caterpillar's club had been shattered. When Theo was discussing the other one he knew of. *The Queen was keeping it in her private chambers...*

"No," I said, with a protest that rippled through me from head to toe. I started to turn, but Theo caught my head with his other hand too, holding my face cupped between them. He walked us back another step, gazing into my eyes.

"I love you, Lyssa. I have to do this. I *owe* you this. I promised I'd get you home."

"Theo—"

He nudged me backward another half a step, and my elbow brushed cool glass. "Just think of home," he said softly.

My body recoiled, trying to throw me forward away from the looking-glass—too late. The mirror's pull was already sucking me through. The last thing I saw of Wonderland was Theo's taut expression before I fell away into blackness.

Think of home, he'd said. As I tumbled headlong through the chilly looking-glass void between my world and his, my skin prickled with the certainty that home was not where I was going but the place I was leaving behind.

I groped into the darkness as if I could catch hold of something that would pull me back there. My body flipped heels over head and spun around. A wave of dizziness washed over me, and I stumbled onto hard wet ground.

I hadn't been focused on anywhere in the Otherland

while the mirror had heaved me here, so it must have spat me out into my former world somewhat at random. Into a drizzly night with a tarry scent in my nose and a pair of headlights bearing down on me.

A horn blared, I scrambled up and stumbled, and a wallop of pain shocked my senses into an even deeper darkness.

LYSSA'S FAVORITE VANILLA-CRANBERRY-PINE SCONES

(Recipe makes approximately 8 scones)

Ingredients:

2 cups flour
2 teaspoons baking powder
1/2 cup butter, cubed
1 cup dried cranberries
2 teaspoons ground juniper berries
1/4 cup sugar plus extra for sprinkling
2 teaspoons vanilla extract
3/4 teaspoon salt
3/4 cup milk, plus more for brushing on top

1. Preheat the oven to 425° F. Line a baking sheet with parchment paper.

2. Combine flour and baking powder in a mixing bowl. Using your fingers, massage in the butter until the mixture looks like fine crumbs.

3. Stir in the cranberries, ground juniper berries, sugar, vanilla extract, and salt. Add the milk a little at a time, stirring until the dough is soft. You might not need all of the milk.

4. Shape the dough into balls about 2 inches thick and roll them on a floured surface. Place on the baking sheet and flatten to about 1 inch. Brush the tops lightly with milk. Sprinkle with sugar.

5. Bake for 15 to 20 minutes until golden brown. Let sit 10 minutes before serving.

Note: For more of a pine flavor, mix 3 tablespoons ground juniper berries with 1/2 cup of sugar and let sit at least 12 hours. Sprinkle the juniper sugar on top of the scones instead of regular sugar.

ABOUT THE AUTHOR

Eva Chase lives in Canada with her family. She loves stories both swoony and supernatural, and strong women and the men who appreciate them. Along with the Looking-Glass Curse trilogy, she is the author of the Their Dark Valkyrie series, the Witch's Consorts series, the Dragon Shifter's Mates series, the Demons of Fame Romance series, the Legends Reborn trilogy, and the Alpha Project Psychic Romance series.

Connect with Eva online:
www.evachase.com
eva@evachase.com

Made in the USA
Columbia, SC
23 February 2019